PENGUIN BOOKS
THE BOYFRIEND

R. Raj Rao was born in Bombay. H̲ ̲ ̲ed in ̲ ̲ ̲ ̲n̲d̲l̲ ̲, and in 1996 attended the International W̲ ̲ ̲ ̲ ̲ ̲ ̲ ̲ ̲ ̲ ̲ ̲ ̲ is the author of *Slide Show* (poems), *On ̲ ̲ ̲ ̲ ̲ ̲ ̲ ̲ ̲ ̲ ̲ ̲ ̲ Soul City* (short stories), *The Wise ̲ ̲ ̲ ̲ ̲ ̲ ̲ ̲ ̲ ̲ ̲ ̲ ̲* and *Nissim Ezeki̲ ̲. ̲ ̲ ̲ ̲ ̲ ̲ ̲ ̲ ̲ ̲ ̲ ̲s̲o̲ e̲di̲ ̲ ̲ ̲Ten Indian Writers* ̲n̲ ̲l̲ ̲ ̲ ̲ ̲ ̲ ̲ ̲ ̲ ̲e̲di̲te̲d̲ *Image of Ind̲ ̲ ̲ ̲ ̲ ̲h̲e̲ Indian Nove̲ ̲ in English (̲ ̲ ̲ ̲ ̲1980).* This is his first novel.

A professor of English at the University of Pune, Rao is also one of Indian's leading gay-rights activists.

the Boyfriend

R. Raj Rao

PENGUIN BOOKS

Penguin Books India (P) Ltd., 11 Community Centre, Panchsheel Park, New Delhi 110 017, India

Penguin Books Ltd., 80 Strand, London WC2R 0RL, UK

Penguin Putnam Inc., 375 Hudson Street, New York, NY 10014, USA

Penguin Books Australia Ltd., 250 Camberwell Road, Camberwell, Victoria 3124, Australia

Penguin Books Canada Ltd., 10 Alcorn Avenue, Suite 300, Toronto, Ontario M4V 3B2, Canada

Penguin Books (NZ) Ltd., Cnr Rosedale and Airborne Roads, Albany, Auckland, New Zealand

Penguin Books (South Africa) (Pty) Ltd, 24 Sturdee Avenue, Rosebank 2196, South Africa

First published by Penguin Books India 2003

This is a work of fiction. Names, characters, places and incidents are either the product of the author's imagination or are used fictitiously, and any resemblance to any actual person, living or dead, events, or locales is entirely coincidental.

Typeset in *Sabon* by Mantra Virtual Services, New Delhi
Printed at Goel Printcolour Scan Pvt. Ltd, New Delhi

Acknowledgements
The author wishes to thank Dilip Chitre for permission to use an extract from his poem 'The View from Chinchpokli'.

For Bharati and Clark

I don't care who you are
Where you're from
What you do
As long as you love me

— *Backstreet Boys*

contents

one

gentlemen

Churchgate station is a tranquil place on a Sunday morning. It doesn't choke with humanity as it does Monday to Saturday. The station is an asylum for Bombay's down and out, but on a Sunday morning one is unlikely to find too many bootblacks. Even they like to forget their Cherry Blossom tins and loll about in bed till mid-day, like the youngsters in high rises on Cuffe Parade and Malabar Hill. On a Sunday morning, one doesn't see urchins greedily finishing the remnants of a discarded bottle of Energee, or a Styrofoam cup of coffee, nor does one bump into skinny pimps and fleshy prostitutes. The only hub of activity is a bookstall run by the famed A.H. Wheeler. Here, newsboys busily sort out bundles of Sunday newspapers to cater to the metro's news-hungry multitudes. (Later in the day, they can be seen hawking *The Statesman* and *The Hindu* that have arrived by air from Calcutta and Madras). Trains, of course, keep zooming in and out. But there are no stampedes on the platform.

Yudi wasn't really sure what brought him to Churchgate that morning. It was a cocktail of reasons at best. True, he came to look up his mother every Sunday, when he alighted at Marine Lines, the station just before Churchgate, as he had done early that morning. But his mother hadn't been in town for over a week now. She had taken the slow train to South India to attend the wedding of one of her late husband's nephews. Yudi had gone to her flat, sandwiched between two old cinema houses—Metro and Liberty—to ensure that thieves hadn't broken in. He had then locked up and walked to Churchgate station. Perhaps he thought he would get a better seat on the train if he boarded it here. After all, he had a long way to travel: his lifestyle demanded that he live on his own, but the only place where he could afford a small flat was remote Nalla Sopara.

Another thing that may have goaded him to go to Churchgate was the newspaper. He was expecting an article he had recently written to be published in *The Statesman*, and he knew that Churchgate was the only place in Bombay where he could lay his hands on it. Perhaps he also thought he'd have a bite at the station before taking his train, so he didn't have to cook once he got home, almost three hours later. Yudi's Sunday afternoon meal was always at his mother's: now that she was away, he was left to fend for himself.

And then, of course, there was the loo. He would be lying if he did not admit that this was the most urgent of factors that drove him to Churchgate. The gents' toilet at Churchgate provided a twenty-four-hour supply of men; the amount of semen that went down the urine bowls was enough to start a sperm bank. But Yudi rarely had any success here, for almost all the young men he fancied and picked up at Churchgate found Nalla Sopara too far. The moment he told them he had a 'place' at Nalla Sopara, they said 'Sorry, not that far, we have to get back home by such-and-such time.' But today the keys to his mother's flat, barely ten minutes away, were in his pocket, and his mother was in faraway Warangal, eating oily laddoos, as one of his luckless cousins tied the fatal knot. Today, Yudi could handpick anyone he wanted;

the guy would be willing to go with him.

The Statesman hadn't arrived yet. Yudi asked a teenager working in the bookstall when it would come. The boy opened his mouth and spoke inchoate things that made no sense. Yudi wasn't surprised. Over the years he had come to the conclusion that Indian men were good only to sleep with, nothing less, nothing more. 'When will *you* come, then?' he said in English, and the boy responded with a brief, blank stare.

Yudi was a prolific freelancer. People in the profession speculated that he made at least thirty grand a month, writing for newspapers and magazines ranging from *The Hindu* to *Debonair*. This, of course, was an exaggeration. Though it was true that some of his stories earned him more than the going rate because they were offbeat enough to titillate the repressed middle-class reader. The article he was keen to see in *The Statesman*, for instance, concerned a homosexual and a lesbian in Pune who had got married, produced a son, and panicked that the boy might turn out to be straight. Alongside, there was a boxed interview with Sunit, who was Sunita, a closet-lesbian, before a sex change operation. He now regretted he had gone ahead with the operation, because he hated being a man.

Yudi moved into the loo—to while away the time, he said to the voice of God in his breast. A man was blowing another to an audience of two. As soon as Yudi stepped in, everyone straightened up and returned to their respective stalls. They wanted to determine if he was a cat or a pigeon. Yudi gave them the Indian nod to indicate it was okay; he was a pigeon. Activity resumed instantly, with Yudi joining in as a member of the audience. In no time, the blown came in the blower's mouth. Yudi waited to see if the latter would spit out the former's cum. To his alarm, the fellow swallowed it.

'Idiot, haven't you heard of HIV?' he said to the man who was still on his knees.

'Kuchh nahi hota hai, nothing will happen,' the chap replied, waving him away.

'Fools,' Yudi thought to himself. 'They'll never learn.'

He came out of the loo and hung around by the showcases that displayed men's apparel. There were shirts, trousers and ties. The name of a Colaba department store, together with its phone number, was prominently advertised. That was for people like him, who would meekly buy the stuff legally, who wouldn't smash the glass and swipe everything that was exhibited. Discerning of the storeowners and the railways to position the showcases just outside the loo, Yudi thought. They served as a brilliant alibi for cruising males. No policeman could accuse a fellow of loitering there, looking for beefcake. The shirts and pants advertised did not interest Yudi. They were made of polyester yarn that didn't agree with his skin. What he invariably wore were cotton casuals, for which he shopped at Fashion Street on Mahatma Gandhi Road whenever he came to South Bombay to submit an article or meet his mother. One could bargain at Fashion Street and bring down the price of an item by half. The Colaba and Flora Fountain shops, on the other hand, were run by nouveau riche Sindhis who proudly proclaimed that they wouldn't reduce prices by even a paisa. Fuckers, Yudi cursed, reminded of a pink-faced queen who had shown him the door when he argued that it was cruel to deny Bombay-walas the small victory of a bargain with which to endure their wretched lives.

Yudi went into the loo again. He hadn't managed to empty his bladder earlier while the game was in progress. The dick is designed to perform only one function at a time, not two; one can either wank or pee. As his piss trickled down, he looked up and saw that the wall before him was full of sketches. All the drawings were in pencil or ball pen and depicted outsized erect penises and generous testicles. Indians will never stop being obsessed by size, he said to himself. The visuals were surrounded by names, mostly of flowers: Gulab, Champa, Chameli. Below the names were phone numbers. 'Do you have ten inch cock?' someone asked. 'Then I am letting you put whole thing in my ass.' He scoured the wall for witty, intelligent graffiti, but couldn't find any. Why couldn't three-fourths of Bombay's copywriters, who came here to cruise, serve as resource persons and contribute to the wall?

Yudi toyed with the idea of writing something on the wall. What? Yudi was here? And what if someone who knew him saw it when he came here to pee? After all, several journalists were Western Railway commuters and not too many people in Bombay had a name like Yudi. No. He would write, 'If you treat me to a chicken biryani, I'll give you a chocobar.' That was tasteful, unlike all the crude stuff with which the wall was defaced. He looked around him. There was always someone or the other playing with his dick. No question of scrawling his desires in their presence.

He checked out some of the men present. Sunday mornings, unlike peak hours on working days, brought the most unappetizing males to Churchgate. There was an old man with freckles on his skin and strands of white hair all over his head. He was dying to exhibit his dick to anyone who wanted a dekko. Unfortunately, no one was interested. Yudi lowered his eyes and glanced at the object on display. The octogenarian was surprisingly hard for his age. But the sight of it revolted Yudi. He turned his head and surveyed what was on the other side. There was a youngish man there who had gone deep into his stall. The fellow looked neither to his left nor right, but fixed his gaze on his own private part. Obviously, there was a price to be paid even to see it. Yudi rarely paid for sex. He believed the time for that had not yet come, although he was beginning to grey at the temples. But he was trim despite his forty-two years and had no tummy. His skin was remarkably free of wrinkles, causing many *chutiyas* to still mistake him for a student. 'You going to college?' they asked him.

The Churchgate loo has two sections. By convention one of them is the gay wing, the other the straight. The hetero wing of course has a better supply of mainstream men, but one dare not cruise in that area for fear of being bashed up. The gay wing gets nice guys only intermittently. As a college student, Yudi often felt like spending the whole day inside the loo to see what it yielded. But that was possible only in theory. There were loo attendants who knew what went on inside; some of them were on the payroll of the cops. They looked at people who hung around in the loo with a great deal of suspicion.

Yudi came out and positioned himself near the showcases again. A guy in his late teens, twenty at the most, was scrutinizing the shirts on display. He had all the characteristics that defined Yudi's type. He was on the thinner rather than the fatter side; his skin was the colour of Cadbury's chocolate (and as smooth too); he had straight (as opposed to curly) hair. If only he *is*, Yudi thought to himself. But the nice ones rarely were. Nevertheless, Yudi inched closer to him and let his fingers touch the boy's. The lad did not withdraw his hand. Yudi's heart thumped. There was success at the end of Step One. Moving on to Step Two, he allowed his fingers to tap the boy's gently. Massage them. Attempt to get entwined in them. The boy turned his head to the left and right to ensure no one was watching them. He looked at Yudi. He had to raise his head somewhat, for he was much shorter than Yudi, his eyes coming up to the level of, say, our hero's tits. Yudi decided it was time to switch to Step Three. He brought his left hand towards the young man's crotch and let his knuckles tap the soft part. As the fellow was wearing a stonewashed bush shirt over his ruffled jeans, Yudi had to grope for a few seconds to locate it. No sooner was he touched there, than the boy started in fear. How could anyone be so shameless! He gasped silently. Yudi, ignorant of the boy's confusion, drew closer. The odour of sweat from the young working-class body made his head spin, but then he noticed the lad's feet. The fellow was wearing slippers. The feet were as shapeless as a leper's, like the feet of most men who came to Churchgate. The uncut toenails were pallid. There were cracks on the soles, especially visible around the heels. Yuk, Yudi burped. The boy abruptly moved away. Yudi noticed that he entered the loo. Taking it as a cue, he followed him inside.

The boy found a stall at the far end of the gay wing and unzipped. As the stall next to his was vacant, Yudi rushed into it before any one else could beat him to the task. Some utterly helpful facilitator had broken the upper part of the wall that separated the boy's stall from his. Consequently, he had an unrestricted view of the lad's member, which was stiff all right. He was disappointed, though, by it's size. Where he wanted to bite into a cucumber, what was on display was a mere chilli. He did not like chillies; they did absolutely nothing for his tongue. The boy played with his chilli. On impulse, he looked over the wall, as if to check out Yudi's vegetable. What did he possess: a cucumber, a carrot, a radish, or a lady's finger? Yudi panicked. Although he owned quite a cucumber himself, it was not quite ready for the bazaar. Yudi attributed this to a variety of factors. Age, certainly, was one of them. Another was that in his youth he did not hoard his semen (like the Brahmans), but freely let it flow into the sewers of Bombay. Up to six times a day. Now his apparatus was taking it out on him by refusing to perform at the touch of a button. Or was all this sheer nonsense, old women's babble? He couldn't say.

While Yudi fondled his cucumber with his right hand, he slowly manoeuvred his left towards the chilli. The embarrassed owner of the chilli looked around once again, hoping that no one noticed.

But that was too much to expect. People went to Churchgate not just to perform, but also to watch. There were at least three men, all Sunday idlers, who were carefully monitoring the action and giving the lovers encouraging nods. The boy was now determined not to let Yudi touch his chilli. He formed a protective cover around it with both his hands. When Yudi pretended not to get the message even after this, the boy zipped up in disgust and left the loo.

Determined not to lose him, Yudi went after him. The boy had halted outside the showcases once again, examining nothing in particular. Yudi sidled up to him and whispered into his ear:

'I have a place.'

There was a pause of what seemed to Yudi like ages.

'Where?' the boy finally asked, in equally hushed tones. Yudi noticed some signs of interest on his face.

'Close by, New Marine Lines, you know Liberty cinema?' he panted, as his excitement rose. For once he did not have to say Nalla Sopara. This was empowering.'Will you come along with me?' he continued.

The boy did not reply; merely nodded to say yes.

They started walking together. As they came out of the station and waited at the pedestrian crossing for the signal to turn green, Yudi slipped a hand into the boy's. It was cold, in spite of the heat outside. The fingers were thin, bony. There wasn't much flesh around them, and this made clasping them an unpleasant experience. The boy did not withdraw his hand, but let Yudi hold it as long as it suited his fancy. Holding hands was an enjoyable preliminary as far as Yudi was concerned. Whenever he picked up people, he began with this ritual long before they actually reached his house. Most men, however, disengaged their hands after the first few minutes, saying, 'People are watching.' To this he would respond by reminding them that they were in India, not

America; it was all right for grown men to hold hands as a sign of friendship. But his partners remained unconvinced. Some of them continued to let him mash their fingers, but only out of politeness. Now, as they walked towards his mother's apartment, Yudi wondered which of these was the boy's scene. Was it mere politeness, or did he actually want Yudi's hand in his? He suddenly realized that he hadn't asked the boy his name.

'What's your name?' he said casually. 'Kishore,' the boy replied. Yudi wondered whether it was the boy's real name. Ninety per cent of the men he pataoed never told him their true names. It was even less likely for them to give him an honest address.

'And surname?' he went on.

'Mahadik,' came the monosyllabic answer. That seemed more plausible to Yudi than the boy's first name. He did seem the sort that would have a surname like Mahadik.

'How old are you?

'Nineteen.'

'How come you are at Churchgate on a Sunday morning?' Yudi persisted with the interview.

'Went to Asiatic to look for a job,' the boy said. 'One of my jaatwalas said there was a vacancy for a servant's post. Someone he knows was dismissed.'

'And you got the job?'

'The manager is out of town. They asked me to come and see him tomorrow. They made me wait outside the store for one hour just to tell me this.'

They walked hand-in-hand. They were now on the road that housed the American Center, the United Lodge of Theosophists, the SNDT Women's University and the Income Tax Office.

'You live in a posh area,' the boy remarked. It was the first time he had initiated a conversation on his own. Yudi grew apprehensive. Was the fellow going to ask him for money? Beware of jobless youth, he frequently told himself.

'Me, I live in faraway Nalla Sopara,' he countered, hoping that this would make the boy realize he wasn't rich. 'We're going to my mother's flat right now. Although it's in South Bombay, it isn't very large. Besides, my mother didn't buy it herself. My grandfather gave it to her as a gift. At that time it wasn't as expensive as it is today.'

'We're going to do it in front of your mother?' the boy asked, after a short pause.

Yudi was relieved that the conversation had shifted from the subject of wealth. 'She's out of the house, silly,' he replied. 'She's gone to Andhra Pradesh to attend a wedding.'

'Are you a Madrasi?'

'My father was, but not my mother. I don't consider myself a Madrasi. I don't even know the Madrasi language. I'm a pucca Bombay–wala.'

'What language do you speak at home?'

'English . . .,' Yudi mumbled, then quickly added, 'and Hindi.'

The boy seemed to ponder on this, then turned and looked up at Yudi. 'Why don't you live with your mother?' he asked.

'We fight when we're together,' Yudi said, hoping that would suffice. 'Besides, I'm not a Parsee.' The boy grinned and Yudi was relieved. He didn't want to be reminded of the scene his mother had created when he finally told her that he would move into a flat of his own, alone and in the same city.

They had reached the dargah of Haji Walad Haji Jamaluddin Asfaraini. Yudi put his finger to his heart and then to his lips.

'Why did you do that?' the boy wanted to know. 'You're not a Mohammedan, are you?'

'No, no, Hindu,' Yudi assured him. 'But why do you ask? You don't like Muslims?'

'They're unclean,' the boy said.

Yudi let that be. He had no desire to educate the boy about the ills of bigotry. All he wanted to do was ejaculate and give him the slip.

He fished out a handkerchief from his pocket. Rolling it into a neat rectangular strip, he brought it to the boy's eyes.

'What are you doing?' the boy yelled.

'Blindfolding you,' Yudi replied calmly. 'Only as a precaution. I always do it to my lovers. The idea is that they shouldn't know what building I live in. What if they came back tomorrow to blackmail me?'

Even as he uttered it, Yudi regretted that he'd used the word 'blackmail'. It amounted to putting ideas in people's heads.

'Do I look like a blackmailer to you?' the boy asked, hurt.

He looked comic as he walked with bandaged eyes, his right hand in his partner's left.

'I didn't say *you* were a blackmailer,' Yudi explained. 'I like to be extra cautious, that's all. In English, we say "Prevention is better than cure."'

They were now on the street on which his mother lived. Her building was the second one on the left. An elderly Sindhi gentleman who wore only white shirts and black trousers, and lived two floors above his mother, was getting into his car. He had known Yudi since Yudi was a boy, when he lived with his parents, and always thought he had a loose screw somewhere in his head. Even so, the sight of him leading a blindfolded fellow into the building was too strange for words. He looked intently at Yudi. 'What's this?' his raised eyebrows asked.

'My servant,' Yudi explained. 'Brought him to Bombay Hospital for cataract surgery. You know?'

'When is mummy coming back?' the gentleman sighed, as he turned on the ignition of his Fiat.

'Couple of days,' said Yudi and hurried away.

He led the boy into Pherwani Mansion (which was what the building was called). He pressed the button for the lift, and was relieved when it came down empty with no more inquisitive neighbours in it. He urged the boy to enter quickly, fastened the 'collapsible' doors in great haste, and took the lift to the third floor.

'You called me your servant?' the boy asked him in the short time the lift was between the first and third floors.

'Only to say something to that fat Sindhi to shut him up,' Yudi responded.

'Does he know about you?'

'Who knows? People don't go around telling you "Aha, I know all about you, bringing pretty boys to fuck in your mother's flat while she's away."'

The boy kept quiet. He didn't like being called a pretty boy. Nor did he approve of Yudi's use of the word 'fuck'. Yudi unlocked the door of his mother's flat and led the boy into the tiny sitting room. He un-bandaged his eyes and brought him a glass of water.

'Here we are, then,' he said, as soon as the boy had finished drinking. 'Shuru karen? Shall we begin?'

Whenever Yudi picked up strangers and took them home, he gladly offered them the active role in bed. He had a theory based on years of experience. As long as men were allowed to penetrate, there was no fear of their returning afterwards to demand money or beat you up. Some even thought it beneath their dignity to accept cash from someone they had buggered. For such a person, according to them, was at best a hijra. And their heroism and sense of valour did not permit them to assault a eunuch. It was only when these men were penetrated that they became wounded tigers. They felt emasculated. They could then even murder.

Currency notes, wristwatches, walkmans, sneakers, were not compensation enough; these couldn't restore their lost masculinity. They accepted the presents with one hand and put a knife in your back with the other.

Yudi didn't mind it if his lovers thought of him as a hijra. It was so much more relaxing if one was freed of the need to perform. Performance meant servicing one's equipment regularly, as one did a car or an air-conditioner. Who had the time for that?

Yudi was now on a coir mat that he had spread out on the carpeted floor, while the boy was over him, struggling to insert his chilli. He was clearly a novice in the art. 'Has it gone in, has it gone in?' he asked every few minutes, compelling Yudi to mutter a 'yes' or a 'no'. Yudi hated it when his partners spoke during sex. Their bad breath made him sick. This boy, however, was a gutkha addict; though the strong, sweet smell gave him a headache, it was preferable to the foul odour of fish or onions. The boy pumped, groaning as he did. Suddenly he said: 'Nirodh phat gaya, my condom's torn.'

'God!' Yudi exclaimed. 'Don't you even know how to use a condom? How old are you? Nineteen, isn't it?'

'We'll do it without a condom,' the boy suggested, instantly reminding Yudi of the suicidal fool at Churchgate who swallowed a stranger's cum. But Yudi did not argue with the boy. He didn't want to play teacher all the time. As it was obvious to him that the boy would never succeed in fucking him, there was no danger. The semen would merely trickle down his buttocks. That's all.

Before long, the boy became still. His groaning stopped.

'Shall I get up?' he asked.

'Not until I'm done, you selfish chap,' Yudi replied. And then he thrashed his body in the north-south and east-west directions, the boy on top of him like a cat above its prey, till he too had spent himself, but on the floor.

Both men rose. Yudi began to dress and motioned to the boy to do likewise. However, the boy demanded that he be shown the bathroom first. Yudi pointed out the bathroom to him, and saw that he went there and put his chilli under the tap. There was a bucket under the tap that he didn't bother to move aside. He emerged from the bathroom wiping his genitals dry with a hand towel. Yudi took the towel from him and put it in his pocket. Nalla Sopara would be its new home now; he couldn't have his mother wiping her face with it after this. Observing the boy closely, Yudi asked him:

'How come you don't have a beard yet?'

'Because when I was a kid, I used to eat my food straight from the tava,' he replied, astonishing Yudi. He had never heard such an absurd answer, although he knew Maharashtrians to be irrational.

'What's the connection between your beard and a hot plate?' he asked, and regretted it, noticing the boy's discomfiture.

'Don't know, but that's what people in my village say.'

'Where's your village?'

'Khed Taluka, Raigad district.'

'Oh, so you're one of Shivaji's descendants!'

'Not at all. I don't like Shivaji,' the boy grimaced.

They were ready. Yudi brought out his handkerchief to blindfold the boy once again. This time he did not resist. Meekly acquiesced in his humiliation. Besides, as he saw it, there was no humiliation here, really, for it was he who had fucked the man. Their roles were quite clear. When Yudi undid the blindfold ten minutes later, the boy found himself outside the Liberty cinema, before a huge poster of *Hum Apke Hain Kaun*. They gazed at the poster that depicted a song sequence featuring Salman Khan. There were other posters near by which they scrutinized in silence.

'Have you seen the film?' Yudi broke the silence.

'Twice. Have you?'

'Not yet. Will you see it again with me?'

'When?'

'Tomorrow?'

'Give me your telephone number,' the boy said. 'I'll call you and let you know if I am coming.'

That was the catch. They always asked for telephone numbers that Yudi couldn't risk giving. What if they made threatening calls at midnight, as one of them had?

'Don't have a telephone at Nalla Sopara,' he lied. 'Why don't you give me your contact number instead?'

'I live in a transit camp at Mahim. There's no contact number there.'

The matter ended inconclusively. What was clear to Yudi was that his boy lover and he were not going to see HAHK together.

'Chai?' Yudi changed the topic.

'Okay,' said the boy.

They entered the Marine Restaurant, one of the area's many Irani joints. Here Yudi took out a pack of cigarettes from his shirt pocket, offered one to the boy (which he gladly accepted), put another to his own lips, and struck a match to light both their fags.

'Do chai,' he said to the waiter, without asking the boy if he wanted something to eat.

They puffed. Yudi noticed that the boy was flicking ash on the marble-top table.

'Don't do that,' he screamed, calling out to the waiter for an ashtray. 'These are old antique tables that you find only in Bombay's Iranis. Don't deface them.'

Though the words made no sense to the boy, he complied, and used the ashtray that the waiter slammed down on their table. He put a question to Yudi: 'What's your name?'

'Oh, didn't I tell you?' he answered. 'Yudhister, the eldest of the Pandavas.'

The tea arrived and they sipped quietly. The boy finished his in large gulps.

'Why did your parents give you a name like that? So old fashioned!'

'Our family is cultured. We like things classical. Names like Rahul or Ramesh or . . . (He was about to say Kishore but checked himself in time) . . . Rajeev are too common.'

The boy asked: 'Is Kishore a common name?'

'Maybe,' Yudi replied. 'But I like your surname. Mahadik. Maha Dick. Odd surname, though, for someone with such a small one.'

There, he'd done it again. He'd slept with a working-class boy and now he had grown tired of the fellow and needed to get rid of him. He hoped the boy wouldn't understand the word dick, that he would miss the insult. But the boy did not.

'You're making kachra of my surname,' he protested and gave him a hard, defiant look.

'Sorry. Was only joking,' Yudi laughed and slapped himself. 'Don't take it to heart.'

'Joker,' the boy said and laughed.

They got up to leave. Yudi asked the boy where he was headed. Lower Parel. That meant they would be travelling on the same route. They walked towards Marine Lines station. The boy was unfamiliar with the area and let Yudi lead him. He noticed that the funny Pandava had stopped holding his hand.

'Where do you work?' he asked.

Yudi wished he would shut up. He was beginning to get annoyingly talkative.

'I'm a journalist . . . reporter . . . you know?'

'Reporter? Which paper do you work for?'

'No particular paper. I'm what we call a freelance journalist. I write for different newspapers and magazines.'

A doubt crossed the boy's mind. Would Yudi expose him by writing about their encounter?

'What do you write about?' he inquired after a few minutes.

'This and that,' came the bored reply.

But suddenly the boy said something that made Yudi's ears pop up in amazement, like a dog's.

'I belong to the working class, and you to the talking class.'

'That is clever! Where did you get that from?'

'From nowhere.'

'How far have you studied?'

'Ninth pass, tenth fail,' the boy said unabashedly.

They had begun to ascend the steps of the footbridge that led to the station. There was a long queue for tickets. Yudi looked at his wristwatch; it was noon. When he went to Churchgate, the time was a few minutes past ten. He would have been at Nalla Sopara by now, trekking home from the station, had he not met the boy: a good two hours wasted. The queue was unusually long now, as compared to the morning. It was as if in the two hours between then and now, all of Bombay had woken up and decided to travel.

The boy spoke in Marathi to the man in front of them. 'There's a problem,' he reported to Yudi, after he was finished with the man. What was the problem, Yudi wanted to know. But no one could tell him. It could be anything: power failure, a goods train derailed, a child run over. What did it matter? The upshot was the trains were late. Living where he did, Yudi was entirely dependent on local trains; he was quite exasperated at the frequency with which these things happened nowadays. 'Shit,' he swore.

There was an announcement. 'Owing to signalling failure between Matunga and Mahim, all up and down trains are running twenty to thirty minutes late.' The announcement was repeated in Hindi and Marathi. It was followed by a commotion among the commuters. Yudi surveyed the queue to see if there were any interesting young men within easy reach. To his disappointment, none in the queue appealed to him. Yudi yawned. The queue inched forward. At last they were at the window. 'Ek Lower Parel, Ek Nalla Sopara,' Yudi said, slapping down a hundred-rupee note. The man at the window issued him his tickets, but made him wait by the side for his change, even as he attended to the next person in the queue, and the next, and the next, and the next. When five whole minutes passed, Yudi blew: 'Are you giving me my money or should I write about you in the newspapers? What is your name?'

His change was returned, but with it came dirty looks.

'Cool down,' said the boy to Yudi, who seemed to have forgotten about his presence.

They climbed down the steps that went to platform number one, the platform for slow trains. It was full of passengers. According to the lit indicator, the next train due was only up to Andheri. A thought crossed both Yudi's mind and the boy's. Simultaneously. Would they be travelling together, or would Yudi cross over to platform number three and board a fast train to Virar? After a while, it was decided that Yudi would take the Andheri local along with the boy, see him off at Lower Parel, and then change trains.

They walked to the far end of the platform. A group of kotis hovered outside the gent's toilet. They blushed and giggled as they saw Yudi with the boy, whose hand he deliberately held, to make them jealous.

'This is another famous cruising spot,' Yudi informed the boy. To which his reply was, 'I know.'

Yudi wondered just how much he knew.

The queens tried to make eye contact with Yudi. They gave up, however, when they realized he was serious about his partner.

When the train arrived, the two of them boarded the very first compartment. Yudi knew this to be the gay coach by convention. Activity, however, was restricted to the empty space between entrances and exits. The train had to be quite full for people to have a go at each other. At Marine Lines, trains were never that full even at peak hour. Now, as always, there were plenty of seats available. Yudi followed the boy and occupied a seat next to him.

More passengers sprang in at Charni Road and Grant Road, increasing the rush in the gangway. By the time they reached Bombay Central, all seats were taken and people were beginning to press on each other in the aisles. In the Virar trains that Yudi caught, this happened all the time, and he was thankful for it. Rubbing his body against someone's was the best way to handle the tedium of the journey—it was much better than reading or singing bhajans or playing cards.

The train left Bombay Central. Only one more station— Mahalakshmi. And then the boy and he would part for ever. However, no sooner did the train leave Bombay Central, than it stopped. Seconds passed, then minutes, but the train refused to budge. Yudi did not bother to answer the question of a fellow passenger, who asked him, 'Kya hua?' Didn't the fool know that the trains were late? He looked out of the window and saw several out-of-Bombay trains parked in the shunting yard. The Rajdhani Express was being washed with hosepipes. The sight of these long-distance trains excited him; Yudi decided he would go on a holiday soon. Not with any of his pickups, as he had done on a couple of occasions in the past with disastrous consequences, but by himself. He loved vacationing at hill stations and beach resorts, although he didn't get much sex there, not even if he was willing to pay.

The train started with a jerk and reached Mahalakshmi. Suddenly Yudi realized he hadn't noted down the boy's address. He took out his pocket diary and asked for the address. The boy hesitated. Realizing there was no escape, as his man friend waited expectantly, note book and ball pen in hand, he blurted out an address: Transit Camp, behind Citylight Cinema, Mahim.

'Is this your real address?'

'Yes.'

'Then how come you're getting off at Lower Parel?'

'Going to have lunch with my mausi.'

'Is the Transit Camp near Citylight well-known?'

'Yes.'

In the past, Yudi had often been duped by one-night-stands who told him that they lived in a particular building and asked him to see them at such-and-such place. The buildings were purely fictional, and the rogues never showed up at the pre-determined spot.

'Can I come there and ask for you?' Yudi asked.

'Yes.'

The boy had gone back to monosyllabic answers. Yudi was silent for a while, as the train ran between Mahalakshmi and Lower Parel at a good speed. A shadow of sadness appeared on his face, making him frown. Casual sex was so strange. You met someone, became intimate with him for a few hours or even minutes, and then bid him goodbye—perhaps for ever. There was little chance of ever seeing him again, especially in Bombay. Yudi tried not to get involved with his lovers, or else life would be nothing but a series of heartbreaks.

His pensive mood changed as the train slowed down. The boy was asking him a question:

'Shall I come with you?'

The question hit Yudi like a thunderbolt.

'No, no,' he said, with irritation in his voice. 'How can you come with me?'

The boy got up and moved towards the door. Yudi felt his heartbeat rise. What if the boy refused to leave until he was paid for his services? He called it his litmus test: if guys lingered on when the moment of parting came, it meant they were hustlers.

The train halted at Lower Parel. Yudi forsook his seat and came to the door of the coach. Not to say good bye to the boy, who had got down without fuss, but to confirm that he didn't hop into the next coach with the intention of following him!

His seat gone, Yudi had no option but to stand in the doorway till the train reached Andheri. At every station he examined faces for Mr Right. But luck wasn't on one's side every time. The gay coach didn't seem to be living up to its reputation. It was stuffed with the most insipid, uninspiring males, entirely devoid of sexuality. Even Dadar and Bandra, that always brought in an army of commuters, did not yield results. The former was famous for its mobs of working men who switched from Central to Western Railway, and vice versa, on their way to office and home. The latter, the queen of the suburbs as it was appropriately called, was the hottest spot in town for queens, but not today. The sight of sweaty old men towards whom he did not feel an iota of attraction sickened Yudi. 'Stand properly,' he felt compelled to say to one of them whose arms were matted with long white hair. Yudi moved closer to the footboard and tried to lean out of the coach, like all his young heart-throbs. The mere sight of these men turned him on, as they leaned out together, in twos and threes, tossing their hair in the wind, and crotches pressed against buttocks. 'You'll fall off,' he heard someone say to him, as he thrust his body dangerously out, and breathed in a shitty odour. Clearly his days for acrobatics were over. No one cautioned the young men who hung out of rakes day after day. He traced the whiff of foul air to its source: four men shitting at a distance of not more than a few feet from each other. Strange hour of day to empty one's bowels, Yudi thought. He glanced at his watch and saw that it was nearing half past one in the afternoon.

Andheri. He alighted, and headed for the gents'. Nothing here. He crossed over to platform number three to resume his journey. There was no train to Virar for another thirty-five minutes. Yudi whiled away his time drinking cup after cup of sugary tea at the platform tea stall. He thought of the boy. There was an innocence about him that made him a lovable kid. Someday Yudi would go to the Transit Camp at Citylight to look for him. Couldn't appearances be deceptive, though? Perhaps the boy wasn't innocent after all, and harboured similar ideas of trying to track him down— and not for love or thrills. Everybody wants a sugar daddy; the difference in age and income between the boy and himself made him a fit candidate for the post. Hopefully the blindfolding would take care of that, since the boy saw neither the street nor the building into which he was taken. Yudi sat on a bench and dozed off. A shoeshine boy tapped his knee. 'Polish, sir?' Yudi opened his eyes and saw the dust on his shoe.

'Okay,' he said. He ordered the ten-year-old to hurry up as his train was announced. Hordes of passengers spilled out of the train when it arrived. 'These people should be beaten up all over again,' Yudi heard commuters who were waiting on the platform protest. 'In spite of announcements on the public address system, they board Virar locals meant only for us!' Although Yudi thought of himself as a democrat, he found himself agreeing. Only those who had to travel to and from Nalla Sopara every day knew how hellish it could be. Not that he couldn't afford a first-class season ticket. But if he travelled first, he would lose out on all the fun he had with young men: only old-fogeys bought first-class tickets.

Yudi didn't have to make an effort to enter the train: the wave of humanity behind him boosted him up. Shortly after the train started, he felt his crotch being massaged. The train was so overcrowded that he had some difficulty in figuring out who it was. When he finally did, he allowed the chap to fondle him for a while, before angrily shaking him off. The man was what he classified as B: he was neither attracted to, nor repelled by him. He met such types on the train every day.

Everyone, including the man he had rebuffed, got off at Borivili. Yudi rushed to catch a window seat. Five times as many passengers, however, got in, and the bogie no longer seemed fit for humans.

The train took off once again. The high rises of Dahisar and Mira Road, the saltpans of Bhayandar and Naigaon, and the span bridge of Vasai Road came and went, even as a rejuvenating breeze lashed against Yudi's face. The train thundered over Vasai creek, and he went into a familiar trance, imagining he was a sanyasi who had renounced the world and now nothing at all mattered. Then, at last, he was home. The diamond-shaped signboard on the platform said: Nalla Sopara. Yudi waded his way towards the exit with some difficulty, before jumping off.

'Goodbye, train,' he said.

His den was only two minutes away from the station. Before he knew it, he was there, entering the building, climbing the stairs, unlocking his door. He made himself a cup of tea and switched on the TV.

two

lost . . .

The studio apartment in which Yudi lived was bought with a housing loan. The finance company, that gave him the several hundred thousand rupees that were required, was initially reluctant. He didn't have a 'permanent' job, they argued. Freelancing, in their opinion, counted for nought. Finally, it was an appointment with the Vice President of the company that got him his loan. The executive agreed to sign on his application form, provided he did him a favour. His wife wrote short stories. Would Yudi help her publish them? That was easy. The subs who worked for *The Democratic Journal* always pestered him for matter; they gladly published the wife's story without reading it even once.

The loan obtained, Yudi had to choose the right builder. The Rahejas and Lokhandwalas were out—they were simply unaffordable. Several builders were said to have links with the underworld; as a newspaperman, Yudi had authentic information on this. The land on which they constructed their buildings often belonged to innocent people who were evicted at gunpoint (and sometimes murdered), kids and all. Yudi didn't want to live in a flat that would be haunted by their ghosts; after all, he lived alone.

In the end, he transacted with a god-fearing builder from

Ahmedabad. Yudi was convinced that this man wouldn't dupe him. His office looked less like an office and more like a temple, with framed portraits of every god and his cousin. There were no files anywhere in sight. The fragrant smoke of agarbattis permeated the room. Whenever Yudi went to see him, he was offered grated coconut as prasad. The gentleman invariably discussed his fears with him, one of which was that if he cheated his customers, he would be reborn as a cockroach.

Yudi did not like the layout of his flat. As the Mahatma sat with him in his temple and unfolded sheets of paper with diagrams, he demanded that the plan of his flat be redrawn. The kitchen was too large, so was the loo. If the kitchen and the bogs were reduced in size, they might even be able to carve out an extra room for him, though the total area of the flat was less than 500 square feet. He could use this room to fuck, though of course to the Mahatma he described it as a guest room. The Mahatma was shocked that Yudi should want a smaller kitchen. 'What about bhabhi?' he said. 'She has to spend her whole day in the kitchen!'

'Bhabhi has run away with her lover,' Yudi told him.

'Shiv, Shiv, Shiv,' the man chanted. 'Kalyug, sir, Kalyug. It is the end of the world!'

Yudi waited to hear him say that bhabhi would be reborn as a cockroach. But this time the man was silent on the subject of sin and retribution.

For the first year, the flat was bare. Yudi was too broke to invest in furniture or household gadgets. He managed only with necessities: a mattress, a hot plate and a writing table and chair (at which he also ate his dinner). By and by, he saved up enough for a gas connection (which he obtained in the black market), a stainless steel cupboard (not Godrej) and a folding camp cot. (When his lovers visited him, he made it a point to sleep on the mattress, not the camp cot, afraid it would give way.) Slowly, a fridge came into the flat, followed by a set of cane sofas, and then a colour TV.

Whenever he went out on assignment, Yudi would pick up curios. They served as souvenirs of the place he had been to, a place he would probably never visit again. He had Nandi bulls, Buddhas, Khandobas, fancy bottle openers, brass cars, bullock carts, paper-weights, earthenware pots, coloured stones, conches, sea-shells, coins, lighters, shivalings, tea-sets, goblets and wine glasses in his collection. Now he evenly spread them out all over the flat, on his desk, fridge, side tables, the ledges of windows, even on the floor. Together with the imitation antiques that he found at Chor Bazaar (mostly sculptures), they gave his flat the look of the Prince of Wales Museum. To complete the picture, he bought a Kashmiri carpet from a roadside carpet seller who hung around at Vasai Road station.

Yudi was fond of music. His mother, to make up for the commotion she caused when he left her home, presented him with a hi-powered music system when he moved into his flat. He classified his audio cassettes into four groups. First, Hindustani and Carnatic classical (instrumental and vocal): Ravi Shankar, Siddheswari Devi, Bhimsen Joshi, M.S. Subbulakshmi et al. Second, Hindi film songs of the 50s, 60s and 70s: everyone from Talat Mehmood, to Asha Bhosle. Third, ghazals: the wildly famous (Ghulam Ali), as well as the almost anonymous (Jutika Roy). Fourth, Western pop music: The Beatles, Boney M, Bryan Adams, Celine Dion and so on. What he listened to at a given time depended on his mood, and on the background of his visiting lovers.

The men Yudi picked up could themselves be put into three boxes. Box 1: English-speaking professionals, all below the age of forty. For them he usually played classical music. Box 2: College students from the Marathi/Gujarati medium. He made these guys compulsorily listen to Western pop music, assuring them it would make them trendy. Box 3: Men from the working class—waiters, hairdressers, motor mechanics, newsboys, auto rickshaw drivers. Needless to say, it was Hindi film music that he played for these chaps. However, most of them being much younger than he, they were lulled into sleep by his choice. What they wanted was fast-paced, action-packed music of the 90s, Anu Malik and company. For them, Yudi switched on to the music channels on TV.

Though he wasn't exactly a collector, Yudi owned a large number of books. Some of them were books he had reviewed (whenever topical assignments did not come his way). Others were books he'd gathered from his BA and MA days, most of them picked up from the pavements of Flora Fountain. And then, if a book shook the world, Yudi went and bought it. All the books were housed in the fucking room in a bookcase made of plywood and glass. Somehow, it seemed right to Yudi, this coming together of sex and the word.

He had plans to write his own book some day. He couldn't say when. Nor did he know what the book would be about. All he knew was that it would be written. Meanwhile, there was life.

A day in the life of Yudi was roughly as follows. He rose early. The morning hours were spent at his desk, reading, writing. Saraswati, the maid, came around 8.30 to do the dishes, the swabbing and cleaning. As she worked, he buried himself in the newspaper—*The Times* on Mondays, Wednesdays and Fridays, and *The Indian Express* on the other four days of the week. After she left, he had his breakfast: cornflakes, omelette, toast. Then he showered and left the house around 11, by which time the peak hour scramble on trains had subsided.

On reaching town, Yudi first had his lunch at an Irani

restaurant. The editors he had to meet were themselves away at lunch till about 2.30, so he wasn't in a hurry.

He spent his afternoons in newspaper offices, discussing the articles he planned to write, accepting commissions. Even as he discussed with the editor and his subs, he engaged in banter. Most journalists he worked with knew that he was gay; and they knew that he knew that they knew. This knowledge helped everyone get rid of those invisible, annoying communication barriers. What he liked about these journalists was that there were no heterosexist assumptions in the things that they said. They talked to him about his boyfriends as they spoke to other men about their girlfriends. It was possible that in their heart of hearts, they thought he was weird; but nothing showed on their faces. Some of them envied him.

Yudi usually had tea with his editors before he left. It was past four by then, and he spent the next three hours going to public lectures, exhibitions or performances that were forever taking place in South Bombay. Although his mother's house was close by, he never went there on weekdays. He had set apart his Sundays for visits to the old lady; in his opinion that was more than enough.

As soon as it became dark, he cruised. He had an A to Z of all the loos in South Bombay where men had sex with men. He bought it from the office of *Bombay Dost*, for which he occasionally wrote. He popped in at all or some of these loos every evening between 7 and 8. The stinking places were always humming with erotic activity. Orgies in the dark, amidst piss and shit. The foul smell, somehow, made the sex more enjoyable. Having spent so much of his life in these loos Yudi had come to the conclusion that there was indeed something sensual about filth. If the toilets were clean, scrubbed with phenyl, patrons wouldn't achieve orgasm. Of course, it wasn't only after dark that Yudi went to the loos on his map. A full bladder always provided him the excuse to visit them even during the day, as he walked from one newspaper office to another. This was why he loved walking.

By 8.30 p.m., Yudi was in a Virar fast on his way home. By 10.30 p.m., he was in his flat, munching the dinner that the dabba-wala had left at his door. A little bit of radio and/or TV after dinner, and he was in bed, snoring.

This was an average day in the life of Yudi. All days, however, were not the same. Days when he brought home a lover, although few and far between now, were different. The lovers sat up drinking late into the night. Yudi chucked the dabba-wala's food into the dustbin, and ordered stuff from a Chinese takeaway on the telephone. He insisted that his lovers showered before they huddled up in bed; he couldn't stand the smell of grime that emanated from their bodies. With all this, it was well past midnight before they switched off the lights and began making love. This did not deter him, though, from waking them up at the crack of dawn (as soon as the locals began plying), and asking them to leave. He didn't want to start a new day with last night's faces. But after they were gone, he went back to bed, and didn't rise until noon. That was the advantage of being a freelancer; one didn't have to write out a casual leave application and timidly approach one's boss.

The lovers Yudi brought home weren't always picked up from the loos. Only chalu, streetsmart guys went there, and he didn't want to spend all his time ensuring his purse wasn't stolen. There were other places, such as Azad Maidan, where he found more straightforward men. Some Hare Krishna folks lectured here to a random group of devotees every evening. As they spoke, pointing out, for example, that 'all other things you read, papers, magazines, etc., are useless yet you buy them again and again; the Bhagavad Gita is precious and you buy it only once in a lifetime', the sun went down. Hurricane lamps were lit; the discourses went on. It was then that bodies connected—furtively at first. The listeners stood so close to each other that fingers unconsciously kissed; crotches dug into backsides. In this congenial climate of spirituality and romance, Yudi found guys he could risk taking home.

Yudi also looked for sex and solace in unusual places and among unusual men. Men who were physically disabled, for instance, turned him on. It could be any handicap: blindness, lameness, a hunched back; he was ready to give anything to sleep with them. Whenever Yudi spotted a blind man on the street, he ran up to him to ask if he needed help, say, to cross the road. The man was usually overwhelmed by the Good Samaritan's kindness. He put away his white cane and gave his hand to Yudi. Yudi clasped the hand firmly. Even if he didn't succeed in getting the poor soul into bed, he at least had a highly charged walk with him, as their hands had intercourse out there in the open.

'Are you a dhakka start?' the man said to Yudi, who had fallen for the thick veins on his erect penis. Yudi had set eyes on the man in the Nalla Sopara loo as soon as he got off his train. He noticed the veins even in the dull light of a zero-watt bulb. After that, he couldn't take his eyes off. They stood in their respective stalls and talked.

'What's your choice?' the man asked him.

'Everything. How about you?'

'Biryani khayega?'

Yudi knew all the slang of working class homos. 'Dhakka start' was gay. 'Biryani Khayega' was rimming.

'Don't worry. I've done it with many famous dhakka starts, including that Ajay Roy Ley-Lund,' the man went on, punning on the name of the celebrated bus manufacturer from London to indicate that the gay activist Ajay Roy was passive.

'Really?' Yudi exclaimed. So these were the man's credentials! He had gone to bed with India's most famous homosexual! Of course, he could be lying. But Yudi was too obsessed with those veins. They clouded his judgement. He would have taken him home any way, regardless of whether or not he had ridden the Ajay Ley-Lund bus. Nor did he blindfold him. The man didn't seem the type who would allow a kerchief to be tied over his eyes.

Back at the flat, they did everything. Yudi ate and relished his biryani, as Asha Bhosle provided the background score. The man's name was Dnyaneshwar. His parents had named him after the revered Marathi saint, Maharashtra's answer to Lord Krishna, in the hope that he too would grow up and show people the Way. Did they know that he would become a dhakka start who would treat the famished to biryani?

Dnyaneshwar was a trainee policeman. That explained those veins. When it was time to leave, what was waiting to happen happened. He took out a penknife from his pocket and began to play with it. Next, he fished out a pen and noted down Yudi's name, address, telephone number (which he saw on the telephone). They were his weapons: pen, penis and penknife. He wanted dough. A thousand rupees. He wasn't going to leave until he was paid. Yudi realized he was conned. But one thousand rupees was way beyond his budget. He started with a hundred, then doubled and trebled it. But Dnyaneshwar was adamant. He spelt out his options. He could shove his penknife into Yudi's belly. He could telephone the cops. He could set hoodlums on his patron. He could find out where he worked, and spill the beans. Finally, Yudi bargained for eight hundred. The saint-policeman didn't leave even after that. He wanted a peg of whisky. That was when Yudi hit upon the idea of taking him to Testosterone, Colaba's gay bar, owned by Mr Pallonji. Not tonight, for it was late already, but tomorrow. He would get all the queens in the bar to manhandle the bugger, strip him naked and take him to The Wall, Gay Bombay's very own Stonewall. From there they would hurl him into the sea. This Dnyaneshwar was no saint. He deserved to die.

Dnyaneshwar didn't leave the flat until he had finished Yudi's khamba of whisky. He teetered as he started his motorcycle. But he remembered what Yudi told him: he would meet him at Nalla Sopara station at 8 p.m. the next day, from where they would go to Testosterone.

The psychedelic lighting in the disco made everyone look as if sprayed with silver dust. Music blared. The dance floor wasn't packed yet, for there were ninety minutes to midnight. Waiters with V-shaped bodies and tight butts, more sleep-worthy than any of Testosterone's regular clients, walked up and down with trays of alcohol. A very fat man was on the dance floor, dancing all by himself. He was so bloated, he looked like the corpse of someone who drowned in the Arabian Sea and bobbed to the surface three days later. He gyrated to the music as if he were possessed. Yudi bought himself a beer and joined the others in watching the fat man's performance. The crowd applauded him, not giving him a chance to realize what a spectacle he made of himself.

A call girl came up to them.

'Hi love,' she said, her jaws dancing as she ate chewing gum.

'Hi,' Yudi replied coldly and looked the other way.

Dnyaneshwar, however, stared at her. The girl felt slighted by Yudi. But she persevered.

'Care to buy me a drink?'

Yudi gave her a dirty look, and fired his favourite salvo. 'Who do you think you are, Meryl Streep?'

The girl got the message and left them alone.

Dnyaneshwar nudged Yudi. He wanted to know why he'd sent this saamaan away.

'This is a gay bar, for heaven's sake,' Yudi told his date. 'A call girl has no right to be here. What's she trying to do, reform us?'

The policeman did not understand, for he believed that men fucked men only when women weren't around.

Dnyaneshwar refused to dance with Yudi. His eyes searched the crowded bar for the call girl. Yudi decided to leave him alone. He would mobilize his army of queens for Operation Stonewall. He spotted Gulab, the undisputed queen of queens, just as the rose is the queen of flowers.

'Hi Gulab,' he hugged him. 'Good to see you again.'

'Hiii!' Gulab drawled. 'Where have you *been*, darling?' As he spoke, he flicked his wrists. 'Meet my twin brother,' he said, and produced a fellow who was his replica.

Yudi was astonished. He had no idea Gulab had a brother who was an identical twin.

'Is he also . . .?'

'You bet he is.'

Yudi told Gulab all about Dnyaneshwar. Gulab loved action; he got to work at once. He approached all his dancing queens, including two in drag, and whispered into their ears. The queens shrieked with laughter. They were all for vendetta. Everyone sacrificed their dancing and assembled at the bar. Here, as they sipped their lager, they worked out their strategy. But there was a long time still for Testosterone to close. They would return to the dance floor, and regroup ten minutes before closing time.

Meanwhile, Dnyaneshwar had located Meryl Streep and taken her to a corner table. The lady didn't seem too keen to be screwed by him. She was used to a more upmarket clientele. A man like Dnyaneshwar appeared to her the Foras Road type. She quoted a price that she knew he simply wouldn't be able to afford—Rs 1000 for the night. Plus he would have to pay for the room. As he haggled over the price, she continued to be obstinate. Just then Dnyaneshwar spotted Yudi, excused himself from the table, and waded through the mass of oddballs to reach Yudi, to request him to buy him two beers—one for himself, the other for his girlfriend.

'You're doing rather well for yourself,' Yudi said to him with puckered eyebrows, as he pushed two hundred-rupee notes across the counter and directed the waiter to serve him his beer.

'Bloody extortionist,' he swore under his breath after Dnyaneshwar left with the frothing glasses.

The music and the dancing reached a crescendo. Couples were wrapped in each other's arms, smooching fast and furious. Some receded into Testosterone's anteroom where they unzipped. Others were having it off in the washroom. No one had any inkling of what the time was, or how it went. Till the DJ announced the last number for the night. Yudi looked at his watch: it was five minutes to two. He went to the bar for a quick beer, before it closed. Gulab came up to him. He and the boys would go to The Wall in advance to set up shop. Yudi and Creepy Crawly could follow. People left in single file. The owner, Mr Pallonji, said good night to each of them personally. As soon as they were out, everyone lit up. They stood in groups outside the front door of their favourite disco, the only place on this lonely planet where they could be themselves, and played the fool.

Dnyaneshwar appeared. He asked Yudi if he knew the exact time of the first train to Virar.

'At 4.15 a.m.,' Yudi told him. Then, offering him a cigarette, he invited him to the Gateway of India. 'We'll take a cab to Churchgate from there,' he said.

Dnyaneshwar might have refused to go with Yudi had he not mentioned the cab. Walking put him off, but the prospect of travelling to the station comfortably in a taxi convinced him that it was in his best interest to hang around with this dhakka start. He could also wangle some more money out of him before they finally parted.

The policeman yawned noisily as they made their way towards Apollo Bunder, past the Radio Club. It was obvious that he wasn't used to staying up late. They walked another minute or so, when Yudi spotted Gulab and his gang.

'Welcome,' Gulab said to Yudi and his guest. 'Welcome, welcome.'

'My friends,' Yudi explained to Dnyaneshwar. 'They're all headed for Churchgate, so we'll go together.'

Dnyaneshwar burst out laughing at the sight of the queens. 'Chhakke log,' he called them. 'Ek dum hijre.' Ignoring his remark, Gulab proceeded to introduce them one by one. First, his twin brother Raat Rani. Then Pinky, Sweety, Badnaseeb, Akash, Hira, Moti, Chandni, Laila, Salma, Salma-ka-Balma. The two drag queens were called Anarkali and Umrao Jaan.

'We're from Mu-lund,' Anarkali said to Dnyaneshwar, giving him a tweak on the cheek.

Yudi lit a cigarette and offered one to Dnyaneshwar. They smoked in silence. Gulab and his friends chattered like magpies, keeping a close watch on their prey. No sooner had Dnyaneshwar finished his cigarette and stubbed it under his leather boots, than Gulab gave his gang the signal to strike. At this, all twelve of them pounced on the cop. One tightly held a hand to his lips so he wouldn't be able to raise an alarm. Others seized his arms and legs to prevent him from boxing, kicking. Still others pinched his cheeks (in the manner of Anarkali), pulled his hair, dug their manicured nails into his flesh. Dnyaneshwar was in a state of shock. Never in his dreams or his waking hours had he imagined that chhakkas, of all people, would assault him one day. He stamped his boots and mustered all his energy to break free from their hold. But there were too many of them, and a couple stronger than him.

There was more humiliation in store. The fellows began to unbutton the saint's shirt and trousers. He couldn't do a thing except look on, as his clothes were torn off his body and untidily bundled, their ironing all ruined. The only garment they left on his body was his underwear. The queens went into spasms of laughter as they jeered at their victim. They held on to him firmly, lest he should escape. A couple of them couldn't resist going for the big thing, so tempting did it appear.

'Check out the veins,' Yudi advised them. Dnyaneshwar looked like Gulliver in the land of Lilliput. He desperately searched the street for policemen on night duty, passers-by, anyone, who could come to his rescue. But there was none at that late hour, save for a few cabbies who were so used to such nocturnal sights that they were too bored to interfere.

While his friends manhandled the chap who'd blackmailed him scarcely twenty-four hours ago, Yudi sat on The Wall and smoked cigarette after cigarette, inhaling the refreshing sea air.

'Serves you right,' he said to the saint with sadistic delight, as he grovelled for mercy.

'Your clothes will be returned and we'll let you off,' he suddenly spoke, taking a puff at his cigarette, 'if you pay back the 800 bucks you took from me yesterday. Or else you'll be thrown into the Arabian Sea.' Everyone grew silent. The queens temporarily suspended their ragging. Dnyaneshwar, who was in a no-go situation, considered Yudi's offer for just a minute, then directed him to fetch his purse. It was in his trouser pocket, he said. Yudi complied. The former took out eight hundred rupee notes from his wallet and handed them over to the latter. Yudi realized at once, from their shape and texture, that they were his very notes; the ones he gave to the fellow yesterday. It was an accomplishment of sorts—the recovery of stolen property. But one problem remained. The bugger had seen his house. He could always come back afterwards and make his life hell. Gulab took care of that.

'See this thing here?' he said to Dnyaneshwar, pointing to Umrao Jaan. 'Do you know who she is? She's the son of Bombay's Commissioner of Police. Trouble my reporter friend again, and you know what will happen to you.'

'Yes,' Yudi added for emphasis, as the policeman wore his clothes amidst tight security. 'If your path ever crosses mine again, I'll see to it that you don't get a permanent job in the police. Not only will I complain about you to Umrao Jaan's father, I'll also write about you in my newspaper.'

Dnyaneshwar didn't say a word. The threats had their effect. He was perfectly convinced that Umrao Jaan, or whatever his name was, was the son of the Commissioner of Police. Hi-fi people were known to be weird. Messing around with them could indeed cost him his job in the police, or at the very least the promotion to which he greatly aspired. He decided to put the whole episode behind him and leave the guys alone.

Realizing that he wasn't held down any more, he started to run. The queens didn't stop him. They only resumed their catcalls as he ran clumsily into the darkness.

Operation Stonewall was a spectacular success.

Post Stonewall, Yudi stopped cruising for a while. He got home early, as everyone did in 1993 due to the riots, and spent what was left of the evening in front of the TV, sipping his drink. He made it a point to padlock the grill door at the entrance, a practice he'd never followed earlier. To put it plainly, the thought that was topmost on his mind was that Dnyaneshwar, who probably had Shiv Sena connections, would come back to the flat for revenge. It psyched him, made him paranoid. Several months passed before this fear was erased from his consciousness.

Sitting by himself in his dimly lit drawing room, a glass of rum in his hands, Yudi often found himself reflecting on his life (solitude does that to people). He was almost forty-two. Most normal men of his age already had teenaged children. They had wives who ran their homes and served them hot meals when they returned from work. The wives and offspring gave their lives an anchor. They felt loved, wanted. In turn, their own emotions found a ready outlet. They were meant for the family, and that was where they were directed. Yudi had journalist-friends who spent all their time talking about the achievements of their kids; about the wonderful parents they themselves were; about the quality time that they gave to their families; and so on.

By contrast, his life was a failure. He had plenty of sex, yes, but he couldn't bring himself to love any of the men he went to bed with, although he carried this great reservoir of love around in his heart. A doomed romance twenty years ago, and the pain that he suffered in its aftermath, had crippled him permanently. No one was worth it, he had taught himself. Moreover, there were no young men who genuinely desired relationships with other men. They were content with a Jekyll-and-Hyde existence, so that they could have the best of both worlds. To all intents and purposes, they were manly men who married women and sired children. Who on earth would know that they also screwed people of their own gender on the sly? But how could an affair that was based on deceit blossom into a thing of beauty? Lies were what thieves spoke; gay love in India thrived on lies.

And yet, as he grew older Yudi felt the need for a mate. Perhaps it was a feature of middle age: one wanted stability. Ten years ago, he was at peace having casual sex. Any sort of commitment would have at that time seemed a bother. Now he wanted someone to care and share his life with. Trouble was, where would he find such a person? There were no swayamwars for homos, where one could choose the man with the toughest muscles, who broke a bow with a soldier's ease! Nor could one issue a classified ad in the matrimonial columns of *The Times of India*.

As Yudi drank and pondered, he grew morose. He began to weep. He wasn't really the wallowing type, but somehow the booze, the old film songs and the diffuse lighting made it all just too much to bear. He sobbed loudly, his nose streamed. It was the prerogative of all those who lived alone. He continued to be in this mood for a long time.

Who is a lover? The person we pine for when we are down in the dumps. That creature alone, we imagine, can save us from drowning. Who did Yudi think of in his most wistful of moments? Not his mother, the only person in this world he could legitimately call his own. He thought of Kishore. It wasn't the first time, of course, that he remembered the boy whom he'd taken to his mother's place, and then packed off in a train. But memories of the kid usually came to him when he was in the bathroom, wanking. Now, for the first time, he thought of Kishore when he was in the doldrums. Strange, how human attitudes change. That Sunday afternoon he was afraid the lad would stick to him like a leech, take his leave only when he was paid. Now, he was about to fall in love with him! Why? Precisely because it wasn't for money that he did it. He was no Dnyaneshwar.

Could Yudi make Kishore his mate? He weighed the pros and cons. Pros: he was attracted to the boy. Cons: he was semi-literate; was only half his age. The semi-literate bit didn't worry him. As for age, he had a ready answer for anyone who called him a cradle snatcher: The boundary-line between filial and conjugal love is as imaginary as that between India and Pakistan. He would pamper Kishore like a son by day, lover by night.

How would he trace Kishore? After all, Bombay wasn't Bulandshahar. Answer: his pocket diary had the address. He opened it and read what he had written. Transit camp, behind Citylight Cinema, Mahim. He wondered why his hand had wavered so much, as he jotted it down, and then remembered that it had all happened in a moving train.

Yudi gulped down his drink, stood up resolutely, and went to the bathroom to wash his face. Tomorrow he would go to Mahim, for whatever it was worth. He would locate Kishore, take him out for a beer, and put to him his proposal: would he be his steady? If he refused, he would take him out to a swanky shopping mall, and ask him to choose what he wanted: shirt, trouser, bicycle, pen, shoes, goggles, wristwatch. And then he would repeat his proposal.

In the eight months since Yudi and Kishore met, Bombay was ravaged by fierce religious riots. In December 1992, Hindu mobs demolished the Babri Masjid at Ayodhya, Lord Ram's birthplace. Then they slaughtered angry Muslims who dared to rise up and give the fanatics a tooth for a tooth and an eye for an eye. What they were saying was that if Muslims wanted to live in India and not be bundled off to Pakistan in another infamous train, they would have to put up with every kind of humiliation, including the razing of mosques. They had lost the right to ask questions the day they converted to the 'conqueror's' faith. What was puzzling, however, was that Bombay bore the brunt of what had gone wrong in Ayodhya, a city with which it has as little in common as pizzas have with pooris.

Mahim was a badly shattered neighbourhood. Muslims lived here in large numbers. As Yudi got off his train, crossed the tracks and began his expedition to Citylight Cinema, he saw gutted buildings everywhere. They looked exactly like the brick structures the Fire Brigade had put up at Cross Maidan to train its fire fighters. Windows were like craters on the soot-blackened walls; shops had their tin signboards and glass windows in splinters. Had he arrived for a walk in Mahim a few weeks earlier, he might have seen limbless corpses strewn on the sidewalks. The streets in this part of the city pulsate with activity all days of the week. But today they resembled a cemetery. So far, Yudi had seen only pictures in newspapers. Now he was witnessing it live. If this was the sort of thing that had gone on here, it was unlikely that Kishore would be alive. Yudi could safely give up his search, make an about turn and catch the first train home.

Thus absorbed, Yudi reached Citylight. He made enquiries and located the Transit Camp, that did in fact exist. He stopped someone who was walking towards the cluster of huts that formed the Camp, and asked for Mahadik, only to be told that no one of that name lived there. 'Kishore Mahadik,' Yudi said, trying to be more specific, as if that would help. The accosted man accosted others to ask if they knew who Kishore Mahadik was. But everyone came out with the same answer: there was no Kishore Mahadik— or any Mahadik—in their colony.

A mob gathered around Yudi and pretended to read the piece of paper that he held in his hands. 'Ikde kon Mahadik nahi,' they concluded in Marathi and dispersed. Yudi was about to ask them if it was likely he was killed in the riots, but refrained.

So he had been conned yet another time. The imp hardly seemed the sort who would lie. But appearances were deceptive. Then, another thought crossed his mind. Perhaps the boy did live in the Transit Camp, but Kishore Mahadik was not his real name;

in which case, all he could do was hang around for a while, hoping he would spot the chap as he came in or went out. Realizing that the people he'd just spoken to would become suspicious if he loitered about near their houses, Yudi returned to the main road a few metres away, and perched himself at a bus stop.

Buses came and went, passengers boarded and alighted. Yudi continued to wait, as one hour, then two, passed. Twice, he thought he'd found his victim. In one case, the point of no return was actually reached, and he had to apologize to the young man, whom he'd slapped on the shoulder, saying, 'Sorry, friend, you look so much like someone I know.'

Such things were simply not done in Bombay.

It was late afternoon when Yudi finally decided to abandon his mission and began trekking to the railway station. He was certain the Maha-dick chapter was over even before it had begun. Life had fluttered into his hands, and then slipped away for ever.

Such things happened in Bombay every day.

three

. . . and found

One Friday afternoon, when Yudi called on the editor of *Metropolis on Saturday*, he was introduced to Gauri, a plump, upcoming painter—upcoming, though she was by no means young. She was dressed in a white handloom sari with a gold border, and wore a bindi the size of a one-rupee coin. She left her hair loose and allowed a part of it to cover her face, creating a magnificent effect of light and shade. Her head shook from time to time, as though a spring were attached to her neck. This gave her the look of a dancing doll. Her appearance overall was seductive: the editor, Bhatnagar, was bowled over. She smoked cigarette after cigarette as she talked to him about her exhibition that was to open soon. On the editor's desk (on either side of which they sat), were catalogues, brochures, newspaper clippings. Gauri was here to sell herself. She wanted Bhatnagar to send one of his 'boys' to review her exhibition, and review it favourably. Yudi walked in at that opportune moment.

'Hi, Yudi,' the editor greeted him. 'Meet Gauri, a woman of extraordinary talent. Gauri's a painter. She's exhibiting, beginning Monday. Can you do a review for us by Wednesday?'

As Bhatnagar spoke, he blushed. He gathered Gauri's publicity material into a neat pile and passed it on to Yudi.

'This should give you an idea,' he said.

Yudi neither accepted nor refused the assignment. He kept mum. It wasn't in his nature to turn down work that came his way. He wasn't an art critic, but it was not as if he couldn't cook up something about a bunch of paintings. Common sense, he believed, was a more useful tool here than all the learned principles of art acquired from books. Whether it was an art review he was asked to write, or a story on massages, to him it was just another article.

Yudi's editors were used to his body language. He wasn't the type who displayed too much (or any) enthusiasm. If he didn't say yes, but not no either, it usually meant that the answer was yes. Gauri, however, took his silence as a personal insult, and assumed he was not interested in her work.

'Would you like a preview of the show?' she asked him, for want of anything more sensible to say. She was smarting inside, but kept a cool exterior: she wanted her review, after all.

'That won't be necessary,' Yudi replied. 'I'll be there.'

Yudi found women, even if they were Madhuri Dixit (which this one certainly was not), so much like uncooked brinjals (that is to say, insipid), that he couldn't bring himself to look them in the eye. Of course he had to during a conversation, but he found the business painful. When he looked at Gauri immediately after he finished speaking, he found that she was ogling him. There was something about the look that frightened him. For Gauri was saying that she was in love with Yudi. He was quite sure of this.

'Oh no, not again,' he sighed, recalling occasions in the past when women had threatened to swallow rat poison if he didn't marry them right away.

Being a witness to the ironic drama that was being played out in his office, Bhatnagar grew insane with jealousy. Here he was, willing to give anything to sleep with Gauri. And she was wooing a man who was gay!

This Gauri wasn't the type who got up to leave the moment her business was over. She was the hanging around type. She continued to smoke till her packet of cigarettes was over, and Bhatnagar offered her his Marlboros. Her eyes continued to kiss Yudi's.

Yudi had no option but to stand up and say he was leaving. 'Another appointment at five,' he lied to Bhatnagar, when for formality's sake he asked him to stay. He'd actually come to the editor's office to complain about a lost cheque. The accounts department insisted that the cheque had been dispatched, but Yudi never received it. He thus wanted the editor to arbitrate. With Gauri in the cabin, however, and Bhatnagar in a romantic mood, this was no time to crab. He would come back another day.

'Be there definitely,' Gauri's hand reached out to Yudi as he left the office. With unnerving passion in her voice she added:

'Have a glass of wine with me at the show.'

The place was full of bearded men, clad either in jeans or kurta-pyjama. Wine bottles and wine glasses were neatly arranged on a side-table, together with five kinds of cheese and nine kinds of chocolate. The guests helped themselves freely. Some of them solicited the services of a young man who was stationed there to serve. To Yudi, the fellow exuded sex from every pore. He was more beautiful than all the paintings on the wall (that he glanced at cursorily). Yudi was in no hurry to meet Gauri who was lost among her admirers, explaining away the intricacies of her craft. It was as he was drooling over the waiter that Gauri spotted him and ran up to him.

'Hi Yudi, I'm so glad you could make it,' she said, her fingers touching the back of his hand.

'Hi,' Yudi replied in a tone that he hoped would deflate her exuberance.

He saw that the woman was short, really short, when pitted against his six-foot frame, so that she had to look up and he down as they spoke.

'Would you like me to take you around and explain what I've tried to do in each piece?' she asked.

'No, thanks,' Yudi said. 'I like to be left alone so that I can respond to the paintings intuitively. Besides, your catalogue contains all the background info I need.'

'That's fine,' Gauri said. 'But have a glass of wine first. Uttam, saab ke liye wine lao,' she shouted out to Yudi's love across the room, causing his heart to flutter.

So the lad's name was Uttam. He was indeed Very Nice. Uttam brought Yudi his wine. This time it was Yudi who allowed his fingers to caress another's, as he took his glass from Uttam.

He gulped down his wine. 'See you later,' he said to Gauri and went to Uttam for a refill, and then, glass in hand, walked round the room to study the paintings. They were mostly landscapes in the abstract mode, with an abundance of blue that seemed to be her favourite colour. On Sundays when he watched TV with his mother on her ancient Sony (gifted by an American cousin), the picture frequently got distorted. All one got to see then was strange shapes in pastel shades. Gauri's paintings looked exactly like the images that appeared on his mother's TV, minus the grating noise that accompanied them. Yudi made a few mental notes, frowned meditatively, and he was finished. He would write his review tomorrow, submit it to Bhatnagar the day after. Getting back to Uttam for a final glass of wine before he left, he said 'bottoms up' to his darling, wished he could inspect his bottom, and slipped out before Gauri could spy him.

The next day, when Yudi put pen to paper, he tried very hard to recall all the picturesque phrases that Bombay's own child prodigy and premier art critic, Manjeet Khote, used in his reviews: harmonious balance, subtle rhythm, vivacious colour. Not because he wanted to plagiarize, but because he had a special responsibility not to sound like Khote, who, after all, wrote for a star paper, *The Times of India*. The *Metropolis on Saturday*, also owned by the Times group, was like a country cousin of TOI. Bhatnagar, the editor, wasn't half as learned as the formidable Mr Khote. If the proprietors of the Bennett Coleman Company suspected that their phrases were lifted, they would sack Bhatnagar and delete Yudi's name from their panel of freelancers. However, as Yudi realized that day, it was a Herculean task to avoid sounding like Khote. There was virtually no expression that he had left untouched, and what was more, his language had seeped into the collective unconscious of the entire fraternity!

It was with utmost presence of mind that Yudi's pen took zigzag turns to evade words previously used by Khote, just as a car swerves to avoid potholes. Bhatnagar was satisfied with his review, promptly delivered on Wednesday, so that it could be published on Saturday. He invited him to a cocktail party at the Press Club. He also promised to retrieve his lost cheque.

The Press Club is situated at the far end of Azad Maidan, a hot cruising spot from times immemorial. Yudi had his first taste of gay love in the Azad Maidan way back in the 1970s. He remembered the incident clearly, as if it happened yesterday. He was on his way home from a 6 to 9 show of *Bobby* at the Excelsior. Instead of making a detour towards Mahatma Gandhi Road or Mahapalika Marg, he decided to cut through the maidan to get home quickly. In no time at all, he was engulfed in pitch-black darkness. As he trained his eyes to see in the dark, one man after another, who all came from the Metro side in an endless stream, approached him. All of them cruised him in their own inimitable ways: some flashed, others had their hands on their crotches. Yudi, only twenty then, was intensely aroused. When he unzipped his trousers to pee, as everyone there did, he was already as hard as a grinding stone. No sooner did his sword emerge from its sheath, than the entire company of cruisers swooped down on him. The crowd began to paw Yudi. He was the youngest among them, and a brand new entrant to their club. Each one wanted to take it upon himself to initiate this lanky boy into the pleasures of banned love. Yudi did not stave off his molesters. He enjoyed what was going on, and the need to get it all out of his system became very strong. Without much ado, he slipped his hand into the hand of someone he found ravishing; together, they went to a quieter part of the maidan. Ignoring everyone else who followed them, cutting out the preliminaries, Yudi and his partner masturbated each other, as many from the cruising company, and the stars in the moonless sky, looked on.

After that, Yudi became an Azad Maidan addict. Come evening, and he would rush off to the maidan as if he were going to answer nature's urgent call. The fact that they lived only a stone's throw from the maidan helped. All he had to do was hop, skip and jump, and pronto, he was there. He didn't have to board cumbersome trains and buses, as many sex-hungry seekers who came to the place did. For a whole decade, from the mid 70s to the mid 80s, there perhaps wasn't a day when Yudi didn't pop in at the Azad Maidan. It astonished him that so much orgiastic activity went on right under the noses of the cops, for the Azad Maidan Police Station is situated bang opposite.

The pattern was broken only when he moved out of his parents' home in the late 80s, a couple of years after his father's death. In the 90s, the maidan lost some of its former glory. The post-Babri riots made the police vigilant. There were reports of gays being thrashed and thrown into the lock-up when they were found loitering in the maidan after sunset. Yudi was an eyewitness to some of these crimes. Like the others, then, he found a convenient alibi in the Hare Krishna bhaktas.

Other hazards, occupational ones, arose. Whenever he went to the Press Club, the restlessness showed. He couldn't resist the temptation to slip out through the backdoor and enter the maidan. Yet he was afraid that fellow journalists at the club would spot him in the darkness. It was one thing to be known for one's sexual proclivities, quite another to be caught in the act by office colleagues.

So, when he arrived at the Metro now on his way to the cocktails, and was faced with a choice, Yudi decided not to take the silk route through the maidan. He resolved to be a good boy and use the Mahapalika Marg to get to his destination, beyond heritage buildings such as St Xavier's College and Cama Hospital.

Guests were already helping themselves to the booze when Yudi entered the Press Club. They sat on sofas and bar stools in groups of four or five and talked. Some of them went out into the garden with their glasses. Bartenders stomped sulkily all about the place with trays of food and drink. Yudi checked out the one who approached him, but found him uninteresting. He picked up a glass of whisky with soda and ice, the first of many he would consume in the course of the evening. Everyone's attention was diverted towards a party of scribes that was having a brawl. The subject was—but of course—the demolition of the Babri Masjid. One half of them were badmouthing the BJP, Shiv Sena, VHP and RSS for trampling on the emotions of Muslims. The other half were saying that it was a good thing the Hindus had at last learnt to pay people back in the same coin, talk to them in their own language, beat them at their own game. They argued in such high-pitched voices that Yudi hoped they would come to blows. What fun to see them flinging knives, forks, spoons, plates and kebabs at each other! His own sympathies lay with the pro-Muslim lobby, but no, he wasn't going to be drawn into the fight. However, to his disappointment, the quarrel ended abruptly with all the bickerers splitting with laughter.

Although nearly everyone at the cocktails knew Yudi, he wasn't on backslapping terms with any of them. They were pedigreed professionals, he a pariah freelancer. They were straight, he gay. Not to appear conspicuous, he joined a couple of people he knew and made small talk. They wanted to know about the living conditions in Nalla Sopara, for they were house hunting and couldn't afford anything this side of Vasai Road. Yudi spoke very highly of his neighbourhood. He promised to introduce them to his builder (if he still existed as a human being, hadn't as yet become a cockroach). The lack of intelligent conversation didn't bother him. His objective was to get drunk, and in this he seemed to be succeeding. He did wonder, though, where his host Bhatnagar was.

The whisky made Yudi pensive as usual. He was rapidly growing oblivious to his surroundings. The house hunters moved away to another table, leaving him to himself. He would have continued to sit there and drink until he passed out, had she not shaken him out of his reverie.

'Yudi, I've been looking for you everywhere,' Gauri's mellifluous voice tickled his ears. 'How are you?'

'Not too bad,' he looked up and replied. He noticed that the woman was laden with tribal jewellery made of copper. Earrings, necklace, nose pin, they all seemed to be part of a set. Even a toe ring, for heaven's sake! She had discarded her starched sari in preference for a khadi chudidar kameez. In her left hand was a cigarette, in her right a glass of gin.

'Thanks a ton for the review in today's *Metropolis*,' she went on. 'All my friends called up to say that they liked it. I think you've been very generous. You know, I told my newsboy to bring me ten copies of the paper.' She laughed.

'You're welcome,' Yudi said, holding his head up with some difficulty. The whisky was beginning to tell on him, especially as the barmen at the Press club were trained to make large pegs.

'When did you get here?'

'An hour ago. You?'

'Just a short while back. I took a ride in Bhatnagar's car. He's a darling, isn't he?'

'Yes, of course.'

So that was why Bhatnagar was late. He had gone to fetch his lady love. Had they had a quickie before arriving, Yudi wondered. Bhatnagar's Maruti Omni was spacious enough, and it had dark tinted glasses. They probably did it in the boot. And now that the rabbit had had his fill, he'd let this woman loose and was consorting elsewhere!

By mentioning Bhatnagar, Gauri hoped to make Yudi jealous. Now she watched his face change colour and thought her ploy had worked.

'Yudi, it's you I want to be with this evening, not him,' she reassuringly said. 'He's a married man with grown-up kids. Not my type, really.'

'What about you? Aren't you married?'

'I'm a divorcee,' she replied.

'Oh, I'm sorry.'

'No, it's all right. It was I who dumped my former husband.'

Yudi wanted to change the topic as quickly as possible. He regretted having asked Gauri a personal question. She would probably take it to mean that he was getting interested in her. That she was a divorcee made matters worse. She was fishing in strange waters, looking for an opportunity to cast her net. Yudi was her Bombay Duck. His main reason for asking the question was of course to tell her that he had no desire to be her surrogate husband. But this, clearly, wasn't something she was equipped to see.

Gauri's next set of words alarmed Yudi. They meant she had been doing her homework.

'You're a bachelor, aren't you?' she asked him. Yudi considered replying in the negative and fibbing about some non-existent wife. But he decided against it at the last minute. The woman would do more homework and find out that he'd lied. So all he brought himself to say was, 'Yeah.'

There was a pause in their conversation. Gauri expected Yudi to ask her how she knew he was a bachelor. He expected her to ask him why he was one. Neither of them fulfilled each other's expectations. Instead, she stumped him further by saying, 'I also know why you're unmarried.' That bitch Bhatnagar had been wagging his tongue! It was perhaps time to slice it off! Just to test whether she really knew, or was only pretending, Yudi said: 'I'm glad you know. But would you like to tell me precisely what you know?'

'That you are attracted to members of your own sex.'

'Members is right,' he replied. Gauri giggled.

There was no objective correlative between Gauri's knowledge of Yudi's sexual orientation, and her behaviour. She continued to think of him as a possible husband. In his private lingo, she was the 'Backbay Reclamation' kind. She assumed that all men were naturally attracted to women. If something about their sex life had gone awry, there was no reason why they couldn't be reclaimed, reformed. They could be made to stop being 'backbay' people. Although Gauri was an artist with shows to her credit, she was no different in this respect from Testosterone's Meryl Streep.

'Your review of my exhibition was very flattering,' she continued, afraid that her tête-à-tête with her reticent man-friend would come to an end if she didn't go on. He had gone worryingly quiet. 'I was so happy to read expressions like "seductive" and "romantic" in your piece.'

And now it was his turn to be worried. 'Excuse me,' he quavered. 'I was talking about your paintings. Not about you!'

'Of course, you were talking about my paintings,' she burst out laughing, taking his remark to be a joke. What she didn't know was that he had reviewed her exhibition favourably not because he liked her paintings, but because he wanted to stay in Bhatnagar's good books.

An hour passed. Yudi was very drunk now. The guests at the cocktail party no longer appeared like individuals to him. They were mere shapes. The world around him was hazy, blurred: he was blacking out fast. Gauri, observing him, felt concerned. While the others neutralized the effects of their drinking by greedily helping themselves to the sandwiches and kebabs, Yudi did not eat anything, except for a few peanuts that he inexpertly popped into his mouth. Gauri had no idea how the man would reach home.

'Yudi, it's time to leave,' she reminded him. 'How do you plan to get home?'

'By train,' he managed to say. 'What's the time?'

'It's nearly midnight.'

'No problem. The locals run till one.'

'Where do you have to go?'

'You mustn't have heard of the place in your life. It's not an aristocratic locality, like yours. It's called Nalla Sopara.'

'That's really the back of beyond!' she exclaimed. Not standoffishly, but only to emphasize that he was in no position to travel that far all by himself.

'I'm used to it,' he drawled.

'Why don't you ride with us till Bandra?' she suggested. 'You can catch your train from there.'

'Not a bad idea,' he said, his head whirling.

In the four hours that they spent together at the Press Club, Yudi was meeting Bhatnagar only now, at the time of leaving.

'Hi Yudi, good review,' the editor said, without gauging his colleague's condition. 'What are you doing for us next?'

It was Gauri who whispered into his ear and made him see how inebriated Yudi was. She also told him that he would be hitching a ride with them up to Bandra.

The trio were among the last batch of people to leave the Press Club. Bhatnagar and Gauri helped Yudi get into the backseat of the Omni, and drove off. The roads being free at this hour of night, Bhatnagar accelerated. The high speed wasn't good for Yudi's belly, saturated as it was with alcohol. They had hardly reached Opera House when he began to throw up. The vomit was on the glass windows, seat covers, rubber mats.

'Oh God,' Gauri sighed. 'Shit!' exploded Bhatnagar. He turned back once or twice to assess the damage done to his upholstery, but didn't think it worthwhile to stop the car. He was in a hurry to get home before his wife threw a fit. Gauri gave him a running commentary on what was happening at the back.

'Yudi, you should have put your head out of the window while vomiting,' Bhatnagar said, annoyed. 'Look what a mess you've made.'

'Sorry, dear,' Yudi replied weakly. 'Couldn't figure out where the window was.' Gauri laughed on hearing this. Bhatnagar did not think it was funny and glared at her. She opened her handbag, fished out a roll of tissue and passed it on to Yudi to clean himself up. She also parted with her bottle of mineral water. Observing that given his state, the tissue and mineral water were of little use to him, she asked Bhatnagar to stop the car, while she got out and went into the backseat. Here, as the jealous editor resumed his driving, Gauri cleaned up her man-friend. They were at Worli Naka now, where, for some absurd reason, the traffic lights were still on. As the car halted at a red signal, the rancid smell of vomit hit Bhatnagar. 'Disgusting!' he swore to himself.

After doing Yudi, Gauri turned her attention to the Omni. She emptied out her bottle of mineral water on the backseat and allowed it to spill onto the rubber mats. She freely used her tissue roll to wipe off the specs of vomit on the tinted glasses. The soaked pieces of stinking paper she chucked out of the car without a qualm, for this was Bombay. Her idea was to keep busy till they reached Bandra, so that she could continue to sit with Yudi at the back. Bhatnagar glanced back from time to time to ask her if she was done, but she always said, 'Not yet.'

When the Omni pulled up into the driveway of Gauri's bungalow on Perry Cross Road, it was from the backseat that she stepped out. Yudi fell asleep after his cathartic discharge. Gauri instructed her editor to put him up at his place for the night, for even if the trains still ran, he couldn't be trusted to find his way home. The editor said he would do as she wanted him to, provided she kissed him before parting. 'Okay,' said Gauri, and they kissed.

On reaching his apartment, merely five minutes away from Gauri's bungalow, Bhatnagar took the watchman's help to bundle Yudi into the lift, and thence into the guest bedroom of his flat. His wife stood at the door, arms akimbo, noticing his every movement without uttering a word. She seemed to be used to such sights. It was the price she paid for being married to the editor of a famous city newspaper.

As for Yudi, he slept like a log until nine the next morning, and then he found that he had a severe hangover. His head was a merry-go-round, his stomach a giant wheel. Even so, he politely chewed the burnt toast and uncooked egg that Mrs Bhatnagar served him for breakfast, before taking his leave and trudging to the railway station.

For a whole week after the Press Club cocktails, Yudi stayed off booze. He knew he didn't own the strongest of livers, and he had no wish to be stricken with cirrhosis. Returning from work, he whiled away his time before the TV, sipping Sosyo (of all things). He felt awfully embarrassed at the way he had thrown up in Bhatnagar's car and had to be looked after throughout the night. He hadn't telephoned the editor still to apologize, though he had intended to do so the very next day. He kept putting it off, telling himself he'd do it later, but now so much time had passed that it didn't make sense to refer to an event about which Bhatnagar himself had probably forgotten. What he would do now was call on the gentleman in his office, agree to write the most boring article, and perhaps buy him a brand new set of car seat covers. This way he would make it up.

On the eighth day after the party, as Yudi sat before the TV with a small rum—for he had only just resumed his drinking after a week's abstinence—the doorbell unexpectedly rang at 9.30 in the night.

'Who could that be?' he asked himself, certain he had not given any one-night stand an appointment. Then his heart began to palpitate as he thought it might be Dnyaneshwar: 'You motherfucker, you stripped me naked that night on a public thoroughfare. Now you won't live to see another day.' Dishoom–Dishoom–Dishoom. Blood all over the floor! Yudi drops down dead.

The bell rang again. He rose from his haunches and tiptoed to the door. When he looked through the peephole, he was amazed to see a feminine shape, no fag in drag but a full-fledged woman! He was relieved. At least it wasn't Yamraj who had come knocking on his door. He opened the door with confidence, assuming it was a neighbour who wanted him to shut his taps.

'Hello, Yudi,' Gauri said.

'You!'

'I've been thinking about you a lot. I don't have your phone number. So I've come to see you.'

'It's past nine at night, for Christ's sake! This is no time to go visiting. Who gave you my address? Bhatnagar?'

'No. I got it somehow. It's not important. Won't you ask me to come in?'

'Absolutely not. I don't see anyone without an appointment.'

'You are being very rude,' Gauri whimpered. 'That's not how you are supposed to speak to a lady.'

A wave of pity rose in Yudi's heart. If a woman left her home in Bandra to travel to Nalla Sopara at an unearthly hour, and that too in a jam-packed local to which she wasn't even used, she was indeed desperate. He remembered how kind Gauri was to him at the cocktail party. She stayed by his side all the while, whereas everyone else, including Bhatnagar who'd invited him, deserted him. And she had cleaned him up with her bare hands when he was sick in the car.

'Okay, come in for a few minutes,' he said to her, his tone softening.

'No. It can't be just a few minutes. I have kept an auto rickshaw waiting downstairs. I will dispose of him, provided you are willing to keep me for the night.'

' What! You must be mad!' he exclaimed, his tone resuming its angry pitch. Yudi ran down the stairs even before he finished talking, leaving Gauri at the door. He met the auto rickshaw driver and told him not to leave without memsaab who was coming down in a few minutes. 'Take her back to the station,' he instructed the driver.

'What station?' the driver shot back. 'Madam has brought me here all the way from Dahisar.'

The implication of the driver's words stunned Yudi. What they meant was that Gauri hadn't come to Nalla Sopara by train, like the aam janata, but in an auto rickshaw, like a princess. She must have hired one three wheeler from Bandra to Dahisar, where Greater Bombay ends and Thane begins, and another from Dahisar to Nalla Sopara! And now she would go back in exactly the same way, spending a fortune in the bargain! And this was what worried Yudi. If a woman blew up so much money just to see him, she would want her money's worth. Yet here he was, about to pack her off.

'Madam is coming down,' he emphasized to the driver again. 'Take her wherever she wants to go.'

Yudi ran up the stairs like a man possessed, without waiting for the lift. Gauri was still at his doorstep. Sweat trickled down her neck; she fanned herself with a hand fan that she carried in her bag.

'The auto rickshaw driver is in a hurry,' he told her, panting. 'Please leave at once. We'll talk tomorrow.'

'So I can't stay over at your place?'

'No.'

'I don't have to sleep in your bed! I can use the guest bedroom.'

'There's no guest bedroom,' he snubbed her. 'It's a small flat. I'm not as rich as you.'

He knew he was being a bastard, but he didn't have a choice. The woman seemed to him to be a lunatic. Only to get rid of her at any cost, he said: 'Here's my phone number. Give me a tinkle tomorrow, and we'll talk.' At this, Gauri burst out crying like a girl of nine. Tears rolled down her cheeks, as if a tap had been turned on. She continued to cry, as she said 'Goodnight, Yudi' and climbed down the stairs.

The night was hardly good for Yudi. He tossed about in bed till the cocks crowed. He was in a schizophrenic state. One part of him felt sorry for the woman he had humiliated and thrown out, when all she sought was companionship. The other was outraged at her audacity. How dare she presume that just because she had cleaned up his vomit, she had a right to his life! Her kindness now seemed like a design, a scheme, by which she hoped to ensnare him. He pitied himself. Was there no one in the world who could love him without exploiting him? Or was love by its very nature exploitative? Wasn't he too an exploiter of all the young men he slept with, even if it was they who screwed him?

Rattled, Yudi fell asleep only at dawn, rose at lunchtime, and decided not to leave the house that day. In retrospect, this was a Himalayan blunder. For when Gauri called him up that afternoon, he innocently lifted the receiver and said 'Hello.' By the time he discovered who the caller was it was too late. There was no option left for him but to proceed with the conversation. After asking her if she had reached home safely, was feeling better, and so on, Yudi found himself inviting this woman who refused to let go for lunch the next day. At The Wayside Inn.

'Thank you, Yudi,' she said in her affected manner. 'I'll be there.'

He knew she would. He was trapped. What was he to do?

Gauri arrived at the venue ages before time. She strolled into the Jehangir Art Gallery across the street, and chatted with a couple of 'fringe artists' whose work was on display on the pavement. She went to the Max Mueller Bhavan to inquire about membership rules. Crossing the road to get back to the Wayside Inn, she entered

Rhythm House to ask if they had a certain song by Jagjit Singh. She walked past Chetana Bookstore and examined the titles in their show-window. She went to Artists' Centre, at the far end of Rampart Row, but decided against climbing the narrow winding stairs that led to the gallery. When she looked at her watch, there were still twenty minutes left for her appointment to begin. So she breezed into Samovar for a cup of coffee. She sat there and she wondered briefly if Yudi had forgotten about the lunch.

Yudi was late. Gauri stood patiently outside The Wayside Inn, putting cigarettes to her lips in rapid succession and igniting them with a lighter. The area being notorious, passers-by mistook her for a strumpet. 'How much?' one of them hissed, and she gave him an amused look.

Yudi arrived a long time after all this happened. 'Sorry, train problem,' he said, and didn't think it necessary to apologize further. When they stepped into The Wayside Inn, he rejected her proposal to sit at a corner table, opting instead for a table in the centre of the restaurant.

'What would you like to eat?' he asked her, but she had no cravings. Told him it didn't matter, she would eat whatever he ordered, or whatever he himself ate. Yudi summoned the waiter and ordered two plates of soup and two plates of veggie sandwiches. 'Can you stop smoking?' he requested her. 'I'm allergic to smoke.'

The food arrived, and they spent the first fifteen minutes or so munching in silence, a silence that only Gauri could break.

'Yudi, I'd like to tell you all about myself,' she said.

'Go ahead,' came the bored reply.

'I'm a very intense person. That's why my marriage failed. I grow possessive of the people I love. Surendra, my ex-husband, he was just the opposite. He wanted his space. What he saw as freedom, I saw as callousness. That's why we parted.'

Yudi was flustered. He didn't know how to react. He wasn't

interested in the story of Gauri's life, was lending his ears only to be polite. About one thing, though, he was certain: he had to maintain a deadpan pose till the end of their date. Any slight emotion on his part, and she would think he was beginning to like her. His apparent lack of enthusiasm did not deter Gauri. She went on:

'My father was in the army. We have lived in such wonderful cities: Delhi, Srinagar, Dharamsala. I shook hands with the Dalai Lama when we were at Dharamasala. In Delhi, our address was 1 Safdarjung Marg. We lived in the very house that would later become Indira Gandhi's! I once drove an Ambassador all the way from Delhi to Pune, with no one by my side!'

Yudi sighed. He was now convinced that the woman he was having lunch with was crazy. She lived in the Prime Minister's house and drove a car from Delhi to Pune.

'Why did you do go on such a long drive all by yourself?' he mocked her.

'Because I fought with my dad. I grabbed the car keys from him and took off.'

'Didn't you have a breakdown on the way?'

'Not even a flat tyre! I drove at 110 kilometers per hour.'

Yes, raving mad, he thought, but said nothing. He merely nodded and waited for her to make her next statement. This wasn't turning out to be so bad, after all. He was deeply entertained by what he was hearing.

'I started to paint when I was eight,' she changed the topic. 'Drawing was my favourite subject at school. I won prizes in drawing and represented my school at various competitions.'

Yudi didn't wish to comment. He had recently been tricked into reviewing her exhibition. Enough was enough. Gauri sensed his embarrassment and switched to the subject of cooking.

'I'm a great cook,' she boasted. 'I'm especially good at making butter chicken. When you come to my house for dinner, eat my butter chicken and judge for yourself.'

The waiter took away their empty plates, asked if they wanted dessert. There was courtesy in his tone, for this was The Wayside Inn. Gauri settled for coffee and said she drank it without milk and sugar. She took Yudi's permission to light just one cigarette, rearranging her posture so that the smoke wouldn't engulf him.

'I also write poetry,' she said, puffing away. 'I have a letter from Mr Nissim Ezekiel praising my poems.'

'What is it that you *don't* do?' Yudi asked her, exasperated.

She burst out laughing. 'I don't water-ski,' she said.

She stubbed her unfinished cigarette in the ashtray. 'Yudi, can't we be friends?' she asked without warning, leaving him momentarily speechless. She was getting personal again. It was time for him to gather all his resources.

'No,' he said, taking more then a couple of seconds to recover.

'Why not?'

'Because it's not friendship that you really want.'

'I do, believe me I do. I'd like to have a platonic relationship with you, Yudi.'

'Madam, can you please explain to me what you mean by a platonic relationship?'

'One in which there's no sex. Although I'm deeply attracted to you, I know that you're out of bounds. Isn't it?'

The question-tag in his opinion was unnecessary. It meant she still hoped that someday he'd go to bed with her.

'I am not convinced you know what platonic love really is,' he told her. 'Hence, I have to reject your proposal. I'm sorry.'

'Give me a chance to prove that I understand it perfectly well,' she replied. 'You won't be disappointed. I promise you you won't.'

'No!' he insisted.

She threw a bait. 'Will you come to my place for dinner,

Yudi? I'll introduce you to my parents. You'll see what a cultured family we are.'

He loosened up a bit. Food invites always had a hypnotic effect on him. They meant freedom in every sense. He was free to eat and drink as much as he wanted, all at someone else's expense. He was also free from household chores. He pretended to mull over the question.

'Sometimes, you do talk sense,' he capitulated.

Gauri was ecstatic. 'I'm so glad you've agreed, Yudi,' she said, her eyes filled with joyous tears. 'Are you free on Thursday? It happens to be my birthday.'

'I don't like birthday parties. I'd much rather come when it's not your birthday, so that we can have a serious chat.'

'It isn't a birthday party in that sense, with balloons and candles. There won't be anyone else, besides you. I don't like birthday parties either.'

Lunch at The Wayside Inn ended with Yudi paying the bill and Gauri parting with her address.

Yudi told the auto rickshaw driver to go into the portico of the two-storeyed bungalow. He stepped out and surveyed the surroundings. There was a lush green lawn. A garden, complete with flowers in bloom, and even butterflies. An 118 NE was parked a few feet away from the porch. The front door of the bungalow was ornate. Exquisitely done up in wood and brass, it looked as if it belonged to an ancient Indian temple or a five-star hotel. He went closer and examined the nameplate on the door: Col. S.S. Wagh (Retd.). He wondered if the gentleman was corrupt. How else had he amassed so much wealth? Only film stars owned bungalows in Bandra. How much did a Colonel earn? Fifteen Thousand? Twenty thousand? Twenty-five? As the Income Tax people put it, the fauji seemed to have assets that were disproportionate to his known sources of income.

Yudi stood before the imposing front door and felt he was about to enter the abode of Lord Venkateswara. Before he could ring the doorbell, the door unexpectedly opened and he was caught unawares as he combed his hair.

'Good evening sir,' the Colonel greeted him. 'Welcome to our humble home.'

Yudi put away the comb into his back pocket and returned the greeting.

'Meet my wife, Mrs Wagh,' the officer said, introducing him to the lady of the house.

'Namaste,' Yudi said to her, joining his hands.

'Namaste,' the lady said and mimicked his action.

They led Yudi to their sitting room where they sat on stylish sofas. There were vases, paintings, Persian carpets and an excess of antique wooden furniture. Yudi glanced at some of the paintings. None of them were by the Colonel's daughter. There was no sign of the daughter yet, and Col. Wagh, guessing his guest's thoughts, said: 'Gauri will be with us in a few minutes. She's having a shower.'

'What would you like to have?' Mrs Wagh spoke for the first time. 'Tea? Coffee?'

'Nothing,' Yudi said. 'I'm fine.'

Her reference to tea and coffee worried him. Didn't Gauri say she was inviting him for drinks and dinner? What if they served only tea and biscuits? He would feel so cheated, he would smash the windscreen of their 118 NE.

The wall-clock ticked. There was an awkward silence that neither Yudi nor the Colonel knew how to break. Gauri came to their rescue, climbing down the stairs at precisely that moment, her high-heeled shoes clicking and clacking. Yudi stood up to wish her a happy birthday, and give her the bottle of perfume he had brought as a present.

'Thank you, Yudi,' she said. 'I'm so glad you made it.'

They sat down. He didn't know what kind of a birthday party this was. There was no cake on the table with forty candles that the birthday girl would put out at one stroke. The absence of other guests made him feel like a solo actor on stage. Gauri tore open the gift-wrapping of her present and started to generously spray herself with the perfume.

'I love Evening in Paris,' she exclaimed.

Yudi prayed she wouldn't discover it was a fake, picked up from the Malayalis on D.N. Road.

The Colonel had by now made up his mind as to what he would say to his esteemed guest. He asked him questions pertaining to his background, and when he discovered that Yudi was an Andhraite, got all nostalgic about the time he was at Waltair. Yudi found, much to his chagrin, that the officer insisted on slotting him as a Telugu-speaking country bumpkin. As the conversation progressed, he even spoke a few words of Telugu himself. Yudi hated Telugu, which he thought was no different from gibberish. At last he decided to put his foot down.

'I'm not that kind of Andhradu, from the depths of Samalkota, you know,' he informed his host. 'My mother isn't a Telugu. We speak English at home.'

Col. Wagh was flabbergasted. He had never met a man who ran down his own mother tongue. He had no intention of offending his daughter's boyfriend, but he did want to tell the man a few things about culture and pride. Gauri sensed danger and swiftly changed the topic. They now began talking to Yudi about freelance journalism. This instantly reminded the father of the charitable review his daughter's exhibition got, and he thanked Yudi profusely.

Excusing himself, Col. Wagh left the room and returned a few minutes later with a bottle of whisky, sodas and three glasses on a tray. Mrs Wagh, who was in the kitchen, came after him with platefuls of pakoras.

'Our maid is on leave,' Gauri explained to Yudi. 'So we have to work ourselves.'

'Good,' Yudi replied. 'Work keeps the body fit.'

As was her wont, Gauri exploded with laughter.

'I didn't crack a joke,' he said, causing her to laugh even more.

The Colonel and Mrs Wagh were pleased that their baby girl was kept humoured. The Colonel made the first round of drinks and served Yudi his glass. The other two glasses were for himself and his daughter. The mother, Yudi observed, didn't drink anything. Her duty was to pester them to eat her pakoras every few minutes.

'Would you like to see my room upstairs, Yudi?' Gauri asked him, sipping her whisky.

He was in a quandary. His honest answer was 'no'. But this was too brazen. Besides, it would have the opposite effect. Instead of taking it as an insult, she would take it as a joke and have another bout of laughter. He decided that the best course was to leave the question unanswered. Gauri was more used to his ways now than she was that first time, when they met in Bhatnagar's office. Perhaps the latter had tutored her: when Yudi kept quiet, he meant 'yes'. Finally, it was her father who resolved the crisis. He advised them to go up, while he followed with the tray of drinks. Against his will, then, Yudi found himself ascending the stairs to Gauri's room.

The room upstairs was as unkempt as the room downstairs was prim. It was strewn with books, newspapers, magazines, paints, brushes, shoes, slippers, bras, panties, and above all, cigarettes. Tobacco was the presiding deity here. Not only were there cigarette packets, ashtrays, matchsticks and matchboxes all over the room, but it also smelled like the warehouse of the Indian Tobacco Company. Gauri was in her element in the midst of all the squalor. She cleared a part of the bed for Yudi to sit on, then went to the aid of daddy dear who was struggling to make space on the table, to lay the heavy tray.

'Here we are,' the Colonel sighed. 'Cheers, once again.'

Unlike the drawing room downstairs, Yudi noticed that the walls here were adorned with Gauri's paintings. Poems were scribbled on the walls in pen and pencil. When Gauri found him making an attempt to read some of the poems, she startled him by disclosing that they were her own compositions. He managed to remark that she was indeed multi-talented. To which he expected her to say 'Thank you'. But she made him choke on his whisky and cough by exclaiming happily, 'Aren't I?'

The Colonel took his leave. He had work to do, he said. After his retirement from the Indian National Army, the Tatas had got hold of him and given him a management consultant's job. He didn't need it, but took it up only to pass his time. It meant no more than spending a few hours every day with his files, for which they compensated him handsomely. Yudi panicked at the prospect of being left alone with Gauri in her citadel. He wanted to ask his host if he could join him, and may be assist him with his paper work. Or else, he could help Mrs Wagh slice the onions and tomatoes. But the words didn't form in his mouth. Col. Wagh said 'See you later' and left, while he sat there like a buffoon, not knowing what to do. Of course Gauri took care of that. She brought out a trunkful of her paintings and poems from under the bed and showed them to him, one by one. Taking advantage of her father's absence, she lit up. Yudi had to stifle his yawns as he went through her work, one yawn for every painting and every poem. In one of her poems, she wrote:

I wait for you
With butter in my hands
As Meera waits for Krishna.
Lick the butter off my fingers,
O lover.
Savour my flesh,
Let my body's juices intoxicate you.

As he read the poem, she drew herself very close to him and said, almost in a whisper: 'This one is for you, darling.' Yudi shot up in a huff and asked her to behave herself. 'Stop getting fresh!' he shrieked.

As usual, she started to laugh.

'It's not funny,' he retorted, livid still. No sitting on the bed with this nymphomaniac, he resolved. A chair should do. Gauri felt belittled by his act of moving to the chair. 'How mean!' she said.

'I'm fine here,' Yudi said.

To avoid engaging with her, he buried himself in the sheets of paper before him, and pretended to pore over them earnestly. She was flattered. Forgetting that she was slighted but a minute ago, she said: 'Unlike my paintings, which are about landscapes, my poems are about people.'

'I can see that,' Yudi remarked, anxious to stop before she ventured to say: 'They are about you!'

The bottle of Mogul Monarch was half empty. Handing over the poems to her, he filled his glass without asking her if he should fill hers too. She replenished hers on her own, and they drank a few sips in total silence. She wasn't the one, though, to keep quiet for very long. She said:

'Yudi, when is your birthday?'

'April,' he replied tersely.

He imagined she would want to know when in April, in what year and so on. He would tell her he was born in the year of the Quit India Movement, and was already an old man past fifty. May be that would put her off. But her intentions were quite different.

'I'll paint for you on your birthday,' she said. 'I'll do your portrait and get it framed.'

'Thanks,' came the skeptical answer. After a minute he added: 'I didn't know you did portraits.'

'Yours will be the first,' she said, and slid into laughter again.

'The bitch is making fun of me,' he thought to himself. 'Must teach her a lesson!'

A prayer bell jingled down below. Yudi thought it was Mrs Wagh, engrossed in her gods.

'It's the dinner gong,' Gauri explained. 'My parents ring the bell when the dinner is ready, so I might go down and eat.'

'Spoilt brat!' he muttered.

His mood changed the moment they went down, and the sight of food captured his senses. On the centre of the dining table was the butter chicken. Surrounding it were rotis, biryanis, salads, vegetables, pickles, papads, raita, and carrot halwa.

'What a gorgeous spread,' he remarked to Mrs Wagh, eager to get over with the formalities and fill his plate with scrumptious helpings.

'The chicken has been prepared by Baby,' said the proud mother. Baby butted in: 'I told you I make excellent butter chicken, didn't I?'

To give it to her, the food tasted as good as it looked. All conversation was temporarily suspended as forks clanged on plates. That it was a buffet meal with everyone standing upright and holding their plates in their hands, made it less obligatory for them to talk. Except for making polite noises about the lusciousness of the food, Yudi said nothing until he was finished. Then he had a hard time suppressing his belches. Each time he tried to conceal his burping, it only became more obvious that he was burping.

Col. and Mrs. Wagh kept advising him to drink water, and also brought him a bevy of digestives to chew, like elaichi, lavang and supari. However, just as he recovered they announced that there was homemade kulfi to be eaten still.

By the end of the feast he was so full he felt he would explode. 'I won't have to eat for the next three days,' he said to Mrs Wagh, at which Gauri went into spasms of laugher: she hadn't heard anything kinkier, she said. Human beings weren't pythons who took a whole week to digest their food!

It is bad manners to leave a host's house as soon as dinner is over. But Yudi had a convenient excuse: he had a long way to go. Didn't Gauri know? She spent three hundred rupees and travelled in five different autos to and from his place that night. In all likelihood, her innocent parents had no idea where she'd gone. He had half a mind to tell them.

'Thanks for making it,' Gauri said to him, as he got up to go. 'Goodnight, goodnight, goodnight,' he said to each of them individually and hailed an auto that was parked just outside the driveway. He was relieved that she didn't ask him her million-dollar question: 'Yudi, when will you meet me next?'

A day after Gauri's birthday party, the accounts department of the *Times* called Yudi to say his lost cheque had been found. Did he want them to post it or would he come there in person to collect it?

'Don't post it. I'll be there tomorrow,' he instructed them, certain they would lose it again if he didn't go.

He reached the *Times* at the stroke of noon; took the lift up;

collected his cheque; took the lift down. When the doors of the lift opened on the ground floor, a long queue of people waited to get in. Yudi walked past them, then retraced his steps to check out a familiar face.

'Recognize me?' he asked.

The fellow blinked, hesitating for only a moment before saying, 'Yes. Mr Yudi!'

Yudi pulled him out of the queue and took him to the Empire Restaurant for a cup of coffee. There, as they sat drinking their coffee, Yudi narrated his saga: how he went to Citylight looking for him and gave him up for dead. 'I thought you were killed in the riots,' he laughed.

The chap told him he had got a job, at last, at Medium Advertising, Bora Bazaar. 'I am only an office boy, but some job is better than no job, no?' he remarked.

'Yes indeed, yes indeed,' Yudi replied.

The coffee over, he walked the boy to Bora Bazaar to confirm that he really worked where he said he did, such was his determination not to lose him a second time. He also took down a string of telephone numbers. Before parting, they made a date: they would meet at six o'clock the next day just outside the boy's office.

Yudi may have gone to the *Times* to collect a cheque, Kishore to issue a classified ad on behalf of his firm. Still they had achieved the impossible, found a needle in a haystack. It wasn't short of a miracle, for this was Bombay, after all, not the set of a Manmohan Desai film, where such things happened every day.

four

testosterone

The next day was a Friday. (It would become the day on which they would routinely meet, week after week. To Yudi, Friday became the light at the end of the tunnel.)

Yudi loitered outside the office of Medium Advertising, surveying the showcases of all the stationery shops with which the street was littered. He loved picking up the latest pens, pencils, sharpeners, erasers and paperweights. Today, however, his mind was not on the things he was buying. His heart pounded when his watch showed six. Was the fellow still upstairs, in the office, or was he hanging around for nothing, like an arsehole? Just then Kishore stormed down the stairs and stood before him. 'I don't believe he's actually here,' Yudi said to himself. To the other he said: 'Hello, Kishore. Good to see you again. Are you finished for the day?'

'I saw you from upstairs and left,' Kishore replied. 'Boss didn't want me to go yet, but I told him I would complete the rest tomorrow.'

'Who's your boss?'

'God.'

'God? But this is Medium Advertising, not Lintas!'

'His name is Parmeshwar. That is why I call him God,' Kishore blushed. The blushing was for Yudi, not for God. The boy was happy to be in the company of someone who had the hots for him, who was so obviously his deewana.

Yudi slipped his hand into Kishore's as they walked towards D.N. Road.

'So, what do we do?' he asked after a while. 'Have a beer somewhere?'

Kishore didn't reply. Instead, he proceeded to give his lover an account of how his boss ordered him about, and didn't pay enough.

'Can you find me another job?' he asked.

'I'll try,' Yudi assured him. 'But I can't promise. Hold on to Parmeshwar for some more time.'

A new pub had opened near Sterling Cinema. It was called The Devil's Church. Yudi took Kishore there and they perched themselves on the high stools.

'Strong beer or mild beer?' he asked him.

'Do you want to make me a bewda?' Kishore looked him in the eye.

'A bottle of beer doesn't make you a drunk,' Yudi told him and ordered to two bottles of Khajuraho. 'You must be hungry,' he continued, studying the menu. 'Have a plate of chicken sandwiches along with your beer.'

Two beers became four, four six. As they chatted, Yudi became high and recklessly sentimental.

'Where have you been all this while? I've been waiting for you. How long you have taken to come!' he said at one point, gazing into the boy's eyes. The boy looked puzzled, so he explained, 'That was what Ramakrishna said to Vivekananda, who was closest to his heart—you are my Vivekananda,' and then, thumping his fist on the table, 'you are my Sudama and I will happily bathe your tired and grimy feet . . . right here, with this beer!'

Both of them laughed: the laughter of drunkards.

'First,' Kishore declared, composing himself, 'My real name is Milind. Milind Mahadik. Kishore is a false name. Is Milind too a common name?'

'You son of a bitch!' Yudi screamed. 'You're just a kid, but you know all the tricks of the rough trade, haan!'

'Secondly,' the other went on, 'the Brahmans will cut off your balls for calling me Vivekananda and Sudama. Let me warn you that we are followers of Gautama Buddha. You know what that means?' He grew serious.

Yudi gulped down his beer, lit a cigarette and offered one to Milind. He knew instantly what the latter was trying to say: that he was an Untouchable; if Yudi felt he would be polluted, he should keep off.

'May I kiss you on the mouth?' Yudi asked him. It was his way of demonstrating that he cared two fucks if Milind was a Brahmin or a Bhangi, whose ancestors cleaned the shit of others.

Milind went red in the face. He was sure everyone in The Devil's Church heard Yudi. He turned around shyly, as he had done in the Churchgate loo, to see if anyone was giving them dirty looks.

'I'm sorry,' Yudi said, noticing he had embarrassed his friend. 'I was only trying to show you it doesn't matter what caste you are. I'll tell you what. I'll call for finger bowls and wash your feet in them and wipe them dry with my eye lashes.'

'Shut up,' Kishore chuckled. 'You're drunk. It's time to go.'

There were a couple of other things that Milind told Yudi about himself that evening. One of them was that his father, who was a ward boy in a B.M.C. hospital, had left his mother and was living with a prostitute. Yudi swallowed each 'horror' story with a sense of triumph. The more down-and-out Milind was, the more they would click. Outcastes, after all, can only expect to be friends with outcastes.

On the train home, they made a pact: they would meet every Friday. Yudi would pick Milind up from work and they would have a beer. 'Don't stand right outside my office,' Milind cautioned. 'Wait for me a few buildings away. I'll be in trouble if Parmeshwar sees you.'

His destination came sooner than Yudi expected. He got up. 'But this is Mahalaxmi, not Lower Parel,' Yudi said.

'Yes, I know,' Milind said. 'We never lived in the Transit Camp. Only some friends of ours live there. We live in B.M.C. quarters at Saat Rasta. My house is on the street that leads to Arthur Road Jail. The nearest stations are Mahalaxmi on Western Railway and Chinchpokli on Central Railway. That day I got down at Lower Parel only to mislead you!'

'Son of a bitch!' Yudi shrieked again.

This time the journalist didn't follow his sweetheart to the door to be sure he didn't hop into the next coach. Milind wouldn't follow him to Nalla Sopara for the life of him. He simply wasn't that type. Tonight, Yudi would believe no wrong of him. He was head over heels in love.

Which was why he couldn't wait till Friday. Friday was seven long days away! He wished he could be with his boy-lover twenty-four hours. He phoned his office the next day, but the fellow had already left. After a depressing Sunday at his mother's, he tried to get in touch with Milind on Monday. Parmeshwar himself came on the line and spoke in a tone reserved for slaves:

'Who are you? . . . What business do you have with Milind? . . . He's not here now . . . We have work to do . . . don't disturb us by calling at the office.'

Yudi slammed the receiver of the public phone down. He could have answered back, no doubt, for like Parmeshwar he belonged to the talking class. But that would have made the damn fool suspicious. Poor Milind might be thrown out of his job for no fault of his. Cooling down, he realized the mistake he had made: he had not left his name or telephone number with the madman. He couldn't even remember if that evening, high as they were, he'd given Milind his number.

The first thing that Milind said to Yudi when they met Friday next was: 'Why did you call up at the office? Boss gave me a big firing.'

'How do you know it was me?' Yudi asked.

'Nobody else has my phone number.'

Yudi's heart skipped a beat. It was as if he had been told: 'I love just you, nobody else.' Apologizing, promising never to ring again, he played with Milind's fingers as they walked. They were heading towards Café Volga, a famous Irani restaurant whose cakes Yudi had been eating since childhood.

The beer bar of Café Volga was situated on the mezzanine floor. A huge signboard warned customers: PAY IN ADVANCE. Taking advantage of the fact that they were the only ones on the floor, Yudi and Milind settled down at a table and smooched. Yudi smacked Milind's lips as if they were sausages fried in pure ghee.

He rang the bell to summon the waiter. A man came up the stairs, took their order and collected his cash.

'Why do they want money in advance?' Milind asked.

'Because people can't find their purse when they are drunk.'

As soon as the waiter left, they resumed their smooching, letting go only when they heard heavy steps treading up the stairs. It was a customer, another beer drinker. Yudi noted with regret that his coming signalled the end of their kissing.

Ten minutes passed, then fifteen. There was no sign of their beer. The new customer frantically pressed the bell for the waiter, to no avail. Finally, the manager, a handsome Irani whom Yudi had once caught wanking in the Churchgate loo, came up himself.

'Whom did you give your money to?' he asked, and informed them that the mezzanine floor waiter was on leave. 'Dandi,' he called it.

Clearly someone who posed as a waiter had made good with their two hundred bucks.

'Inside job,' Yudi told the Irani, hinting that they shouldn't be charged again. But the latter would hear none of it.

'Not our fault,' he argued. 'You should be careful, no, about whom you pay money to?'

Yudi had half a mind to blackmail him: serve us our beer or I'll tell old man Irani what his son was up to in the Churchgate loo. But he liked the place, and he was warm and happy after the lusty kissing, so he kept his cool, and as if in reward, a waiter brought a tray with three glasses and two bottles of Arlem beer and a plate of wafers.

'Cheers,' they clinked glasses.

Yudi watched Milind drink his first gulp. A tube ran down Milind's neck. Yudi mistook it for a vein.

'How prominent your veins are,' he remarked.

It wasn't a vein but a plastic tube Milind let him know. 'Two years ago I had TB Meningitis. I was going to die.'

The tube, apparently, was fitted by doctors to drain away the excess fluid from his brain.

'How terrible to go about with a contraption like that inside your body!' Yudi exclaimed.

Milind told him what he'd heard from the doctors who treated him at the Out Patient Department of the hospital where his father was a ward boy: it was either the tube or death. The operation was painful and lasted over eight hours.

So the boy was ill. It surprised Yudi that he hadn't noticed the tube when they made love in his mother's flat. He now knew the reason for the somewhat garbled way in which Milind spoke: his brain had been messed with. One more thing that put him in the company of the wretched. The thought made Yudi feel more secure about their love.

'What about the riots?' Milind suddenly asked, popping a wafer into his mouth.

'What about them?'

'What did you do during those days?'

'Nothing. Stayed at home and read all the newspapers.'

'What sort of reporter are you?'

'The lazy sort. And you, what did you do?'

Milind gave Yudi a long account of one of his experiences.

'I was working as a Brasso-Master in CIPLA. It was a leave vacancy. The factory is in Vikhroli. My job was to polish the brassware, keep it shining. As usual, I left home early in the morning and caught a train at Chinchpokli, to reach the factory at nine. I didn't know that the factory was closed because of the danga. I came back to Vikhroli station, but the trains had stopped running by then. Like other passengers, I started walking along the railway tracks. I knew it would take hours and hours to reach Chinchpokli, but then what choice did I have? From time to time, people gave us hool. "They're coming, they're coming," they yelled. We ran for our lives till we realized it was only a joke. Two hours later I reached Kurla. Had a cup of tea at the station, and enquired when the trains would start running again. No one knew. No announcements either. I left Kurla and walked on the tracks towards Sion. "Bachao, bachao," I heard people scream as I reached Dharavi. I looked back and saw a frightened group of Muslims in lungis running towards me. Each one had a small bundle in his hands. There were women among them also. I realized that if I didn't run, I might be killed by the mob that was chasing them. So I started running and became a part of the group. An empty local train stood on the next track. I went under it and hid. A few minutes later, the mob caught up with the scared Muslims, got hold of a couple of them, and in front of my eyes, slaughtered them, as goats are slaughtered at Deonar!'

'God,' Yudi gasped, putting his hands on his head.

He ordered another beer.

'So I wasn't very wrong in thinking that you had been killed in the riots. You nearly were! How did you finally get home that day?'

'The mob dispersed after killing those chaps. I got out of my hiding place and resumed my trek. I walked on the other side of the empty train, to avoid stepping on the dead bodies. There was no other incident. I only had swollen ankles when I reached Chinchpokli.'

'You should be given the Padma Shree for your patience and courage,' Yudi said. 'But tell me, what do you think of the demolition of the Babri Masjid? Are you happy or unhappy that it was destroyed?'

'Of course I am unhappy. The Muslims are our friends, even though they are dirty and I wouldn't really spend time with them. I hate the Brahmans and the Marathas, the VHP and RSS.'

Yudi was about to respond when Milind interrupted him.

'You must hear this. When I was thirteen, I was in the RSS. I used to wear khaki shorts and go for their drill at Shivaji Park every morning. We had to bring our right hands to our chests to salute. They ordered us to stay in that position for very long. My hand ached. When no one was looking, I quietly brought it down. I even played their games. The gandus enrolled me in their party, although they knew I was a Dalit. If I bunked they came to my house to get me.'

Yudi forgot what he wanted to say. The image of Milind doing the RSS salute in khaki knickers was too funny for words. Guffawing, he closed his eyes and tried to picture his boy-lover there, at Shivaji Park. What were they trying to do? Baptize him? Ask him to shed his Bhangi skin, so that new Brahman skin might grow in its place? The snakes!

Milind tapped Yudi's knee. He opened his eyes and saw Master-Baiter standing before them.

'Boss, old man said not to charge you for one beer. Not your fault, after all. It is a security lapse on our part.'

'That's better,' Yudi replied. 'Those who live in glass houses mustn't throw stones.'

'What?'

'Nothing. Just remembered my favourite proverb.'

The lovers smooched one last time after his exit. They walked to Marine lines, boarded the same train, Milind alighted at Mahalaxmi, Yudi earned his freedom aeons later, when the train reached Nalla Sopara.

The free beer succeeded in ensuring that Café Volga wouldn't lose two of its loyal customers. It was Friday again and they were wondering what beer bar to visit. Yudi put it to the vote, and Café Volga won by a huge margin. Yudi hoped it would be empty, like the last time: he had more or less made up his mind to have it off with his cock-throb up there on the mezzanine floor.

They settled down on the hard wooden chairs and switched on a table fan. Yudi ordered a pitcher, and was touched when Milind opened his wallet to pay the waiter.

'You can't pay every time,' the smaller told the bigger. Yudi told Milind to not be silly and put away his wallet. This was the first and the last time such a thing would happen; henceforth it would be assumed that Yudi was the treasurer with an endless supply of easy money.

A group of college boys from St. Xavier's smoked at another table. Some of them had long hair, others wore earrings, still others had obscene graffiti scribbled on their jeans. Yudi compared them to Milind, all of them being of the same age. 'Privileged kids of crorepati parents,' he said to himself. He wished they would leave soon. But the boys seemed to be in no hurry. They ordered beer after beer, paying the waiter by turns.

The pitcher arrived, accompanied by wafers. Milind enjoyed pouring the frothy liquid into tumblers and clinking the glasses. Then he picked up each wafer on the plate, bit into it, and threw it back on the plate.

'May I ask what you are doing?' Yudi said.

'Testing if my caste really doesn't bother you. Eat my jootha if it doesn't.'

'Oh no, not again,' Yudi replied, infuriated. He took a half eaten wafer and popped it into his mouth. 'There you are. Are you convinced now?'

'No! Eat the whole lot!'

'Stop it!' Yudi howled, causing the Xavierites to look in their direction.

'Cool down,' Milind said. 'I was only joking.'

'Homos are no different from Bhangis. Both are Untouchables. So why should I have a problem eating your jootha?'

'But you are a Brahman, aren't you?'

'No, I am a homosexual. Gay by caste. Gay by religion.'

'I don't understand what you are saying.'

'What I am saying is that homosexuals have no caste or religion. They have only their homosexuality.'

'How can that be?'

'That's how it is. Straight people are Brahmans, gays Shudras.

So you see, both you and I are Shudras. That's why we are best friends.'

At some intuitive level, Milind suspected that Yudi was talking sense. He was in no position, however, to understand the intricacies of the argument.

The Xavierites abruptly got up and left. Yudi lost no time. First he brought his mouth to Milind's and kissed him till the boy pulled away; then he ducked under the table, unzipped Milind and blew him to finish. A new set of customers arrived just as Milind fastened his trousers and Yudi went to the sink at the far end.

'You're too bindaas,' Milind said disapprovingly, as soon as Yudi got back. 'Supposing these people came a minute earlier? They would have caught us red-handed.'

'This is Bombay, my love. People mind their own business.'

'That's true only as far as high society is concerned. For the middle class, indecent behaviour is a crime.'

'What about me? Where do I belong? The middle class or high society?'

'You? High society of course! That's why you're a gone case!'

Yudi laughed. The ice was breaking, and that was a good sign. If Milind was disrespectful, it only meant he was beginning to think of Yudi as his own. They bantered for quite some time, Yudi perceiving it as dillagi.

'Repeat,' he said to the waiter each time he appeared to ask if they were done. So absorbed were the lovers in each other, that they lost track of who came up and went down the stairs. When they were alone again, Yudi asked Milind to return the favour: blow or shag him. But he refused.

'Sorry,' he said.

'Why?' Yudi demanded. 'Don't you love me?'

'I do, but I don't take in the mouth. I don't take it in the arse either. I don't mind fucking you, but not here. Let's go to your mother's house. It's close by, isn't it?'

Yudi was upset by this reference to his mother. He didn't expect Milind to remember where exactly her building was.

'And where do we send my mom, to your place?' he asked.

'Forget it, then,' Milind said. 'We'll see next time.'

A doubt crossed Yudi's mind.

'Tell me honestly,' he told his boyfriend, 'are you really a homosexual?'

'Who knows.'

'Do you enjoy having sex with women?'

'I've never had sex with a woman, so how can I tell?

That was too neat, and despite himself Yudi snapped, 'But you seem so sure of what you will do and what you won't.'

This provoked Milind to snap back, 'If you're that horny, ask the bawaji to suck you,' referring to Café Volga's masturbating proprietor.

'If I want to I will,' Yudi replied tersely.

Milind turned his attention to the menu painted on the wall to their right and decided to try out the fried eggs-and-chips. The dish took ages to arrive; when it did finally, he asked the waiter for sauce, and emptied half the bottle of tomato ketchup on his plate. The red sauce and the yolk ran into each other, like paint on a painter's canvas. Milind soaked each potato chip in the red-and-yellow admixture before chucking it into his mouth.

'Nauseating,' Yudi whispered to himself, hoping he wouldn't be heard. But Milind had sharp ears. His mouth was full of the stuff when he opened it and said: 'Come on, kiss me, why don't you kiss me now?'

Yudi didn't reply. He took out a copy of *Bombay Dost* from his bag and browsed through it as Milind ate.

'What's that?' Milind asked to break the silence.

'Gay magazine. India's first and only.'

Milind grabbed the magazine from Yudi's hands and flipped through the pages hurriedly. He stopped whenever he came upon pictures of half-naked men, and looked at them intently. Yudi observed his reactions closely. He had no doubt that the boy was turned on by people of his own sex. When Milind returned the magazine to Yudi, it was full of oily fingerprints.

Opening the magazine to the 'Swayamwar' page, Yudi explained that gays could advertise for partners here, just as heteros did in the matrimonial columns of the *Times of India*. Milind was nonplussed; he had absolutely no idea that such things happened in his city.

'You hi-fi guys and your crazy ideas!' he exclaimed, wide-eyed.

Yudi read out what was written and boxed at the top of the page:

CAUTION

Swayamwar is for homosexuals who wish to meet other homosexuals and for lesbians. Transvestites, transsexuals and hijras can also advertise in swayamwar. This page is not for heterosexuals. Heterosexuals, that is men who like women and women who like men, already have innumerable opportunities to meet each other. We therefore urge Heterosexuals Not To Abuse This Precious Space.

Milind heard with interest, asking Yudi what transvestite and transsexual meant. He urged him to read out a couple of the ads. He was dipping the last of his finger-chips in the orange goo.

'Okay,' Yudi obliged. 'Here goes . . . *Hi! I'm Raja, age 25, slim, slightly hairy, of brown complexion. Would like to meet gays of my age or below. I am eager to meet gays from Tamilnadu,*

Kerala, or Bangalore. South Indians turn me on. Write to Raja, BD Box No 109/23.

'And here's another . . . Slave man seeks dominant master between 30-35, to service. Willing to travel. Come to my service station. Write to C. K. BD Box No 109/28.

'And listen to this one . . . Young, 28-year-old Transvestite Drag Queen loves the feminine life. And still a virgin, homely, passive. Offers himself for a lifelong relationship with a wealthy, aggressive, sincere, honest male from any part of the world. Willing to settle anywhere in the world with you when we learn to get along. Write to R.M. BD Box No 109/4.'

'Do you want to respond to any of them?' Yudi said, putting away the magazine in his jhola.

'Rubbish!'

'You don't need to because you've found the love of your life?'

'Rubbish!'

Milind washed down his fried eggs-and-chips with a Pepsi before they left. They decided to catch their train from Churchgate, instead of Marine Lines.

'Does your mom know you are gay?' he asked Yudi, as they walked.

This was the second time he had referred to the old lady. Yudi wondered why. Just what was on the boy's mind? Then he felt foolish for being so suspicious.

'Well, she both knows and doesn't know,' he replied.

'How can that be? She either knows or she doesn't know.'

'You're too clever to be an office boy.'

'Find me the job of a Managing Director then!'

Branching off from the well-lit Mahatma Gandhi Road, Yudi decided to walk through Cross Maidan. 'Short cut,' he called it. His real idea of course was to feel his mate all over in the maidan's darkness. Just as they squatted on a grassy patch and Yudi began to do Milind, a policeman came charging at them, blowing his whistle. Milind put away his maha-dick just in time. The policeman let them off with a warning: 'If you are ever caught sitting here again, I'll put you in the lock up.'

'I told you, madman,' Milind said, as they resumed walking, 'the police are always around to make money.'

'Money's not what most of them are after,' Yudi laughed. He proceeded to inform his boyfriend that policemen went after gay couples only because they wanted to be sucked off; he had first-hand information on this as a journalist. Milind found that hard to believe.

'I don't believe half the things you say,' he said. While on the subject of disbelief, he also told Yudi that, in his opinion, all those ads in *Bombay Dost* were fake.

'In that case, respond to one of them and see for yourself,' Yudi told him.

Milind suddenly felt inclined to take up the challenge.

'You won't mind?' he asked his lover.

'Not as long as you don't get serious about it.'

'Why, are you jealous?' Milind giggled.

'I'd swallow rat poison,' Yudi said dramatically and they laughed as they entered Churchgate station.

They didn't go to Café Volga the next weekend. Instead, they went to Fashion Street to buy clothes. They had made up their mind to go to Testosterone, but not before Milind chucked his old-fashioned clothes that would make him a laughing stock. Yudi bought him T-shirts and jeans at bargain prices and paid for the lot. They looked for shoes and landed up at Churchgate's Shoe Bazaar. Both of them had heard of the aggressive marketing strategies of hawkers here. However, even Yudi was unprepared

for the way they grabbed him, dragged him into their stalls, and
didn't let go of his arms, legs, and shoulders till he sat down to
try out their shoes. The ruffians virtually raped their customers
into buying their wares. Yudi enjoyed it while it lasted, for the
stalls were manned by smart young men under twenty-five,
probably from the slums of Dharavi, and it was with great
reluctance that he broke free from the grip of the last chap, saying
'Bahut costly hai.' But he had his fill before leaving. Milind
followed him from stall to stall, fully aware of what was going
on. The vendors were less keen to paw him, for they knew it was
Yudi who paid the piper and called the tune. In spite of the heavy
discounts the buggers offered, quoting a price of, say, five hundred
rupees for a pair, and then bringing it down by more than half,
Milind felt they were swindlers. He didn't want his obsessed friend
to be ripped off on his account. So he persuaded him to leave the
guys alone.

'Come with me to Ded Gali early tomorrow morning. We'll
get the same shoes for just fifty rupees.'

'Ded Gali? One-and-half-streets?' Yudi exclaimed. 'What's
that? And where?'

He thought he was an authority on Bombay; but Milind was
to give him a glimpse of shady Bombay, of which he knew next
to nothing.

He woke up at two the next morning; an hour later he was at
the station to board the first train to town. Ded Gali, Milind had
explained to him, was a division of Chor Bazaar. The vendors set
up shop early every morning, around five when the milk vans
plied, and by half past seven all their goods were gone. The police,
who posed as customers and whisked them away into waiting
police vans, lock, stock and barrel, frequently harassed them.
Hence they were suspicious of clients, whose faces they tried to
discreetly read in the early morning light. A deal was struck only

when they were convinced that so-and-so was a genuine buyer. If there was one thing that worried Milind, it was that they would mistake Yudi for an agent provocateur, what with his bossy air.

Yudi alighted at Bombay Central, as his streetsmart friend had instructed him, and walked towards the notorious Alexandra Cinema where they'd arranged to meet. Stray dogs chased him on one occasion, pimps on another. Milind was already there when he reached the cinema. They entered a ramshackle restaurant for a quick cup of tea, and were sickened by the smell of kebabs that were being fried at this ludicrous hour.

'See that lane there?' Milind asked him, as soon as they got out of the restaurant. 'It leads to my school.'

'What's the school's name?'

'Anthony D'Souza's English Medium Night High School.'

'Why did you drop out of school?'

'After my meningitis operation I lost my memory. Couldn't by heart lessons for the exams. I appeared for my tenth, failed, and did not appear again.'

'Would you like to give it a shot this year? I'll pay your fees.'

'No thanks. I still can't by heart anything.'

It was strange, thought Yudi, that they should engage in this sacred digression concerning Milind's studies at a time they were going to buy stolen goods. He allowed Milind to lead the way, losing track of where they were as they left the main road and entered narrow lanes and by lanes. He recovered his bearings all of a sudden, when he saw a signboard that said SHUKLAJI STREET.

'Do you know we are in the middle of the red light district?' he asked his friend, and proceeded to inform him that Shuklaji Street was famous for its hijra prostitutes. Milind was no ignoramus. He knew everything. What he was interested in, though, was whether Yudi ever visited any of the hijra-whores.

'No,' Yudi lied. It was only a half lie: he'd been there several times, but that was all so long ago, he barely remembered the thrills and the squalor.

Another five minutes, and they were in Ded Gali. Only after getting there did Yudi understand why the place was called one-and-a-half street. There was a longish alley that led to a shorter one at right angles to it, where the hawkers sat. The long road was one, the short road half, the sum one-and-a-half.

Everything was exactly as Milind had described it. The shoes were there, spread out on the road, and there were mobs of buyers at every pavement stall. Unlike the shoe-sellers of Churchgate, the vendors here didn't outrage their customers' modesty. They touched only shoes, not bodies. Yudi stood at a stall and discovered that the footwear indeed went for a song. After much haggling, not over the price but about the kind of shoes he wanted Milind to wear, they settled on a pair of suedes with large buckles. Quoting a price of Rs 100, the seller readily gave it to them at a twenty-five-rupee discount.

'Amazing,' Yudi said. He wanted to survey the other things sold at Ded Gali: bags, belts, clothes. Milind told him that in that case he'd have to be on his own. It was nearing office time; these days that harami Parmeshwar screamed if he was even five minutes late.

Yudi complied. Hugging Milind as if he were taking off for the United States, congratulating him on the purchase of his shoes, he bid him goodbye. 'Have a nice day,' he said, American style. On his own now, he went from stall to stall, stopping only if something caught his fancy. There were more shoes. And shirts and trousers and wallets and belts and pens and ashtrays and lighters and vests and perfumes and goggles and key chains and cassettes and hip flasks. The entire range of men's things found in swanky stores like Benzer's. Yudi picked up a folder here, a buckle there, but in the end did not buy anything. As darkness gave way to light, he noticed manufacturing defects in all the items. Some goods were dented; others had scratches on their surface. The vendors, he realized, set up shop before dawn not just to prevent their wares being confiscated by the police; it was equally important that buyers did not detect manufacturing defects in the half dark. His only prayer was that Milind's shoes should last them their session in Testosterone.

They swung their bodies to the rhythm of the music, stepping up each time there was a fast number. This left both Yudi and Milind exhausted. From time to time they spoke to each other, as heteros do while dancing, but gave up half way. For one thing, the music was deafening. For another, not being the same height, the taller had to bend, the shorter stand on tiptoe to follow what the other was saying. In a disco, gestures were preferable to words, Yudi felt.

In between numbers, someone came up to Milind and whispered: 'Are you a plug or a socket, love?' Milind frowned, looking puzzled, so the fellow switched to Hindi: 'Koti ho ya panthi?' But the boy didn't make sense of this either, and looked at Yudi who was about to raise a fist to strike the bastard.

'Keep off,' he yelled at the top of his voice. Leading Milind by the hand, kissing him on the way, he marched off to the bar.

'What was the harami asking me?' Milind was impatient to know.

'He wanted to check out if you're the fucker or the fucked.'

'So that's why people come here? To pick up guys and take them home?'

'Obviously.'

'May I go with him and make some money on the side?'

'Fuck off!' Yudi sulked, forcing Milind to stop laughing and apologize.

They left the dance floor, beer mugs in hand, and sat down on two chairs, the last that were available. Milind looked ravishing in his Fashion Street clothes and Ded Gali shoes. No wonder he was propositioned. Yudi looked around to see who the other occupants of the tables and chairs were. On spotting a familiar face, he froze. The face was Dnyaneshwar's. He was cuddled up in a corner, with a nymphet as usual, but this time it was Faye Dunaway, not Meryl Streep. Yudi looked away quickly, and made sure he sat with his back towards the hooligan. But Dnyaneshwar spotted him and walked up to him, extending his right hand.

'Hello, saab, mujhe pehchana?' he asked.

Yudi shook the policeman's hand, but lukewarmly. He had no idea what the blackmailer would say to him next; Gulab and company weren't in the pub tonight, in case a fight broke out. To his utter relief, however, Dnyaneshwar took his leave on his own, saying, 'Okay, saab, bye.' Yudi's eyes followed him; discovered he was sandwiched between two folks, Faye Dunaway on the right and some man on the left who played with his balls.

'Who was that?' Milind asked Yudi, without bothering to keep the jealousy out of his voice.

'Don't know really,' he answered evasively. 'Some guy whom I picked up before I met you, just as you were about to be picked up by Plug-and-Socket.'

'You never told me about him before.'

'Who all can I keep telling you about?'

Yudi saw that his boyfriend was hurt. He assured him that whereas in the past he gave only his genitals to lovers, to Milind he had bequeathed his heart. 'I love you,' he said to him for the first time since the start of their affair. Milind blushed, fumbled in his shirt pocket and offered Yudi a cigarette, lighting it himself with a disposable lighter picked up on the streets. They smoked in silence. Yudi flicked his ash into a cute shoe-shaped ashtray on the carpeted floor. As he took it in his hands, fingered it, played with it, he wondered where Pallonji got his curios from. This one was most unusual, perhaps a gift from abroad, he mused. The fellow went on foreign jaunts at the drop of a hat. And why not! With all the money he minted, charging each homosexual guest a cover charge of Rs 100, it didn't seem difficult. Testosterone, after all, was Bombay's only gay bar, and the city had more homos than the populations of London and Paris put together.

Yudi kissed Milind full on the lips, the latter allowing it only because he saw everyone else kissing. Even so, he didn't want it to be an endless affair. As he pulled away Yudi thought of complaining but was interrupted by tremendous shrieks.

They came from Faye Dunaway.

'Oh God,' Yudi put his hands on his head, as he realized his folly. That was no ashtray! It was a real-life shoe, the Hollywood clone's, and the poor thing had just put her foot into it, singeing her sole on the hot cigarette ash.

Dnyaneshwar and his accomplice rushed to the lady's rescue. They blew air from their mouths on the underside of her tiny white foot, appearing like a pair of circus clowns in the process. Luckily for Yudi, they had no idea he was the culprit.

After a while, the confusion died down. The blonde's discomfort was drowned out by the music. Her heroic knights literally carried her to the drinks bar and bought her a gin-and-tonic. The money couldn't be Dnyaneshwar's, Yudi speculated; it was undoubtedly the other chap's. Who was he anyway? The Inspector General of Police?

Yudi took Milind by the hand and led him to the dance floor, now packed to capacity. A marathon dancing session followed, Milind demonstrating that he was a graceful dancer. Not bad for a lad from Chinchpokli, thought Yudi. Having abandoned the idea of parleying while dancing, he directed his attention to the graffiti on the walls. BACKDOOR ENTRY IS BEST, one painted slogan said. ADAM WAS MADE FOR ADAM JR., said another. A third reversed the laws of Physics: LIKE POLES ATTRACT, UNLIKE POLES REPEL.

Sweat poured freely down every neck; as freely as the booze in the bar that actually wasn't free but cost twice as much as it did outside.

Ten minutes into the dance, there was trouble again. A fat guy, whose frenzied dancing had held everyone spellbound till he tired and slowed down, began to eye Milind. He explored every possibility, optically speaking; staring now, now winking, now rolling his eyes upwards and downwards. Desire was writ large on his face. Yudi observed him for a bit, and when he could take it no longer, seized him by the scruff of the neck.

'What do you think you're doing, baby?' he asked.

'Eye exercises,' came the repartee. 'You see, I have been diagnosed with cataract, and have to do my exercises at all times.'

'Oh yeah?' said Yudi. 'I'll have your cataract removed right now. You won't have to see a doctor.'

As he spoke, he punched his rival in the stomach and on the nose, a la Hindi film style. All hell broke loose in the bar. Mr Eye Exercises returned the compliment, striking Yudi on the chin. Had the dance floor been less crowded, they would have lain flat on the ground and rolled over each other in a passionate fit of hate and love. However, that being impossible now, they rewarded each other with fisticuffs and abuses. Fucker. Asshole. Son-of-a-bitch. Faggot. Both bled from the nose.

Pallonji and his bouncers rushed in to forcibly draw the wrestlers apart. Both Yudi and Eye Exercises were part of Pallonji's upmarket clientele (EE came in a Mercedes). So he couldn't order them out of his bar, as he doubtless would have done had the contenders for Milind's hand been taxi drivers.

The fairies on the dance floor broke into a loud chorus. 'Hai, hai,' they screamed, as the blows went from this side to that and that to this. 'Blow each other, but not like this!' Then they joined Pallonji's pehelvans in their tug of war to separate the adversaries.

In the middle of all this, Dnyaneshwar surprised Yudi by joining the fight, entirely on Yudi's side. He thrust a knee into fatty's balls, as policemen perversely do, causing him to squeal in pain.

Pallonji was livid. He ran Testosterone at considerable risk to himself, and was frequently hassled by pandus who demanded their hafta. By getting into brawls inside the pub the gay community was only digging its grave; it was needlessly drawing attention to itself. If not the Greater Bombay police, the Shiv Sena would beat them all up and shut down the place once and for all. He ordered his DJs to announce that they were closing for the night; if anyone wanted a quick drink for the road, they had better hurry.

Milind was highly embarrassed by Yudi's behaviour. If he knew his Shakespeare, he might have referred to it as much ado about nothing.

'So what if he was—'

'Ogling you?' Yudi helpfully filled in the blank.

'Yes. Don't you trust me?'

Embarrassment, however, was something the boy could deal with. What he couldn't handle was the blow to his manhood. In his scheme of things, men fought over women, not over men. Did he appear like a woman to Yudi? To Fatty? He compared himself to the heroine of a Hindi film, sandwiched between hero and villain, and felt emasculated. Why didn't anyone get possessive about all those effeminate boys he saw in Testosterone? Was it because, as Yudi explained to him, most gays preferred manly men to womanly men? That sleeping with womanly men was as revolting to them as sleeping with women? He didn't know. All he knew was that what happened should never have happened. He was no woman to be fought over. He was the one who fucked, wasn't he? And yet, he felt elated. Seeing Yudi's bloody face, he realized that here was someone at last who cared for him. Or else, would he have got into a scrap on his account?

His mother and father had four sons to divide their love amongst. Yudi had just Milind. Only him.

They were on Colaba Causeway now, walking towards Regal cinema. They spoke little. Yudi was in pain, and also regretted the scene he had created. Milind was still confused about it all. Just then they heard footsteps behind them, loud and clear at this hour of night. Turning round, they saw it was Dnyaneshwar.

'Kya saab?' he said. 'Mera chai pani?'

At which Yudi gave him a hundred bucks and thanked him for his help.

'Chalta hoon saab,' he snatched the dough and hurried away, as though afraid that Yudi and his boyfriend might strip him naked a second time.

As they walked towards Churchgate, Yudi told Milind everything about Dnyaneshwar. A to Z. The mutiny in the gay bar had instilled a new trust in both their hearts. Both felt that the other was his, over whom he had a right, towards whom he had a duty. No mean achievement for a couple who had met in the Churchgate loo.

When they parted at dawn, that most holy hour of day and night, Milind said words he'd never said to anyone before:

'I love you, Yudi.'

mate house

When Yudi went to see his mother on Sunday, she entrusted him with a task. A cousin of hers, now settled in the US, was in Bombay, staying at the Taj. She wanted Yudi to see him and hand over the gifts she'd bought for his kids. He was leaving for the States tonight, so the job had to be done immediately. Yudi had no desire to hobnob with his mother's long lost cousin. At the same time, he didn't wish to incur her displeasure. The lady was getting old; if anything happened to her, he would have to live with the guilt for the rest of his life. Moreover, he was his mother's sole support. Whom could she rely on other than him, her only son? He told her, but once, that he couldn't go to the Taj as he was busy. But when she thumped her fist on the table and gave him a Sunday sermon on filial duty, he capitulated.

His dilemma, however, was genuine. Milind was coming to his place to spend a week. They had arranged to meet on platform one of Mahalaxmi station (under the clock) at 2 p.m. sharp. How would he inform Milind, who didn't have a phone at home, that he would be late? If, not finding Yudi at the station at the appointed hour, he went away, Yudi's week would be ruined.

He thought for a moment—only a moment—and hit upon an idea. He would go to Mahalaxmi, pick Milind up, and then get to the Taj before heading homewards. It meant, no doubt, that he would be travelling back and forth: Marine Lines to Mahalaxmi to Churchgate to Nalla Sopara. But then, what choice did he have?

On meeting Milind at Mahalaxmi, he gave him the once over to see if he was suitably dressed for the Taj. His shirt was ruffled, his jeans frayed at the edges, and the rucksack he carried was about to give way. They went to the Taj all the same, where Milind waited in the lobby as Yudi took the lift to the fourteenth floor to see the old uncle.

The interview took longer than he expected, the cousin insisting that Yudi taste the Taj's club sandwiches, migrate to the US, and get married to an NRI woman who would pay him an immense dowry. Yudi kept looking at his watch and farting. Milind was the only thing on his mind; he wished he could smuggle out a few sandwiches for his hungry mate to eat on the train. When, otherwise, would his poor Sudama get to savour Taj food? Gobbling up his sandwiches, saying no to a luscious glass of badam milkshake, promising his host that he would seriously consider relocating to the US and marrying a wealthy NRI, Yudi hurried into a lift that brought him to the lobby at rocket speed.

He reached the lobby, the doors opened; he was overcome by a sense of deja vu. Some months ago, it was the opening of lift doors at the *Times* that had brought him his lost friend. But the friend seemed to have got lost again, for he was nowhere in the lobby. Not on the fluffy sofa. Not at the reception desk. Not in the loo. Yudi panicked. He looked everywhere; Milind wasn't anywhere. Just as he concluded that the fellow had slipped away because he didn't really want to go to Nalla Sopara, he looked beyond the Taj's glass doors and found him sitting on the Apollo Bunder Wall (the very Wall on which a bunch of queens had stripped a macho policeman).

Yudi waved his hands to draw Milind's attention. He was in the porch now, but didn't cross the road to go to the other side.

Although Milind noticed him, he didn't budge from his perch. Suspecting that the afternoon sun had affected his brain, Yudi crossed the busy street much against his will and went up to his love, who had a horror story to tell: he had been thrown out of the Taj. Smarting still, he gave Yudi the gory details. A durwan came up to him, asked him what his business was, and when he fumbled with his answer, caught him by the collar and hurled him out the glass doors. In full view of dozens of people, mostly foreigners! As the fanatic manhandled him, he also said: 'The Taj is not a refuge for the city's urchins. Go to the Gateway of India instead. You will find many of your kind there.'

Yudi was enraged. The thought that Milind was disgraced while he sat in air-conditioned comfort, munched club sandwiches, and indulged in bourgeois talk, filled him with remorse. He had half a mind to go up to that durwan and slap him across the face. Or else he could expose him in tomorrow's papers. But would it really matter? The man who had just been thrown out of a five star hotel was only Milind Mahadik, a ward boy's son. He was no Aubrey Menen or M.F. Husain.

Yudi stroked his friend's back. He took him to Fashion Street, asked him to choose a shirt, then paid for it, saying, 'A gift for you.' A shirt, of course, couldn't restore Milind's lost dignity, but Yudi was trying to assuage his own guilt by making it up to his wretched friend.

They didn't speak much during the train ride to Nalla Sopara. Both of them privately brooded over the incident. Unless Yudi evolved a strategy, such episodes would constantly plague their lives. This was India, after all, and Milind a working-class Dalit.

Sights, sounds and smells have so much to do with mood. As the train went past the saltpans and trundled along the Vasai Bridge,

Yudi and Milind managed to put the offensive thing behind them. They regained their lost spirits.

Soon after they got out of the station and walked towards his building, Yudi showed Milind a bungalow called 'Mate House'. It was an exquisite bungalow, elegantly done up in mustard and yellow, its Nottingham windows significantly contributing to its beauty. No, Yudi didn't dream of owning the house some day; he was a man of modest aspirations. What amazed him about the bungalow was its name.

'I've started to call my own apartment "Mate House",' he said to Milind. 'Isn't it most appropriate?'

Though Milind wasn't a matriculate, he had enough common sense to reckon that the word wasn't supposed to be pronounced as 'mate'. 'It's "Maa-tey", the owner's surname, silly,' he educated Yudi, who retorted, 'But what's the harm in reading it the way I please? In any case, "mate" sounds much better than "maa-tey".'

'You are an expert at making kachra of people's surnames,' said Milind. 'Remember what you did to mine?'

Engaged thus in verbal foreplay, Yudi's arm around Milind's shoulder, they reached their own Mate House. The sun hadn't set yet; it was the pleasantest hour of day.

'Welcome, my dear,' Yudi said, as he unlocked the front door.

'Where's the aarti?' Milind giggled. His next move was to ask where the bogs were, rush in and emerge distraught.

'You have an English-medium toilet!' he exclaimed, referring to Yudi's western-style loo. 'I won't be able to shit for a whole week!'

'I'll teach you to,' Yudi said. ' If you still find it hard, you can squat on the shit-pot, as you do in your sandaas at home.'

They freshened up. Yudi opened a bottle of whisky and fixed their drinks.

'Is this the first time you're drinking hard liquor?' he asked

Milind, to which the boy answered with a cackle. Milind needed something to munch with his drink, so they went to the kitchen and fried a dozen papads. Then they returned to the drawing room and clinked glasses, as they did Friday after Friday at Café Volga. Milind switched on the TV. He was used to having it on at all times, even if the programme aired was boring. At least, there were people on the TV, and voices. Coming from a family that lived in a one-room tenement (four sons and a mother), he found the quiet of Yudi's flat unnerving. 'How do you live here all alone?' he asked him several times that evening. 'It's as silent as a graveyard.'

While they were on their second round of drinks, Yudi called his favourite take-away and ordered dinner.

'Do you fancy Chinese food?' he asked Milind. Then: 'Well, we have no choice, even if you don't. These guys don't do Indian stuff. I'll take you to a nicer joint tomorrow. As for now, you must learn to like what you get, since you can't get what you like.'

Milind burst out laughing: 'What's the point of your lecture? When did I say I don't like Chinese?'

They completed two more rounds of drinking before the doorbell rang and a Nepali waiter brought them their meal. A thought flashed across Milind's mind: this guy has all the freedom in the world. I'm sure he has it off with all and sundry, with people like this waiter here. Can I really trust him?

They kept drinking. Milind was hell bent on finishing the bottle. He seemed to be in no hurry to eat the food, which was now clammy. As for Yudi, it suited him fine to get Milind drunk. He was looking forward to a night of febrile sex. It was well past midnight by the time they teetered to the kitchen, undid the wrappers, and swallowed all the fried rice and Chicken Manchurian.

As soon as dinner was over, they crashed. Yudi, normally

fastidious, forgot even to clear the table, giving fat black cockroaches a chance to feast on the leftovers. Then there were ants that fed on the cockroaches' leavings.

The sozzled duo fell fast asleep within seconds. As a consequence, the sex didn't begin till much later, say 3 a.m. or thereabouts, when Yudi woke Milind and they mounted each other by turn (the boy too drunk still to insist that he alone would do the fucking). Milind still hadn't learned to wear his condom.

Afterwards, they huddled and cuddled up to each other; didn't rise till the sun was high in the sky.

'My God!' Yudi screamed, looking at his watch. 'It's ten o'clock. Saraswati will be here any minute.'

Saraswati, Yudi's cleaning woman, was got with much difficulty. 'Our marad log don't want us to work for single men,' most women told him and left. He couldn't risk losing the only maid who had stayed on, even when she suspected the saab was not quite normal.

Yudi had spent part of his night worrying where to hide Milind when Saraswati came. Not in the bathroom, for that was where she washed clothes . . . Now, minutes before Saraswati was expected to arrive, he had no definitive answer yet. He woke Milind up in alarm, tickling him all over when he refused to get out of bed.

'Take a long walk,' he ordered him, 'and come back after an hour. There'll be hell to pay if Saraswati sees you here.'

'What a moosibat,' grumbled Milind, as he wore his trousers and searched for his toothbrush.

Not being the walking type, the boy whiled away his time at a nearby bus stop, while the Goddess of Learning did Yudi's dishes, scolding him for leaving things so dirty. Cleaning women, Yudi reminded himself again, are the mothers-in-law of unmarried men.

Milind sat at the bus stop for exactly an hour, and when his time was up, walked back to the flat, missing Saraswati by scarcely a few seconds.

Later that day, they trekked to a nearby saloon for a haircut and a shave. A sort of ritual cleansing, Yudi laughed, for he was a fussy Brahmin and it wouldn't do for the Dalit boy to be unkempt and long-haired in his house. Milind asked if, in that case, the barber would also trim his pubic hair. There were barbers who did that, his learned friend informed him, but they weren't in Nalla Sopara. They were in Shuklaji Street. 'The next time we go to Ded Gali, remind me to take you there.'

The radio at Rajesh Khanna Hair Cutting Saloon was on at full blast. A song from the film *Baazigar* enraptured customers:

Yeh kali kali aankhen
Yeh gore gore gaal

These black black eyes
These fair fair cheeks

Milind wondered why the saloon had such an old-fashioned name. Why wasn't it named after the latest sensation, Shahrukh Khan? Yudi explained that it was founded in 1970, when Shahrukh Khan was still in his short pants. Rajesh Khanna was the phenomenon then, and so were his films. *Aradhana*, *Amar Prem*, *Kati Patang*, where he wore yellow pants. 'But wait a minute,' he cried. 'How should *you* know? You weren't even conceived then!'

'Old man, old man,' Milind paid him back in the same coin.

As they waited for their turn, more *Baazigar* songs filled their hearts with joy. So it wasn't Vividh Bharati, but an audio cassette of the film. A barber summoned them to his throne. Yudi asked Milind to go ahead for he was still busy flipping through the pages of *Filmfare*.

Half an hour passed, Milind completed his purification rite; Yudi was in the process of being shaved. Suddenly, Milind looked at him in the mirror and was shocked to find him sucking his barber's fingers. The barber, like all Indian barbers, had put his thumb on Yudi's lips for a firmer grip. Yudi licked the thumb, sucked it, then licked the man's other fingers.

'Gone case!' Milind said to himself.

On their way home, he asked, 'What do you think you were doing?' A certain mad professor, Yudi replied perfectly seriously, had this theory that Indians who spoke English were so alienated that they couldn't relate to the language of barbers in a barbershop. 'I was merely disproving his thesis, by relating to the barber's body language. I mean, how dare he rest his thumb on my lips!'

'You unfaithful bastard!' Milind's response might have been. But it wasn't. He was merely confused.

Seconds after they got home, Yudi switched on the radio, then the immersion heater in the bathroom. When the water was hot enough—Milind dipped a finger in the bucket to satisfy himself—they undressed.

Milind had a hard on, which pleased Yudi, who happily poured mugs of water on the boy's body. They soaped each other copiously, till both looked like astronauts, just back from the moon, and scrubbed every inch of each other's bodies, being partial to the dick, bums and tits. By the time they had washed off the rich lather, so much water had seeped out from under the door that a part of the flat had been transformed into Vasai Creek.

For Yudi, a purification rite wasn't complete till one's nails had also been cut. He looked at Milind's fingernails and was repelled by the sight of the black rim of muck crowning them. The toenails were jagged.

'Pare your nails,' he said, managing to smile indulgently. 'And pare them not with a pair of scissors but a nail-clipper. Do you know what a nail-clipper is?' He was reminded of rustic servants in his parents' household who chewed their nails to trim them.

Milind was offended by the insinuation. 'Am I from Alibag or what, that I don't know what a nail clipper is?' he snapped.

'From Alibag!' exclaimed Yudi, impressed by his wit. 'What's that supposed to mean?'

He passed on a nail-clipper to his boyfriend, and saw that he used it with great flourish, collecting the severed pieces on a newspaper and chucking them out of the window. The lad was spruced up now, his hair was groomed, and the stubble on his chin had disappeared; his fingers and toes looked good enough to have for breakfast. Only one thing remained, and that was his nose, more or less similar to a clogged drain, which he picked far too often for Yudi to ignore.

'Blow your nose and get the snot out,' Yudi told him, 'and then you are good enough to be Mr Universe!'

That night, they gave each other nicknames. *Jhop Mod* (Sleep Breaker) was Milind's for Yudi. He thought it suited him well because he had a way of rousing him from slumber and pleading that they make love. Yudi reacted by calling his young lover a *Palang Tod* (Cot Breaker). More than once, he had worried, even as they fucked furiously, where he would find a carpenter if the double bed gave way.

When it was time for Saraswati to come in the following morning, Milind refused to run off to the bus stop. 'I look respectable now,' he explained. He froze on the bed like a mannequin when she arrived, and as a consequence got assaulted with a yellow dusting cloth, the bai mistaking him for a new curio her saab had picked up.

Thus the days passed. Mate House became a delightful holiday resort for Yudi and Milind, a prelude to the vacation they would soon take. In Milind's company, what little unfamiliarity Yudi had with the ways of 'menials' disappeared. People were no different from each other, he often declared, and now he could say that with absolute conviction. Having conceded that, however, he had to admit Milind's gutkha-eating, that left red blotches all over his bathroom tiles, nauseated him. In the end, he put this to erotic use too, asking Milind to kiss him when his mouth was full of the juice so that the stuff was transferred to his gob, and he hygienically disposed of it in polythene carry bags.

This was Milind's outing in every sense of the word. Hence Yudi very kindly took him to the saltpans of Nalla Sopara, not far away, and to Nirmal, a strange monument for which the place is famous. Meagre though these pleasures would seem, they were happy. Milind proved this one morning by calling Yudi Jaaneman, the life of his heart, which made old Yudi's head spin with joy.

The middle of the week was dominated by food. Milind, Yudi discovered, loved to eat and made no bones about it. Yudi's hot plate was on for longer than usual; the plug burned in the socket one day and let out a fishy odour. Indeed, that morning, misled by the smell, Milind thought it was fish his jaaneman was cooking for his lunch, and was so disappointed to be told it was only a burning socket, that he went on a hunger strike. The fast didn't last for more than a few minutes. He pounced on his breakfast the moment it was laid on the table, never mind if the boiled eggs had disintegrated in the hot water. As he ate, he explained to Yudi that his father earned so little, and had to feed so many mouths, that he always went hungry to bed. Was he mad to look a gift horse in the mouth by criticizing an egg for being improperly boiled? It was in Yudi's home alone that he ate without a sense of guilt. In his own, he was always seized by the feeling that by swallowing an extra morsel he was depriving one of his brothers, and definitely his mother.

Yudi was moved. The sadder he was, the more ravishing Milind looked, though it was also true that he had a divine smile. (Just looking at those even, white teeth, scrubbed, he presumed, with Colgate danth manjan, gave Yudi a hard on.) Yudi decided to treat his starving friend to a hearty non-vegetarian meal at a nondescript place where they paid only for the food, not for the paintings on the walls and the piped music. Milind opted for beef, saying beef-eating was in his blood. After all, his forefathers ate the carcasses of cattle with gusto. These were 'gifted' to them by Brahmans, who were actually using their stomachs as dustbins: what a lot of expense and labour they saved, not having to bother about the cremation of animals! Yudi wasn't shocked. He had read the autobiography of Laxman Gaikwad, who ate live pigs as a child to quell his hunger, only a few feet from the spot where women shat.

Milind's beef and rice were tasty. These were modern times, not the days of his forefathers, or of Laxman Gaikwad's childhood. The meal over, they rushed home, for he badly needed to crap, having eaten so much that his stomach bulged.

Their lovemaking began early that day, in the afternoon itself, and stretched well into the night. The beef and rice pumped Milind with a new vigour. Yudi, conversely, was weakened by too much food and sex; so much so, that he had no strength to beat an egg to make Milind an omelette (he was still hungry). He went to his medicine chest to pop some vitamin pills, dropped one on the kitchen counter, and after a while, saw it being carried away by retinues of ants. Had it not been for the incredible good fortune of having a boy half his age for a lover, Yudi would have wept at the loss of his youth.

Yudi didn't leave Mate House that whole week to meet his editors in their downtown offices. He managed with daily phone calls.

He didn't think it was a good idea to leave Milind alone in the flat, while he gallivanted around town. Not that he expected the guy to break open his cupboards and walk away with his life's savings; but money *was* a big temptation. Asking Milind to accompany him to Greater Bombay and then return to Nalla Sopara was like wishing for a rocket trip to the moon. The boy was that lazy! Instead of converting him, Yudi adapted to his way of living. That essentially meant watching every episode of every serial on TV. He sat by his side and feigned interest in *Tara* and *Swabhimaan*, his real interest being Milind's body on which he feasted his eyes with shocking greed.

When he couldn't bear TV anymore, Yudi suggested an even better diversion: they would get married. He even wrote out a wedding card: Mr and Mrs Maha-Dick request the pleasure of your company at the wedding of their son MILIND with YUDI, son of the Old Lady of Pherwani Mansion, on Thursday, 25 November, at Mate House, Nalla Sopara, Bombay.

Shehnai music from Yudi's collection of cassettes created the right mood. They lit a fire in the fucking room, and were about to go round it seven times, when a major dispute arose between them. Each wanted to be the engine as they encircled the fire. Each had a strong case. Milind's was that he was 'active' (a word he had discovered only recently, at Testosterone), Yudi's that he was the breadwinner. In the end, of course, Yudi capitulated. At his age, love rarely came without sacrifice. He fished out a chiffon sari that his mother had once left behind, draped himself in it, and became the bride. Milind made him up with Vicco Turmeric paste, bindi, kajal, nail-polish. Put sindoor in his maang. Tied the pallu of the sari to his own jabba. When they were done, they went round the fire seven times, with Yudi saying these words and Milind repeating them:

'I promise to be your humsafar, trust me, till death do us apart.'

Yudi set his automatic camera to click the historic event, and they went around the fire again, this time for the camera. Milind, though, wasn't as keen as Yudi that their wedding be photographed. He wasn't afraid of blackmail; but the studio that would develop their roll might think them loony. But he too made his little sacrifice, and the ceremony over, the photos taken, they ate laddoos and laughed and hugged and smooched, and said 'I love you'.

They spent their wedding night fucking like rabbits. Who would be pregnant with the other's child, Yudi wondered aloud, and in Milind's grin he saw the obvious answer. He began to see Milind as his tender gender bender.

The first thing that gender bender thought of doing, the moment the sun rose, was to decorate the house with rangoli. Newly-weds did such things, didn't they? It was a way of spreading happiness. However, there was no coloured powder or even coloured chalk anywhere in the house. And neither of them was willing to go to the corner shop. Finally, Milind decided to draw his rangoli with the Krazy Lines Cockroach Poison that he found in Yudi's kitchen.

However, when he opened the door to draw with the Krazy Lines, he found that a cat had torn open their garbage bag. In the litter strewn all over the floor, was a condom with his semen! Milind picked up the condom and slipped it into Yudi's trousers, hanging on a wooden peg.

After the wedding, the honeymoon. Yudi and Milind could have gone to the Vasai Fort for theirs. Instead they went to the movies. A recent flick, featuring a sensational new superstar. The Bollywood Movie Industry presents Shahrukh Khan in and as *Baazigar*. Husband and husband went to the movie, first day first show, with tickets bought in black—Bees ka chalis, bees ka chalis. Milind had read all about the film in *Mayapuri*. Shahrukh Khan became a baazigar for vendetta's sake: the world had ill-treated his mother, and he had to give them a tooth for a tooth and an eye for an eye.

Milind too had a miserable mother, and all on account of his father, who had found himself a younger woman and came home every once in a while to check on his brood or beat up his wife.

'I once returned from school and saw my father on top of my mother, not making love to her, but hitting her. I tried to grapple with him, but he was much stronger than me. How do you think I felt, seeing my mother lie there, all broken and helpless?'

His principal reason for seeing *Baazigar*, then, was to draw inspiration from Shahrukh Khan and become the local baazigar of Saat Rasta.

'What's the name of the talkies where the film is showing?' asked Milind.

'Bajrangbali,' said Yudi, who had grown up in an area flanked by the flamboyant Liberty and Metro. But Bajrangbali wasn't bad if you ignored the name. It had air-conditioning; it had pushback seats. Yes, cockroaches and mice sometimes nibbled at the patrons' toes; but then that happened even at Metro and Liberty.

Baazigar began. Milind's concentration was entirely on the film. Yudi's, mostly on Milind, whose fly he had undone. 'Have you no shame? What if someone sees us like this?' Milind hissed. Yudi assured him it was too dark even for the most committed voyeur to notice anything, as long as he kept quiet.

Then came the crucial scene where Shahrukh Khan brought Shilpa Shetty to the office of the Registrar of Marriages, Worli, and pushed her off the terrace. Both Milind and Yudi forgot all about sex; both bit their nails and watched the scene with concentration. Milind thought: mustn't ever go with Yudi to the terrace of Mate House. What if he pushes me down? Yudi thought: this bloody movie might give Milind ideas. And this too was love, for isn't love thinking the same thoughts at the same time? Ditto ditto.

Baazigar ended. Milind knew now how to avenge his mother's grief. Yudi was already planning other diversions for his boyfriend.

Time flew faster than an Air India Jumbo. Before they knew it, it was Saturday, end of the week, and Milind's last day at Mate House. Tomorrow he would return to his one room tenement where four sons and a dumped mom slept in a row. Depression gripped Yudi as he woke up and thought of Milya's imminent departure. But he gathered himself quickly, roused Milind from bed, and resolved to make the most of their last day together. What did he know of the rival plans fate had in store?

The doorbell rang. Throwing all caution to the winds, Yudi opened the door without looking through the peephole, certain it was Saraswati. It was not. It was a bolt from the blue.

'Hi Yudi,' said Gauri, looking rather corpulent in the T-shirt and jeans she wore in a bid to look like the men who turned Yudi on. 'I've come to see you because I didn't hear from you for so long.'

Yudi, who didn't want Gauri's shadow to fall on his Milya, flew into a rage: 'I can't see you now. My boyfriend's with me in the flat. Please go away at once.'

Saying this, he tried to shut the door on her face. But she wasn't the one to give up so easily. She clutched the door from the outside with exactly the same force with which he clutched it from the inside, so that it stayed were it was, making the two of them look like Kolhapuri wrestlers. Five full minutes went by with neither of them speaking a word to each other, but playing tug-of-war with the door. Then Milind, who was till now in the bogs, came to the door to see what the pandemonium was about. No sooner did Gauri set eyes on him than a pang of jealousy sliced her heart.

'You there,' she screamed, contempt twisting her face, 'it's because of *you* that he ignores me!'

Scarcely had she finished saying her lines than she thrust a hand through the half open door and grabbed Milya's collar. The poor lad was stunned. He hadn't a clue who this madwoman was or why she should want to break his neck. He knew he could overpower the witch, whoever she was, so what if she was fat; but his values didn't permit him to beat up a woman. So, obeying Yudi's orders, he joined him in his tug-of-war with the door, and now that they were two versus one, they managed to slam the door shut in Gauri's face.

Mortification, of course, wasn't a word in the painter's vocabulary. Where anyone else would have left the scene, possibly in the name of self-respect, she balanced herself on the banister and began to sob. Milind and Yudi took turns to view the spectacle through the peephole. Much time passed; the lady had a never-ending supply of tears that streamed down her face inelegantly. She also carried many hankies in her handbag; as soon as one was drenched with tears and mucous, she brought out another. Yudi suspected Gauri knew they were watching her through the peephole. Those tears were crocodile tears, he told an uneasy Milind, whose values also didn't permit him to make a woman cry.

It was Saraswati who came to everyone's rescue. Reporting for work, she was astonished to find a memsaab sobbing outside her saab's door. Not once in her five years with Yudi had she witnessed such a sight. Her first thought was: must go to Pandharpur and thank Lord Vithoba for making saab normal. Then, taking charge of the situation, she assumed the tone of a head nurse and asked Gauri to go away.

'Women are not permitted to enter the flat,' she scolded her in Marathi. 'They destroy my saab's tapas, he's a brahmachari sadhu, a celibate.'

Gauri, who found that outrageously funny, tittered through her wet sobs. Obeying Saraswatibai as if she were her mom-in-law, she rose quietly and plodded down the stairs. Yudi and Milind, still at the peephole, almost coming to blows over who's turn it was to see the tamasha at the door, sighed in relief.

Saraswati walked in, muttered to her saab that this was no way to treat a possible wife, and got down to dusting and cleaning and glaring at Milya, whose provenance she had no doubts about: he may be well groomed but he couldn't fool her; he wasn't even of *her* class, leave alone the saab's.

After she finished the housework and left, Yudi had a lot of explaining to do.

'So you claim you're gay?' Milind said, pointing a finger at him accusingly. 'Then who was that woman? A wife you divorced? A mistress you made pregnant? She did look pregnant. Why did she come here? To blackmail you?'

Yudi calmed his boy-love down and told him the story of Gauri from scratch; the way B.R. Chopra narrated the *Mahabharat* on TV. Milind was convinced. He felt sorry for Yudi; thought hard about what he could do for the friend who was doing so much for him. At last he hit upon an idea.

'Will Gauri marry me?' he asked. 'Although she's as old as my mother! But if she does, we can be a nice three-in-one.'

They broke into laughter. The tension of the morning was eased. It was Milya's last day at Mate House and they were going to have a ball.

Sunday. A mosquito bite woke Milind up. Throughout the week, they had successfully managed to keep the wretched things away, thanks to an assortment of Odomos, mosquito coils, and Good

Knight mats. But now it was as if the insects had resolved to give Milind his parting bite.

'If I get malaria, you'll have to pay for my treatment,' he jokingly said to Yudi even before he brushed his teeth. Jokingly, because even if he got malaria, he would be treated free of charge at the hospital where his father was a ward boy. Yudi thought for a minute, and said: 'One mosquito bite giving you malaria is like one insertion making you pregnant. It happens only in movies.'

Somehow, the word 'pregnant' instantly reminded Milya of Gauri.

'What's the matter?' he asked. 'You are thinking a lot about making someone pregnant!'

As the time for Milya's departure approached, Yudi regretted that they couldn't live together although they were married. Milind advised him to buy a kholi where he could keep him. Keep him! Yudi chuckled to himself. The poor, innocent kid's role model here was his own daddy, who shamelessly lived with his keep in a kholi at Kandivili which he'd bought with his meagre salary. By connecting Yudi to daddy, what Milind was unconsciously saying was that he was unhappy with his father, badly needed a substitute, and who other than Yudi could bring his search to an end? Daddy had eloped with a whore and left them high and dry. In his place Milind had found a sugar daddy! That was what gay men all over the world looked for anyway: sugar daddies. So why should Yudi be surprised or sad?

Playing the part, Yudi gave the boy a hundred bucks as pocket money. 'Ask me for money whenever you need it,' he said, kissing him on the cheek. Milya, unfamiliar with 'pocket money', was more inclined to see it as 'petty cash', the sort Parmeshwar gave him for day-to-day expenses.

Yudi went to the station to see Milind off. They pretended he was going on a long journey, oh such a long journey, from Nalla

Sopara to Nampally Road, say, not just to Mahalaxmi barely an hour-and-a-half away. They acted like lovers whom fate was cruelly separating for years. Yudi had tears in his eyes. The week had shown him that human beings were not meant to live alone; there was something to be said for being in a relationship. If he valued his privacy (or thought he did) that could merely be a case of sour grapes.

A Virar-Churchgate local came into view. Yudi hugged Milind. 'Kaha suna maaf karo,' he said, as Hindi-speaking people do.

Milind: Thanks for everything.

Yudi: I love you.

Milind: I love you too.

Yudi: Call me when you reach Bombay. Did you jot down my phone number?

Milind: Yes. I'll call you.

Yudi: When do we meet again?

Milind: Friday.

Yudi: Shambar Takka!

Milind: Nakki-Pucca.

Nakki Pucca-Shambar Takka. It would become the theme song of their meetings and partings.

The train halted, Milya got in, the train started. Yudi returned to an empty Mate House. There were calls from his mother and Gauri, and Saraswati rang the doorbell.

shravanabelagola

Milind had taken with him all the joy from Yudi's bachelor life in wretched Nalla Sopara. Yudi kept thinking of the sunny time they had together during that golden week at Mate House. He rarely felt this nostalgic about any of his pick-ups. But then they were just one-night stands. Memories of Milind were so intense that as he had his lonely drink that Sunday evening, Yudi found himself close to tears. Rather than taking hold of himself, he allowed himself to cry into his whisky, thinking about how Milya and he had bathed together, how Milya had drawn rangoli with Krazy Lines Cockroach Powder, how he had joined on his side in the battle with a crazed nymphomaniac at his door. There was another burst of weeping the next day when he collected his wedding photos from a Nalla Sopara studio, and saw how happy they were. But his alter ego stepped in soon enough to admonish him. What was this? How sentimental could he get! And it was not as if his Milya lived hundreds of miles away, in faraway Jhumritalayya. Why couldn't he evolve a strategy that enabled them to live together?

This of course was easier said than done. There were problems galore on both sides, his as well as Milya's. What was possible was to find excuses to be together more often. Friday evenings at

Café Volga no longer meant much to Yudi. He wanted to be with Milya days and nights at a stretch.

It was during these brainstorming sessions with himself that he hit upon the idea of an outstation tour. To some place where they would be in a train for over a day! A place where they could stay in a hotel or lodge, and no one would suspect they were lovers, because only men and women were lovers. There were hundreds of places like that in India, this ancient land of forests and temples. True, it would cost a packet and the penniless boy wouldn't be able to contribute a paisa. But he would foot it all; it was the price he had to pay for his Milya's company. Nothing, after all, came without a price.

Yudi phoned Milind in his office and asked if they could meet *before* Friday as he had something urgent to discuss. He took care not to tell him what it was, for he had a nagging feeling that if he did, Milind would ask him what the hurry was: why couldn't it wait till Friday?

'Sure! I'll have all the time to travel since you'll make me lose my job anyway,' Milind screamed at him when they met at Café Volga that evening to discuss plans for their forthcoming tour.

'As soon as you put the phone down, Parmeshwar gave me a warning: "Tell your friends not to phone you at the office. Or else I'll chuck you out of your job."'

'Fuck him!' said Yudi. 'I'll look after you if you lose your job.'

'No thanks,' Milind replied, fuming still. 'I don't want to be your ghulam.'

For exactly half a minute Yudi thought of the delicious prospect of having the boy as his devoted slave. Then patted Milind's shoulder and ordered beer.

The beer cooled the boy down. Sipping it, Yudi came to the point. It would be a long picnic. All expenses would be borne by him, so the boyfriend had nothing to lose on that score. To be sure, Milind, who had never gone anywhere except to his village in Marathwada, was delighted at the prospect of a free trip. What dampened his spirits were thoughts of Parmeshwar: the bastard would never give him leave.

'Talk about being someone's slave!' Yudi scolded him. 'Don't you know your rights as an employee? All workers are entitled to leave!'

'You fool, don't you know I'm tempo-vary? If I ask for leave, the man will say go and never come back.'

'Tell him you're going to attend a cousin's wedding in your village. No one says no to weddings in India.'

Milind wasn't convinced. However, putting aside the question for the time being, he allowed Yudi to come to the main point: where would they go?

They shortlisted a few places and found that all of them had to do with nudity. Except Bodh Gaya to which Milind (but not Yudi) wanted to go. Milind suggested Bodh Gaya because it had the Bodhi tree that inspired the Buddha, who in turn inspired Ambedkar, the messiah of the Dalits. But Yudi objected that it was too boring and too far, and too much was made of what was after all only a tree. They considered alternatives. The first among these was Goa, with its nude beaches where hippies roamed about in the altogether. But Yudi rejected this right away as 'too touristy.' The Kumbh Mela was another option. Naga Sadhus, according to Yudi, looked sexier than naked hippies. Unfortunately the Kumbh Mela happened once in twelve years, and there had been one only five years ago. Option three: the Soundatti temple of Karnataka. This was a hijra shrine, where on festive days eunuchs were said to pray without clothes. However, this too was ruled out. Milind wasn't interested in hijras, and even though Yudi would be the one paying, he didn't feel strongly enough about naked eunuchs at prayer to overrule his touchy young lover.

The fourth option, agreeable to both, concerned nudity not in the flesh, but in stone. If naked hippies, naked hijras and naga sadhus were out, they would settle for a naked Gomateshwara. They would go to Shravanabelagola to see the statue of the Jain saint, seventeen metres in height.

Yudi was thrilled. Milya and he would be spending another week together. He sat up with train timetables all night, planning, planning. They would first take a broad gauge train to Miraj, then a metre gauge train to Arsikere Junction. Parting company with trains at Arsikere, they would travel by road to Hassan, and onwards to Shravanabelagola. The whole operation would take them close to two days: the longer the better. Consulting more travel guides, Yudi found that the Karnataka Tourism Development Corporation (KTDC) ran a hotel at Shravanabelagola. The rates were steep, but it would assure them of a modicum of comfort. Besides, if he did a story on the place and sent it to *India Magazine*, he would recover all his costs.

They went to VT to book their tickets, and to KTDC at World Trade Centre to book their room. Milind approached Parmeshwar for leave.

'I'm going to my native place in Aurangabad to see a girl,' he told his boss. He improved upon the yarn Yudi told him to spin, making it virtually impossible for the old man to turn down his request. Marriage in India was a fundamental right: no boss could tell a subordinate, howsoever lowly, not to tie the nuptial knot. On returning, if pressed for details, Milind could always say he didn't like the girl. Of course, Parmeshwar did try to dissuade his peon from getting married, or rather, from taking leave:

'What's your age, you are too young, haven't got a beard yet. This is no age to marry and have kids.'

To which Milind had a suitable answer: 'Mind your own dick,

harami.' But this wasn't what he told his boss. What he said was: 'In my caste, we marry early.' Again, the boss couldn't contest that. But he was an educated Brahmin, concerned about his country, so he couldn't help thinking: 'You stupid untouchables!'

Coincidentally enough, the day of their departure was a Friday. They met at Café Volga, around 6.30, as they always did on Friday evenings. This, however, was a Friday that Yudi would remember for life. For they didn't part after their beer, but trekked to VT with their backpacks to board the Mahalaxmi Express, their honeymoon train, that left at 8.30 p.m. sharp. Only one thing upset an otherwise ecstatic Yudi: the edges of Milya's rucksack were frayed.

'They betray your lower middle-class origins,' he brusquely told his travelling companion.

Milind's response worked brilliantly to shut Yudi up. 'There is time for the train to leave. Come, buy me a brand new VIP suitcase. Hurry up, hurry up.'

Hardly had the train started, when Milind disappeared into one of the sleeper's many toilets. Between VT and Kalyan he went to the toilet twenty-one times.

'Are you all right?' Yudi asked him, worried that the journey was having an adverse effect on his bladder.

'I'm okay,' he mumbled incoherently. It was only after the train left Kalyan, and everyone made preparations to sleep, that Yudi discovered the truth. Milind, quite inebriated now, kept slipping into the loo to take a swig at his bottle of rum!

'Swine,' Yudi whispered into his ear. 'Why didn't you tell me you had booze on you?' Milind laughed loudly, causing the Maharashtrians in their cubicles to ask him to shut up.

In spite of the rum, Milind had a bad night. Not particularly fond of train journeys, hardly having taken any in his life, he had hoped the rum would help him doze off. But now there were problems. First the window. Yudi, who took the lower and gave Milya the middle berth (to assume, he said, more or less the same positions they did in the bed), wanted the window open for fresh village air. Milind shivered. It was February, not May, and February in the Sahyadris is still winter. Finding his daft friend fast asleep, Milind jumped off his middle berth to shut the window. However, half an hour later when his teeth chattered, he discovered that the old fool had opened the window once again.

He shut it. Yudi opened it. This went on all night.

Secondly, his air pillow. It had a leak. Each time he inflated it, put his head on it, and fell asleep, he awoke to find his head at mean sea level. When this happened half a dozen times, he angrily flung the air pillow away, and slept with his head on his forearm. (The pillow landed on a squat Maharashtrian lady, putting an end to her snoring.)

Throughout all this, Yudi slept. Being a seasoned traveller, he had cultivated the art of crashing anywhere—on narrow railway berths, dusty platforms, smelly waiting halls. In his twenties he had roughed it out, ruthlessly, even when he could afford to pay for some comfort. Now in his forties, that early experience came in handy whenever the situation demanded it.

'Did you sleep well?' he asked Milind, as they alighted at Miraj Junction. It was a rhetorical question that enraged the boy so much that he developed lockjaw. To him, the discomfort had been Yudi's fault. Nothing would appease the wronged boyfriend, save the steaming hot idlis sold on the platform. Yudi bought him three quarters of a dozen, the idlis being half the price they were in Bombay. While a ravenous Milya ate, Yudi explained: 'When idlis and dosas are cheap, when tea is costlier than coffee, you can be sure you are in South India.'

Like scores of passengers, they boarded a metre gauge train that pulled up on the other side of the island platform. It was headed for Bangalore.

This time round the two had window seats that faced each other. The sun had quietly risen. Once he was done with surveying the dicks of trackside squatters, Yudi turned to Milya to talk about the landscape. The boy was asleep. Yudi woke him up despite his protests.

'You can sleep any time,' he said. 'If you miss the scenery, you won't see it again.'

For every station they passed, he had a tale to tell. Gokak had waterfalls. Ghataprabha was on the border of Maharashtra and Karnataka. Belgaum was full of colleges: medical colleges, engineering colleges, MBA colleges that charged exorbitant capitation fees. From Londa, they could branch off to Goa. (Milind's ears popped up at the mention of Goa. Still sore that they weren't going to the nude beaches, he said: 'Come, let's get down here and go to Goa.') At Dharwar, Yudi told Milind the legendary love story of Siddharth and Sudhir. It happened, he said, twelve years ago. Like Romeo and Juliet, Shirin and Farhad, Heer and Ranjha, Laila and Majnu, the two men were tragic lovers, united in death.

Milind, still displeased with this and that, said, 'Good.' Then he closed his eyes and was silent.

It was dark when the train pulled into Arsikere. The porters and paanwallahs who hung about at the station advised them against travelling to Shravanabelagola at night. The roads were dark and constricted, the cabbies unwilling to risk their lives. Left without a choice, they checked into a lodge opposite the station, where Milind didn't allow Yudi to touch him all night, because he was exhausted and 'not in the mood'.

While Milind slept, Yudi strolled out into the night for a beer, and found the town's only beer bar, Hotel Vaishali, with much difficulty. A smart young waiter led him by the hand into the underground bar, causing his heart to flutter and momentarily forget Milya.

In the morning, they first caught a bus to Hasan. Here they saw rows of black-and-yellow Ambassadors that took tourists to Sharavanabelagola. Among all the Ambassadors Yudi spotted a very old Fiat, and decided it was this one they would hire. As they approached the taxi, he told Milind it was a classic, manufactured in 1957; because its back was shaped like the snout of a pig, it was popularly called Dukkar Fiat. Having uttered the word, however, he regretted it instantly. For the driver of the cab, who was standing near by, heard him use the abusive word, and introduced himself sullenly as Abdul Chacha. 'Dukkar means pig; avoid speaking the word with Muslims,' Yudi whispered into Milya's ear. From then on Yudi referred to the car as Pig Fiat, assuming that Abdul Chacha didn't know English.

Arsikere Junction, unlike Malgudi, may not have had its Railway Raju, but Abdul Chacha was definitely Hasan's answer to Driver Ghaffur. Yudi and Milind were his first passengers, his 'bouni' in Hindu parlance, so he offered them the front seats. However, as they soon realized, he wasn't going to start his cab till he had loaded it with a dozen passengers. When they finally took off, with luggage crammed in the boot and piled high on the roof carrier, it looked as if there was an orgy in progress in the Pig Fiat. Half the passengers in the taxi were squirming and bobbing on others' laps.

Not only was the ride bumpy, the road was the narrowest Yudi had seen in his life. As slender, as winding as the back of a serpent. On this road heavy vehicles plied up and down at full speed. Every time a tourist bus or truck came at them from the opposite direction, Yudi said his prayers, certain there would be a smash-up. But they were always saved by the skin of their teeth.

Abdul Chacha told them about his proud possession. It was an Italian Fiat manufactured in 1957, 'before you were born.' It was stronger than all modern cars put together. He picked it up in Bangalore many years ago, for just Rs 10,000. It served him faithfully—hadn't conked even once.

'Isn't it rather noisy, though?' Yudi, who was seated next to Abdul Chacha, asked.

'All Fiat gaadis are noisy,' the driver said defensively.

Milind nudged Yudi: 'Why don't you buy a Pig Fiat? You can drive it from your house to Nalla Sopara Station!'

There was a squawking sound. The Pig Fiat came to an abrupt halt.

'Hat teri ki!' Abdul Chacha swore. 'Puncture!'

'I thought the Pig Fiat never gave you trouble,' said Yudi.

'Nazar lag gaya,' said a passenger in the back seat.

For the next half hour, Abdul Chacha struggled with jack, nuts and bolts, as single-handed he changed the Pig Fiat's flat tyre. The passengers didn't assist him. Instead they sauntered into the bushes for a leak. Then lit up. There was a strong breeze. Yudi followed some of the peeing passengers into the fields. Milind, thoroughly familiar now with his friend's idiosyncrasies, left him alone. When he returned, they walked some distance away from the punctured Pig Fiat, where they located a tea-shack. Other passengers did likewise.

Abdul Chacha, kind man, drove up to the tea-shack the moment he'd changed his flat tyre. 'Get in, get in,' he cried. Yudi bought him a cup of tea, for which he was grateful. The sun was pretty high in the sky now, impelling the sun-shy Bombay boys to take out their dark glasses.

For the next twenty minutes on the road, Yudi and Milind enjoyed the scenery. However, when Yudi casually turned his head to have a glimpse of Abdul Chacha, he found the man dozing off even as he drove. He froze, and remembered his Maker. Take me to Heaven O Lord, not to Hell!

But the Pig Fiat had its own inbuilt safety mechanism. When Abdul Chacha combined driving with napping, it's engine simply cut out. For the second time during their one-hour ride to Sharavanabelagola, the car stalled. Hat-teri-ki.

This time Abdul Chacha couldn't fix the car on his own. He went looking for a mechanic. Scores of Ambassadors zoomed past gaily, filling the ancient Pig Fiat's passengers with envy. If only they'd opted for one of those 'fat women' they might have been in Shravanabelagola already, staring up, open-mouthed, at Gomateshwara.

Milind, who was tired of walking, decided to stay put in the Pig Fiat till it took them to their destination. On the other hand, Yudi, whose natural condition was walking, found it taxing to sit in one place. He wandered off into the fields with his bottle of mineral water, sporting a red-and-yellow cap. A villager who saw him, bottle in hand, tried to be helpful (as villagers always are). He asked Yudi something in Kannada, which Yudi didn't at first understand. It was only after he had smiled and walked on that he understood what the villager's question was: 'Are you looking for a place to shit?'

Despite the odds, they reached Shravanabelagola. So what if it took them three hours to cover a mere fifty kilometres? This was India, rural India, where time too preferred to crawl. They thanked Abdul Chacha and bid goodbye to the ancient Pig Fiat. The KTDC Hotel at which they checked in was called Hotel Hill Slopes. Milind went straight to the TV in their plush, carpeted room. Yudi ordered him to switch off the TV and dress, so they could go say hi to Gomatesh.

The seventeen-metre-high statue of the naked Gomateshwara was more dynamic than Yudi had imagined. As soon as they set eyes on it, he forgot Milind, hurried towards the saint with his Pentax and started clicking from all angles. Milya was amazed. When friends went on picnics they took photos of each other—in various poses. That was what he and the yaars of his neighbourhood did when they went to the Powai Lake. And now, here was this other friend, wasting expensive film roll on a mere statue! How could he bear to have photos without people in them? Observing him closely as, camera in hand, he assumed the strangest positions before the statue, Milind realized he had temporarily lost his boyfriend to Gomatesh. He busied himself with his surroundings. A tourist guide was lecturing to a group of credulous tourists:

'. . . Lord Mahavir was the founder of Jainism . . . This statue is thousand years old . . . The hills between which Shravanabelagola is wedged are known as Indragiri and Chandragiri . . . This shrine is situated on top of the Indragiri hill. . . .'

There were some foreigners in the group. Fascinated by the sight of white flesh, Milind became engrossed in the spectacle. He tried to imagine who these firangis were, where they came from, why they allowed the third-rate guide to take them for a ride. Doubtless they had tons of money to blow up, he told himself. Yudi startled him by approaching from behind and blindfolding him with his fingers.

'Yudi!' he yelled, pissed off with his lover for abandoning him, but not wanting to make it an issue. Then he asked for a favour:

'Tell those foreigners to pose with me for a photo.'

'I'll do nothing of the sort,' said Yudi, 'have you no self-respect!'

Holding him by the waist, he weaned him away from the firangis. They sat down under the shade of a tree, where Yudi took on the role of a tourist guide himself.

'Did you know,' he began, 'that Jainism and Buddhism are sister religions that have much in common? Both the Buddha and Mahavir rebelled against Hinduism, which had degenerated into an inventory of rituals, and founded their own religions.'

Yudi took Milind's yawning to mean he didn't want a history lesson. He tried to say something lighter.

'Do you know why Gomatesh is always naked? Because he had conquered lust! Looking at this mighty statue, though, it's clear he hadn't stopped thinking of his physique. Doesn't he look like he worked out everyday? In fact, I think he . . .'

Milind frowned at Yudi to shut him up before he said something blasphemous. The man loved to make provocative statements, like an extra-smart kid he knew in school.

'Shut up!' Milind snapped. 'Have some respect for a sacred place. You're so educated, yet you talk such rubbish!'

'Let me put it this way,' said Yudi, not accustomed to being snubbed. 'I talk rubbish because I'm educated. At least I have something to say. You illiterates are slaves. You only say what people allow you to!'

Milya said nothing to that. This was worse because it didn't give his anger an outlet. What eased the tension was the arrival of two sadhus who approached them for alms. One was a teenager with a Hanuman mask. The other was a middle-aged man who wore a necklace of his own fingernails. Each fingernail, mostly from his little finger, was about an inch long. Yudi tried to make a deal with the sadhu.

'Give me that necklace and I'll give you fifty rupees.'

The wise man refused to part with his treasure.

'I won't give it to you, even if you pay me five hundred. Many foreign tourists have offered me US dollars, but I haven't given them the necklace. It belongs to Sri Gomateshwara.'

'Fuck off then,' said a slighted Yudi, disappointed at his failure to obtain the wonderful drawing-room souvenir.

They returned to their room at hotel Hill Slopes. Milya continued to be in a bad mood. He had been called an 'illiterate' and a 'slave' by a man who went down on his knees before him like a whore. He vented his anger on the mosquitoes in the room, grabbing them madly with his fists, then examining the blood on his palms.

Yudi poured out the booze. He tore open a packet of moong dal and laid it out on a paper plate. He was aware his friend was pissed off, but didn't wish to humour him.

Saying his customary 'Cheers,' he began drinking, while Milind continued to watch the newly installed colour TV, complete with remote control. After a while, he joined Yudi at the drinks table. However, he still remained engrossed in his TV, lapping up all that was aired even if it didn't interest him. Yudi, who expected that they would look into each other's eyes and drink, began calculating the expenditure he had incurred on the trip, thinking of it as a colossal waste. This certainly wasn't his idea of a holiday with a boyfriend. He wondered why KTDC was stupid enough to have TVs in hotel rooms. Didn't people take the trouble to travel thousands of miles to Shravanabelagola to get away from the fascism of TV?

'You can watch TV in Bombay,' he ventured. 'There are better things to do here.' On hearing this, Milind got up and switched the TV off, but he continued with his vow of silence. They sipped their whisky without exchanging a word. Although at the end of his tether, Yudi took hold of himself and swore not to explode.

They'd come here to have a good time, not to bicker. Perhaps if given time, the fellow would recover his mood. But alas! Their small bottle of whisky was drained off to the last drop; the last grain of moong dal went into their stomachs; but Milind didn't open his trap.

It was at the KTDC dining hall, where they went for lunch, that he temporarily broke his silence. A cat lurked under their table. 'Go away, cat,' Yudi said to the creature. Milind found that preposterous.

'It isn't from the *Times of India*,' he said. 'It doesn't understand the meaning of "go away".' Saying this, he gave the animal a solid kick. She scampered, seeking refuge under another table, from where she gave him a terrified look. Yudi ruminated. First it was mosquitoes, now the cat: Milind was getting progressively violent. A Jain pilgrim centre was hardly the place to squash mosquitoes and kick cats. The Jains walked barefoot on the streets to avoid trampling on ants and such like, who might be their kin reborn! They ate their dinner before dark, so that they didn't inadvertently swallow a dead brother back on earth as a fly! And here was this heretic flouting every rule in the book.

The food arrived. Milind resumed his satyagraha, eating so slowly that Yudi nagged him to hurry up. There were things to be seen still, before sunset. Milind was quite sure he wasn't going anywhere. He saw no point in visiting old monuments about which Yudi spoke as if he himself had lived in them.

But he was compelled to break his resolve. And follow Yudi wherever he went, like a sorry dog follows its master. At the end of the day, it was Yudi who held the purse strings. He had their room key deep in his trouser pocket. But every word Yudi spoke set his teeth on edge, till finally, driven to desperation by Yudi's haranguing (lectures, lectures, more lectures), his ego shattered, Milind could take it no longer. 'Will you shut up?' he asked by way of warning, raising a fist. But Yudi wasn't the one to take heed of a warning. The next thing he knew, as he continued blabbering, Milind's fist came crashing down on his shoulder. There was silence. Yudi was dumbfounded. The blow was excruciatingly painful. He made mental notes. Milind's brain operation, evidently, had resulted in a complete loss of self-control. In other words, he was crazy. First, the mosquitoes; next, the cat; now Yudi! No, he wasn't going to retaliate. He could assault only with his pen.

Though he had delivered his blow, Milind's anger didn't subside (Yudi thought it would). He remained in a rage for quite some time, not saying a word. It was this that got Yudi's goat. Swallowing his humiliation, he tried to pacify his boyfriend. But each time he cajoled him, touched him affectionately, Milind wrenched himself free.

'Don't touch me!' he screamed.

Now Yudi lost his temper.

'You beggar!' he exclaimed, gnashing his teeth.

Milind was glad he had succeeded in drawing the older man into a fight. He could deal with an equal.

'You *chhakka*—fucking faggot!' he hit back.

They walked quietly, lost, neither certain where their hotel was. Then came the calm that follows the storm. Milind cooled down. Remorse replaced anger, and he decided to behave respectfully towards a man who was old enough to be his father (his father, after all, had sired two offspring by the time he was twenty). Besides, in this case, the man was paying for the entire trip.

The quarrel's aftermath saw them seated in an open-air café by the highway, Milind plucking the white hair on Yudi's head.

'Even I have white hair,' he tactfully said, not wanting his boyfriend to feel offended.

The last night of their Shravanabelagola tour, having seen the little there was to see, Yudi and Milind had sex on the double bed, adding to the vulgar stains decorating the blue bedspread. They slept till late, way past breakfast time, bathed, and ordered beer and a hot chicken curry, so hot that their noses ran. Yudi let Milind eat in peace. They were in no hurry now. The only thing left to do was to pack their bags and go.

They checked out at noon. Taxi drivers called out to passengers at the taxi stand. Milya hopped into the first available Ambassador, pre-empting his possessed friend's attempts to look for the Pig Fiat. As the car snaked through the country road, the driver chatted with the passengers in the front seat. Yudi gathered from their conversation that there had been a collision somewhere; a driver had been killed. Straining his ears, he discovered to his horror that the vehicle in question was none other than Abdul Chacha's Pig Fiat.

'Oh God,' he sighed. 'May his soul rest in peace.'

Milind wanted to know how the accident happened.

'Brake-fail,' said the taxi driver.

'Supposing its brakes had failed while we were in it?' Yudi asked.

'We would be dead, what else?' said Milya matter-of-factly.

Gloom marked the rest of their journey as Yudi and Milind brooded about the kindly old man who reached them to their destination. Yudi wondered if Milind felt the same dread at the thought of death as he did. The young had no reason to.

A train packed with pilgrims and peasants took them to Miraj. The crush of bodies and beedi-smoke gave Yudi a headache; he felt old. Milind seemed quite at home and calmly read a Marathi newspaper, laughing at a report which said that the RSS, VHP and Bajrang Dal were offering Maruti 800 cars to those who converted to Hindusim.

Snoring and dreams marked the night journey from Miraj to Bombay by Mahalaxmi Express. Everyone snored and farted. Indian trains were like that: they brought out the beasts in men. Yudi dreamt: Milind had left him for a man with the face of Gomatesh. Milind's dreams were less predictable. He saw Gomatesh put a hand on Abdul Chacha's forehead and revive him. Grateful for the new lease of life, the taxi driver converted to Hinduism and exchanged his Pig Fiat for a brand new Maruti 800!

When their eyes opened, the train was already passing through Sion. The odour of human excreta wafted in through the windows: the slum-dwellers of Dharavi had woken up. Yudi and Milind got off their sleeper berths and went towards the lavatories, toothbrushes in hand. But the train rolled into Dadar before any of the toilets were free.

Groggy, they alighted with their rucksacks and followed the herd of passengers to the footbridge. Yudi asked himself his favourite question: why must we arrive?

They parted without fuss on the Dadar footbridge. For all the time they had spent together, each went his own way now, vanishing unceremoniously into the crowd.

wanted

The office of Medium Advertising, situated in one of Fort's back lanes, was undergoing a facelift. Workmen, with distemper all over their bodies, were busy scraping walls, levelling them, painting them anew. Brushes and cans of paint were strewn all over the tiled floor. The office wasn't large. Rentals in Bombay's business district being what they were (higher than rents in New York City) all that the company could afford was a tiny room in which people could fit only sideways. A part of this rat hole was partitioned off with teakwood and glass for Parmeshwar, the boss. This was God's cabin, air-conditioned and all, from where he transacted with clients. Those outside had to contend with a hot blast of air from God's AC, fitted into an internal wall. The company boasted a staff of twelve—secretaries, accountants, artists and peons—so brisk was its business. However, the exigencies demanded that at any given time half the employees be sent out on errands. If not, there would be a stampede.

That morning as Milind climbed the narrow stairs that led to the office, he was sickened by the smell of paint. His brain surgery had made him allergic to odours, or so he thought. Parmeshwar was at the door, frenetically instructing painters. He stood there, arms akimbo, not noticing Milind, blocking his passage. Milind positioned himself just behind the boss, so that the man had no chance of seeing him till he took an about turn. The fact that he was much shorter than the boss helped: it prolonged his game of hide-and-seek. It was Rekha, one of the boss's secretary-cum-concubines, who spilled the beans. She giggled—at first, putting a hand to her mouth so as not to give away the secret. But the sight was so funny that soon she burst out laughing, alerting Parmeshwar instantly, causing him to turn around and face his peon.

'Welcome, welcome,' said the boss, as sarcastically as he could. 'See, we're renovating the office in your honour, and in honour of your Mrs. Where is she? Didn't you bring her along? For griha pravesh?'

Milind was deeply embarrassed. The boss had no business to slight him in front of so many people.

'What wife?' he managed to mumble, only to save face.

'Why? Didn't you say you were going to get married?'

'The girl was too fat.'

'Enough!' Parmeshwar screamed. 'You didn't go to see any ladki-vadki. I telephoned your brother in his office. He said you went on a picnic!'

'Okay, I went on a picnic. What's the harm? I have come back, no?'

'What's the harm? You asked for three days' leave and remained absent for a week! This won't do. If it happens again, you'll be fired.'

Not the kind who believed in dialogue, Parmeshwar left the office immediately. A smarting Milind did nothing for the first ten minutes; merely sat in a corner and brooded. To add to his woes, the fumes gave him a coughing fit. It was Rekha who came to his rescue. She placed a comforting hand on his shoulder, and then made him a cup of tea. Her sympathy caused him to bury his face in her lap and sob. For five whole minutes he sobbed, drenching her sari at the waist.

Having no clue as to what was going on, a senior peon, Subayya, approached Milind. He was twice his age, and like Parmeshwar, a 'Madrasi'. He had done Milind's work for a whole week, without a murmur of protest, while the fellow picnicked with friends! Now it was he who was going on leave, and he wanted Milya to assure Parmeshwar that work in the office wouldn't come to a standstill.

Milind wiped the last of his teardrops and went to the sink to blow his nose. There was no love lost between Subayya and himself: the man was anti-youth, anti-Maharashtrian, anti-Dalit. Milind reasoned it out for a minute. Why should he do the chutiya's work? He refused point blank. To the man's face.

Subayya, known for his bad temper, lost it. Anyone doomed to be a peon till forty is bound to be disgruntled.

'Bhadva!' he abused Milind.

The war of bad words began. Milind called Subayya a gandu. Subayya called him a Bhangi. When it was Milind's turn again, he told Subayya he was an impotent ass who got Parmeshwar to fuck his wife.

That did it. Subayya, who had cups of tea in his hands (for the painters), flung one of them at Milind. It didn't scald his skin, for the tea wasn't very hot. It spoilt his Heera-Panna clothes, no doubt, but the stains could be washed away with Surf detergent, sold at four rupees a pouch. But the tea also landed on the newly painted walls, and those were ruined beyond redemption. Even the painters (for whom the tea was anyway meant) couldn't do a thing to get those caffeine stains off! They remained on the off-white walls as faint blotches, giving them a gangrenous look.

There was more to come. Insulted for the second time that morning, this time by a chutiya peon, Milind flung himself on the

Madrasi (just as the tea was flung on him), grabbed his collar and punched him in the belly, Kader Khan style. The fighting duo fell on a side table full of papers, toppled it, and caused it's glass top to break into splinters. The blood on Milya's elbow notwithstanding, they rose and began a round of fisticuffs. Rekha, and everyone else in the office, tried to intervene and bring the fracas to an end. They failed. The fighters went on grappling with each other, Subayya obviously being the loser in the unequal fight. A commotion ensued. People from neighbouring offices came to view the boxing match. Such entertainment didn't come their way every day: it gave them a chance to leave theirs seats a whole hour before lunch.

Had Parmeshwar known about Milya's sexual leanings, he would have surmised his two peons were shamelessly making love in full view of dozens of people. Because by the time he returned the fight had progressed to a stage where the fighters were on the floor, rolling on each other. True, there wasn't much space in that matchbox of an office for orgies or acrobatic feats. But then, a fight is not a fight without a tight clinch or two and reckless rolling around on the floor. Rather than draw them apart, the spectators actually applauded them, most of the applause going to Milya, the young and winning horse.

Parmeshwar arrived at precisely that moment, when the excitement was at its height.

'What's going on!' he yelled at the top of his voice, in order to make himself heard. But no one heard him. His ego was immensely wounded: was *he* the boss, or those peons lying obscenely on the floor? It took everyone a while to realize that the boss was back. The moment they did, the tamasha came to an end. The neighbours went back to their offices. The employees of Medium Advertising resumed whatever work they had left half done. As for our khiladis, they rose at once and pretended everything was okay; they were not guilty. But God would not be fooled. He demanded an explanation from both of them. Isi waqt, right now. Was the office a place for a wrestling match? And what, anyway, had fuelled the duel? Both Subayya and Milind spoke at the same time, not giving Parmeshwar a chance to understand what either was saying. Each pointed an accusing finger at the other, blamed him, said he was the villain. Their words clashed and tumbled on the floor before the boss could grasp their meaning. This wasn't communication; it was noise. Parmeshwar raised a hand. He was about to ask them, in all fairness, to speak one at a time, single file, when his eyes fell on the tea stains on his expensively done up walls, and that settled it all. He didn't need to say anything more, or find out who was right and who wrong. Summoning Milind, he fired him that very minute.

'Get out! Out!'

Milya, naturally, wanted to know why it was he and not the other who was being shown the door. But God would hear none of it.

'Get out before I kill you!' he said.

In tears again, Milya managed to ask for his dues.

'Collect them after three days,' said a snarling boss.

None in that office spoke up for the poor boy. Not even Rekha, who genuinely felt sorry for him, but depended on the boss's favours to bring up her kids.

Milya had no choice but to leave. But he didn't go home till late in the evening. Instead, he went to Gateway of India and sat on the wall, facing the sea. Boats bobbled sadly on the filthy water. He felt his world collapse before his eyes.

A bad workman finds fault with his tools. Milind looked for an alibi that could be blamed for his dismissal. He readily found one in Yudi. It was he who had tempted him to go to Shravanabelagola, quite against his will. What did the guy have to lose? Nothing! He wasn't a regular employee anywhere. Why did they have to go that far for a picnic? Weren't there enough places around Bombay where they could have gone over the weekend?

What Milya didn't know was that of late, Parmeshwar's business wasn't doing well. He was looking for ways to trim his fleet, and the tea stains on the wall gave him a convenient excuse. If Milind had some inkling of this, he wouldn't have borne a grudge against Yudi. Wouldn't have vowed not to see him till he got another job.

The boys in Milya's chawl advised him to go back to the office and apologize to the boss. Perhaps he'd fired him in a fit of rage. Once his anger cooled, he would reinstate his peon, especially if he was repentant. If he still didn't, all Milind had to do was fall at his feet and say he was 'Garibaldi', a poor man. The most stonehearted of bosses were moved by these words.

Milind did exactly as his chums told him, but, alas, it didn't work. Indeed, Parmeshwar's rage had vanished and he had a hearty laugh when Milya prostrated before him and held his ears. But these antics didn't impress him. Paying the boy whatever money he owed, he said, in reply to Milya's request for an explanation, that Subayya wasn't being fired because he was permanent.

'No,' said Milind, 'not because he's permanent, but because you fuck his wife.'

Having spat this out of his mouth, he stormed down the stairs at lightning speed, denying a reviled boss the opportunity to assault him in word or deed.

That was the last time Milya saw the Medium Advertising office. But he took his revenge. Every other night, he stole out to the local phone booth and called Parmeshwar's flat in the wee hours and asked if it was the Bombay Fire Brigade!

Yudi hung around outside Café Volga for a whole hour that Friday. There was no sign of Milind. Violating his ban, he telephoned the office of Medium Advertising. Unaware of what had transpired between Milya and his boss, Yudi was taken aback to hear the choicest abuse on the phone, after which the boss slammed the phone down without letting Yudi say a word. Fear gripped Yudi. Despite repeated requests, Milind had refused to give him his address. Did this mean he'd lost him a second time, now that the fellow had been chucked out of Medium Advertising?

Upon getting home after a tired drink at the Press Club, he found someone asleep outside his flat. It was Milind. Rising as soon as he heard Yudi's footsteps, he let him know that he'd left his house and come to stay with Yudi.

'It's because of you that I lost my job,' he said. 'Now you'll have to look after me for the rest of my life.'

Yudi heaved a sigh of relief. At least he wouldn't have to go on another manhunt.

'My Chickoo,' said Yudi. 'Don't worry. I'll find you another job, and increase your pocket money.'

The word 'Chickoo' astounded Milind. Was he a baby or what to be addressed so!

'My name is Milind,' he reminded his lover. 'If you don't mind, please call me by my name. My full name, not even Milya.'

As Milind had suspected, now that he was jobless again, Yudi began to 'daddy' him. If he touched him in bed, it was only to protectively pat his cheeks or possessively stroke his hair. The word 'Chickoo' escaped from his lips several times that week.

Still, Milind felt indebted to his lover. Here he was, providing him with boarding and lodging, and pocket money too! Yudi also insisted that Milind send a message to his parents, telling them he was safe and sound, and would be returning home in a couple of days. Milind realized that if a friend did so much for him, he too had a duty towards that friend. It was this noble thought that inspired him to polish Yudi's brassware with brasso one afternoon.

'It's something I'm good at,' he told his host when he returned home that evening. 'Remember I was a Brasso Master at Cipla?'

Train services, yet again, had been thrown out of gear. Milind waited and waited on the platform along with millions of faceless others, but no train graced the station. The announcements too were infrequent, and said nothing about when the next train was due. No one complained. Nalla Sopara was a wayside station that didn't enjoy the status of Borivili or Virar. Passengers didn't troop into the office of the Station Master here and smash equipment. If Milind had his way, though, he would have liked to do precisely that! For today's was no ordinary journey: it was a question of life and death. He was on his way to Dadar to meet Ashish Shah, owner of a coaching class called College of Knowledge. Yudi knew Ashish, he had telephoned the man and set up an appointment for Milind—half an hour from now! And here he was, stuck on the platform!

When the train finally arrived, Milind charged in and found a window seat on which someone had left a leather folder. Taking it as God's gift for his patience, he picked up the folder, unzipped it and found the death certificate of a man named Ashish Shah! If Ashish Shah is dead, what am I going to the interview for, he asked himself. Then, poring over the piece of paper, he realized it wasn't the same Ashish Shah. This one was seventy-nine years old. He decided to keep the folder but post the death certificate to the unfortunate relatives of Ashish Shah (the first).

He landed up for the interview one hundred and twenty-one minutes behind schedule, because, as he explained to Ashish Shah (the second), not only did the train move at snail's pace, but he also had much difficulty locating the College of Knowledge.

The interview commenced without much ado. Milind was caught on the wrong foot. The man interviewing him was a stickler for time, with NRI uncles in London and New York.

'If you're late for the interview, how can I expect you to come to work on time?' he asked his candidate, not in a mood to entertain excuses. Moreover, as if being two hours late wasn't bad enough, Milya committed a serious gaffe. Instead of giving his interlocutor the reco letter that Yudi had written (which he had put into the leather folder on the train), he gave him the death certificate of Ashish Shah, the first; not, of course, on purpose. He realized his faux pas a little too late, and only when he saw his interviewer go white in the face.

'What's this?' the man asked, terrified. Milind apologized, retrieved the wrong piece of paper and gave Shah the right one, but altogether it mattered little. The man asked him a few token questions, just so the whole exercise didn't seem farcical. Then he said he was sorry but he couldn't give Milind the job, 'because you are both unskilled and unschooled.'

There was more to the interview than what was spoken. This Ashish Shah was a queen, literally, to his manicured fingernails. One look at him, and Milya knew how Yudi knew him. It was no different with Shah. If Yudi recommended someone, he had to be gay. What bothered Shah (the real reason why he rejected Milya) was that the boy wasn't a she-gay but a he-gay, the sort he liked to have sex with. But if he had sex with Yudi's minion, the forty-year-old would surely break into his office and chew his balls like boiled egg.

Milind returned to Nalla Sopara in a huff and gave Yudi a blow-by-blow account of all that happened since he stepped out of the house that morning. He wasn't sure how Yudi would react. Luckily for him, there was no love lost between Yudi and Shah.

He was wholly on Milya's side, though he did think Milya shouldn't have given Shah his own death certificate.

'I shouldn't have got the *Metropolis on Saturday* to give the bogus College of Knowledge a write up,' he said consolingly. Furthermore, he felt it was time to expose the racket—how Ashish Shah did everything from charging exorbitant fees to awarding fake degrees to leaking question papers. But what had poor Milya got to do with this? The fact remained that he was back to square one, jobless, parasitically living off his lover.

Yudi persuaded Milind to return home after giving him his address (in case prospective employers wished to meet him). He promised he would go through his address book very carefully to see which of his friends he could contact to get him a job.

'Tell them my caste before hand,' Milind said unexpectedly. Deep down he had the nagging feeling that Shah threw him out of his office because he was a Dalit.

'Don't romanticize your condition,' Yudi advised him, giving him a five hundred rupee note to alleviate his guilt, for, the real reason why he sent Milind packing was that the fellow ate gutkha on the sly, spat the juice in his bathroom sink, and clogged it so badly that a plumber had to be called.

Yudi was a true friend. True friends, unlike fake ones, say what they mean and do as they say. Yudi was serious about scanning his address book to zero in on the right contact. In fact, he began working on it minutes after Milya's departure, pen in hand. Half an hour later, he was ready with a shortlist of twenty names, whom he planed to contact one by one. He was about to lift the receiver to phone the first guy on his list, when the instrument rang.

It was Gauri. 'Yudi, if you can't propose to me, at least

proposition me,' she said, forgetting whatever had happened at his front door the last time she went to see him.

Acknowledging she had a way with words, Yudi quickly went over his shortlist to see if Gauri's name figured anywhere on it. Mercifully, it didn't. Even so, he ventured to impetuously ask her if she could find his boyfriend a job. Instead of answering with a simple yes or no, Gauri began to moan:

'You do so much for your boyfriend but so little for me!'

'Oh no, not again,' she heard Yudi fret, and afraid that he would slam the phone down and bring their lover's quarrel to an end, she informed him that she had taken to eco-feminism, and worked with an organization that protected the rights of animals.

'Your boyfriend, or whoever, is welcome to come and work with us, and we will pay him a modest salary.'

'Now you're talking sense,' Yudi mellowed down.

Gauri's munificence, however, was conditional.

'I'm not finished,' she said, readying him for battle again.

'What is it now?'

'I'll ask my group to employ your boyfriend, provided you too join our movement and, like me, become an animal rights activist.'

Yudi was impressed by the way the lady thought out schemes to ensure he would always be by her side.

'Okay,' he said, 'but I'll protect the rights of only the gay animals, not the straight ones. You'll have to tell me which of them have come out.'

As usual, Gauri found this screamingly funny and she had a laughing fit on the telephone. When her laughter subsided, she said:

'Yudi, I'm glad you've not lost your sense of humour.'

She then wanted to know what he'd had for lunch. 'Two pegs and two eggs,' he said blandly.

'You're not eating properly,' the mother in Gauri chided the son. Conversation tapered off with the mother inviting the son to The Yellow River, a new restaurant in Bandra, for a meal.

Bandra is infested with restaurants. Gauri always chose the latest one to entertain her friends. She was lonely and she could afford it. The Yellow River scored over other restaurants in the neighbourhood in that it had adventurous stuff on the menu, like cockroach and rat curry. The host arrived much after the guest, having (by now) perfected the art of arriving late. Her neighbours, after all, were Bollywood stars.

On entering the restaurant, Gauri paid Yudi a compliment, though a left-handed one.

'Your eyes still have a radiant look in them,' she said, and wanted to know the secret of his youth.

'How do you mean "still"?' Yudi asked, offended.

'You're forty plus, sir,' the spurned woman reminded the man she was head over heels in love with.

The answer came to Yudi in a flash.

'You know why my eyes sparkle? Because I'm an ammonia-queen, that is to say, toilets addict. I keep entering public loos with an expectant look in my eyes, hoping to find a new face and a new dick each time. That's the secret of my youth.'

'How promiscuous!' a scandalized Gauri said. 'And here I am, going frigid from non-use.'

They placed their order, passing on the weird stuff and settling for conventional things.

As they waited for their food—they were rather slow at The Yellow River, giving couples enough time for starters and preliminaries—Gauri found an ingenious way of touching Yudi, who had told her more than once that he was allergic to the touch of women. She grabbed his hand under the pretext of reading his palm. She had scarcely begun tracing her fingers along its contours, and telling him how self-centred he was, when he wrenched himself free.

'Read my fortune,' he said, 'provided you can read the lines of my feet. I believe that that's where our life stories are really contained.'

'How perverse!' cried Gauri. Pausing for a moment, she said, on second thoughts she wouldn't mind looking at his feet, but for that they would have to go to his flat.

The banquet arrived. Seconds after he bit into a chicken bone, one of Yudi's molars began to throb. A couple of his teeth were already missing, and still others were loose.

'Your teeth give your age away, even if your eyes don't,' said Gauri, determined to have her revenge.

Yudi bared his teeth at her.

The waiter presented them with the 'check' and Gauri paid by credit card. It was a status symbol she had newly acquired. Guilt-pangs struck Yudi. He realized that not once during his 'dates' with Gauri had he offered to pay even half the bill. An inner voice told him it was okay, for it was she who hungered for his company. However, it also reminded him that, for a change, he needed her help now to find his Milya a job. On the advice of his inner voice, Yudi took out his wallet and made a pretence of paying. He wouldn't have done so if he hadn't been absolutely sure that Gauri would have none of it, would insist that since she invited him to dinner, *she* would foot the bill. His calculations worked. The Prima Donna not only used her credit card, but also assured him that an occasional dinner with the man she adored wouldn't make a hole in her purse.

Gauri kept her word and got her group to hire Milind. The word Non Governmental Organization, NGO, was only just coming into use in 1994. In the past, they were simply referred to as the private sector. However, since so many of them were formed or funded by wealthy Indians who lived abroad, they invented the term to describe themselves, especially as it sounded similar to that other epithet, Non Resident Indian. Gauri's group was an NGO that took it upon itself to save the environment—from pollution, deforestation, over population and plastic. They had researchers who provided the statistics: Such were the pollution levels in India's major cities, that every time we left home, we shortened our lives by a day! Two thousand four hundred plastic bags had been found in the stomach of a cow when it was cut open! For every human being born in India, half a dozen cats and dogs lost their lives! And so on. The environment to these activists (another fashionable word that replaced the boring 'social worker') was a woman violated by men. Hence the members of Gauri's group saw themselves as eco-feminists, people who, even as they protected the environment, made a statement about women's rights.

So far so good. Trouble was, for all their noble intentions there was nothing concrete that the eco-feminists seemed to do. They had an agenda, yes, and funds in plenty, but no clear sense of where they were going. Milind was given all sorts of assorted tasks. If on a certain day he went with other 'field workers' to put up posters all over Azad Maidan, the next day he was asked to stand outside Churchgate or VT and distribute leaflets to every single commuter who emerged from the station. Most people, already burdened with life's conundrums, glanced at their leaflets cursorily before chucking them away on the street. In course of time, the pavements were so thoroughly littered with the pink and yellow sheets, that the efforts of the eco-feminists were self-defeating. But the activists carried on undaunted. They even went round with tin boxes collecting money from office goers, college students, everyone, in the name of this and that cause. Milind worked with the eco-feminists not out of conviction, but because it brought him a monthly income. Also, as other field workers of his ilk taught him, it was easy, in the circumstances, to pilfer and appropriate.

One day Yudi decided to accompany Milind on one of his assignments. It was Milind's third anniversary at work, meaning he'd successfully completed three months with the eco-feminists. The boys were given a set of posters and told to paste them on every single lamppost from Metro to VT. Though he was bored stiff, Yudi pretended to view their activities with great interest. Passers-by thought he was their supervisor. The well-built boys carried barrels of glue and a ladder. One of them applied the glue to the posters with a paintbrush, while it fell to Milya's lot (as the youngest member of the team) to climb the ladder and stick the posters on the lampposts. Yudi felt concerned. What if he lost his balance and fell? 'Be careful!' he heard himself scream each time Milind went up the ladder.

At the end of a hard day's work, Milind and his compatriots needed to relax. Their chosen form of relaxation was to repair to a paan-shop on D.N. Road and empty sachets of gutkha into their mouths. The paan-shop was just a stone's throw from Medium Advertising; it was from here that Milind bought his monthly stock of Manikchand during his stint with Parmeshwar. Naturally, he knew the paan-wala well. Yudi felt like a fish out of water. As the working-class boys talked and laughed and spat, he grew fidgety, like a bride in her husband's childhood home. Finally, our bourgeois journalist could stomach it no longer. He summoned Milya aside and asked him if he was finished. One look at the expression on his face—a mixture of anger, jealousy and disgust—and Milind knew what was coming.

'Why did you come with me then?' he tried to be reasonable. Then, discarding reason, he said: 'My friends are like this only.

They are not hi-fi, like *your* friends. If you don't like them, don't come after me.'

Yudi said nothing to that. But in his heart he called Milind an ungrateful wretch. Not that he expected gratitude. He was convinced that poverty made people mean; the truly generous were those who were well off. Milind would have had his way: rather than go with Yudi, he would have stayed with his yaars for more gupshup and more gutkha. What wrapped up the issue was the attitude of his yaars. Shocked to see their pal crapping with a stranger, and that too in the middle of the street (and that too with English words thrown in!) the guys took up positions on the battlefield, ready to strike. At least that was what the menacing glint in their eyes seemed to suggest. Milind sensed danger. The fellows were the rada baazi type all right, who didn't need an excuse to start a riot. He abruptly bid them goodbye and drew Yudi away. While Yudi waited at a safe distance, Milya went back to his comrades and whispered to them. What he told them was: 'I've borrowed money from the pimp and he now wants it back. Since I don't have the money, I have to go sweet talk the bhadva, assure him that I'll repay his loan later.'

Nothing could convince the boys better. Each one was himself up to his neck in debt.

That Yudi had won didn't mean, of course, that Milya was going be sociable. On the contrary. On his vow of silence again, he sulked all the way to Café Volga, and didn't open his mouth to utter a word even as they drank their beer. Yudi didn't speak either, although he was tempted to give the boy a long lecture on love, friendship, duty, respect, reverence, gratitude and conviviality. His seven deadly sins.

When they finished their beer and descended the steps of the mezzanine floor, the weather turned. A sunny day suddenly became dark, cloudy. It was June and here were the city's first pre-monsoon showers. Both Yudi and Milind felt rejuvenated by the raindrops that lashed against their skin. Their anger melted away, and they hugged each other as if they were in Yudi's bathroom, showering together. They allowed themselves to get drenched to the bone. Yudi even managed to kiss Milind in public—their first kiss in weeks—because when it rains cats and dogs in Bombay no one is bothered about anyone but himself.

The easy affection that Milind felt for Yudi that rainy day survived till the following Friday, and then the next, for hadn't the guy got him a job, and a decent job too, where he got to be on familiar terms with perfumed upper-class women who spoke in English? The high point came two months later, when the eco-feminists had a big do at the Crystal Ballroom of the Taj. Delegates came from all over the world. As the most 'presentable' handyman in the organization, Milind was posted outside the hall to give them folders, brochures, notepads, and anything else they wanted. He alone, among all the helpers of the group, had a smattering of English (having studied for a year in the English medium). But the speeches that everyone gave were full of bombastic words that went clean over his head. He was amazed at the way they talked for hours at a stretch. Didn't their mouths ache? After the foreigners (the kind he had wanted to pose with at Shravanabelagola) it was the turn of the Indians to speak. Gauri's name was announced, and he had a better view of the lady this time, as she stood under the lights, before the mike. She was pretty, though stout and ageing. Her clothes were weird, though. He couldn't figure out whether she was wearing a sari or salwar kameez. It looked like a combination of both. And she wouldn't let go of her cigarettes even while speaking. What if he took her to his mother and said he wanted to marry her!

Waiters approached Milind with sandwiches and glasses of tomato juice. They addressed him as 'sir'. It was the fulfilment of a vow, for when he was thrown out of the Taj, not long ago, he had promised he would return one day and make them touch his feet. Of course it wouldn't have flattered him to know that the waiters offered him the victuals only because the delegates were full. Better the stuff went into the poor peon's stomach than into the bin.

The conference went on and on and on. Milind reached home very late that night, his eyelids drooping with sleep but his heart full of song, for he felt upper-class himself, and important.

In September 1994, Bombay was visited by the plague. It came to the city from Surat, 260 kilometres away, hitching a ride on the Flying Rani. There were some who dismissed it as rumour. The chief characteristic of the disease was that one saw dead rats all over the streets, but the rats in Bombay were in the best of health, slithering up and down the sewer pipes of buildings as if they were landlords. True, one saw the occasional dead rat in some quarter of the city, but there wasn't any proof that it had died of the plague. It could simply have been poisoned, or run over by a Maruti, or killed by a cat.

Most Bombay-walas, however, are a cowardly lot prone to panic. Any small thing distresses them. If it was the riots and bomb blasts last year, this year it was the plague. People stayed away from the Flying Rani and in fact from most trains on Western Railway, because they brought in hordes of outcastes, each one a potential transmitter. Others stopped buying diamonds because they were made in Surat. Yudi was badly affected by the entire hullabaloo. Nalla Sopara, as everyone knows, is half the way to Surat, so unlike before, he easily found a window seat on the train home now. But with the trains and stations deserted, just as they had been during the riots, there were no men to ogle, no crush of bodies, no hungry-eyed boys in the loos.

The newspapers, especially the tabloid press, took advantage of the situation by printing sensational headlines that jacked up their sales. One of *Mid-Day*'s banner headlines read: HALF OF BOMBAY TO DIE OF PLAGUE.

The worrying kind himself, who had once told a fellow journalist he was worried he didn't have any thing to worry about, Yudi now felt concerned about Milya, and about his mother, not to speak of himself. His mother was in what they called the 'low risk' category for she rarely left the house. Even so, he made it a point to drop in at her place every other day to see if she developed symptoms. Milind was a different problem altogether. For one thing, his work kept him out on the roads for most part of the day. For another, he lived in a chawl where hygiene wasn't the most important word in anyone's vocabulary.

Determined to ensure his boyfriend didn't die of the primitive disease, Yudi gave Milind some of the Tetracycline capsules he had bought for himself and his mother. 'Take them if you have a vomiting fit,' he advised. But Milya wasn't perturbed by the goings on in the city. 'In my family we worship the plague,' he told Yudi.

'You do what?' Yudi asked, baffled and a little fearful.

'You see, it's the plague of 1962 that gave my father his job. People were running away from the hospital in fear. Suddenly there were a whole lot of vacancies. My father stayed back and that's how he got permanent.'

The story didn't impress Yudi. He insisted that Milind should wear a protective mask, the one that they distributed free. 'Otherwise, you won't get your pocket money.' The threat worked. Milind was heavily in debt and needed every extra penny that came his way. The salary he got from the eco-feminists was hardly sufficient. If he antagonized Yudi by disobeying him, the man might indeed terminate his dole and land him in a soup.

The next few days saw the boyfriend go about everywhere in a black mask. On the fourth day he was picked up by the cops and taken to the police station. The police were on a rounding-up spree, having been tipped off by their espionage department that Pakistani terrorists had infiltrated the city. The plague, apparently, enabled the gunmen to strike gold: as everyone wore black masks, there was no telling who was a terrorist and who was not. They thus got away literally with murder. Both Yudi and Gauri were summoned to the police station to identify Milya and bail him out. Trembling with fear, sobbing like a child (the cops have that kind of reputation) the poor thing had barely managed to give the inspector their phone numbers.

'Does he look like a Kashmiri militant?' Yudi asked the inspector point blank, trying to stuff common sense into his head. 'Anyone can tell his ancestors were Maharashtrians who trekked up and down the Sahyadri Mountains.' But the inspector didn't go by inferences and deductions. The only word in his dictionary was duty and he knew it backwards.

'Hey mister,' he said to Yudi. 'Please keep quiet. I know you and also *about* you.'

Yudi was stunned. Had that bastard Dnyaneshwar been talking? Unwilling to tempt the Indian law, he cooled down. Inspector saab finally released Milind after Gauri signed a bail bond of Rs 5,000 on behalf of her organization. She extracted a dinner from Yudi for the favour, dragging him once again to The Yellow River, where she sampled cockroach fry.

If it was a toothache the restaurant dinner gave him the last time, this time it was anal warts. Yudi discovered them in the bogs, and freaked out. Could it have anything to do with the plague? Milind made him an emergency call to report that he too was decorated with warts. In his case they were on the tip of his dick.

'You swine,' Yudi swore. 'You transmitted them to me. You STD booth!'

Milind denied it was he who was the wart-giver:

'What's the proof that you got them from me, and not I from you?'

They argued for a while on the phone but didn't come to any conclusion. This much Yudi knew: if it was a sexually transmitted disease, it wasn't the plague. And STDs weren't a big thing any more; they could be cured with a shot of penicillin.

The doctor to whom Yudi and Milind jointly went for treatment was disgusted. How could the two men be so shameless as to openly admit they had contracted the warts through anal intercourse?

'No unnatural sex, no warts,' he kept telling them as he injected them, assuming the manner of a high school master.

It was only because he was the friend of a friend of a friend that Yudi resisted the urge to ask him to fuck off and mind his own business!

Milind understood him better. 'Don't you see,' he told Yudi, 'that he wants one of us to have unnatural sex with him?'

The eco-feminists terminated Milind's services. What was worse, they didn't give him any reason. Milind called Yudi who consoled him and asked him to keep his cool. Then he did the one thing he hated from the bottom of his heart—he telephoned Gauri. She took ages to come on the line. Music from a device fitted to her phone entertained him while he waited. The tune was familiar: 'Hum tum ek kamre mein bandh hon' from *Bobby*. When Gauri came to the phone finally, she apologized profusely, both for keeping Yudi waiting and for asking Milind to quit. It had nothing to do with his performance or for that matter his character, she assured Yudi. He was a 'cute kid'. It was just that as they had no projects going, they were cutting down on excess staff. The axe naturally fell on temporary hands like Milind.

Yudi went through his address book again, and this time telephoned Sadiq, an Iraqi gentleman who was married to one of his classmates (whom he had helped in the exams). Sadiq ran a recruiting agency at Bhendi Bazaar to which Muslims who wished to migrate to the Gulf flocked. As his business flourished, Sadiq prospered. He told Yudi he could easily give Milind a job—'Send him, send him,' he said. Knowing him to be the snobbish type, Yudi took Milind to Fashion Street to spruce up his attire. Responding to the lecture Yudi gave him on good dressing and personal hygiene ('You stink most of the time'), Milind reminded him that he was poor, and that his mother couldn't wash tons of clothes every day. The new clothes that Milind wore there itself, changing virtually on the busy street, and the matching dark glasses he sported, coupled with his soldier haircut, so transformed him that some hawkers began to address him as 'Crorepati Saab'. Yudi was thrilled. At least Sadiq wouldn't look down upon the fellow now.

There was only one thing Sadiq asked Milind at the interview— how was Yudi his friend, considering the difference in their age and social status. Although he hadn't been coached, Milya fielded that one well.

'Both of us have been living in the same locality since our childhood,' he lied. 'It's not just I who know Yudi. Our families too know each other well.'

Sadiq didn't believe Milind's story, but gave him the job all the same. His snobbery and pride in his wealth ensured that he couldn't refuse favours, even to a man who fucked other men— men like this fellow from the gutter! He wanted to puke when, his crorepati attire notwithstanding, he saw Milind wash teacups in the sink (his first assignment) and tried to imagine how Yudi and he made love. How could anyone cohabit with menials, he wondered, especially menial men! Wasn't the offensive smell that emanated from their bodies enough to put one off for life?

Milya stuck on with Sadiq for all of forty-eight hours. During this time the only thing he was asked to do, was bring jarfuls of sugarcane juice for his master from a nearby ganna-seller.

'Sugar-can' he called it, amusing even the not-so-literate Milind.

On the third day, Sadiq called Yudi to say Milind had disappeared after the lunch break. 'What kind of boy did you send me?' he asked, sounding as if he'd been betrayed. 'He says he's going for lunch and doesn't come back at all. I'm still checking my cupboards to see if he's embezzled any cash.'

Yudi wore his acting costume again. He found himself pacifying Sadiq, assuring him Milind wasn't 'that type', while in truth he went pale with worry: was the boy still alive or had a BEST bus crushed him to pulp?

chaitya bhoomi

Paranoid about accidents, having witnessed the most maiming ones while commuting by train, and having heard nothing from Milya for over a week, Yudi was convinced his lover had gone under the wheels of a car/bus/lorry. He saw visions. Of Milya's body lying unclaimed in the J.J. Hospital morgue. Of his family performing the last rites without informing him (whom they didn't know from Adam). He grew neurotic with worry. This helped, because he was the type who worked well under stress. He sat down with paper and pen and charted out his course of action. The first thing was to contact Sadiq and ask him to elaborate. What exactly happened on that fateful day?

A long line of carpenters, masons, waiters and fitters stood outside Sadiq's Bhendi Bazaar office, desperate to go to the Gulf. (Yudi checked each one of them out but wasn't attracted to any. They were too obviously middle-aged). Gatecrashing his way into the office, he was greeted by Sadiq who offered him a refreshing glass of sugarcane juice. It wasn't the juice of course that Yudi had come there to drink. He wanted details: the details of Milind's disappearance.

'Damn it,' swore Sadiq who didn't wish to broach the subject again. 'Didn't I already tell you what happened? He worked here till noon, told me he was going out for lunch, and didn't come back. But what is the point of your coming here? Why don't you go to his house and ask them where he is?'

Some questions can't be answered and this surely was one of them. How could Yudi tell the homophobic Sadiq that their relationship was a secret, with their families nowhere in the picture? Heteros seemed rather dumb when it came to sensitive matters of the heart.

Sadiq's demeanour provoked Yudi to ask him another question:

'Are you sure you haven't bundled him to Muscat, or some such place?'

He asked the question half seriously, half in apparent jest. Had it been otherwise, Sadiq might have asked him to leave the office at once. For it was an allegation with grave repercussions: he was calling the man a kidnapper.

'I'll let that pass,' said Sadiq, 'only because you are Veena's friend.' After a short pause, during which he lit a cigarette, he added, 'It is I who would like to accuse you of sending me a rogue and a cheat, whom I employed purely in good faith.'

Phone call after phone call interrupted their exchange, all of them from Gulf hopefuls. The carpenters and masons and waiters and fitters who waited outside in the sun grew restless and banged on the glass door. 'Jaldi karo, saab,' they cried. While Sadiq lifted the receiver to take yet another call Yudi slipped out without saying good-bye. There wasn't much he was going to get out of the Iraqi. Time was running out: he had better move on to stage two.

His next act surprised him. As soon as he got home, he found himself calling Gauri. But wasn't Gauri an enemy in this matter? Why, then, was he seeking her advice in this calamitous hour? He knew the answer even before he asked the question. Gauri alone would hear him out fully; meditate upon his every utterance, just so that she could stretch her conversation with him on the phone. She was in love with him, with his voice, and would feign interest, even if in her heart of hearts she were very glad that Milind was out of the way.

He was as right as the Big Ben. Not only did Gauri empathize with him as best as she could (she kept saying, 'Yudi, I know how you feel'), she also took the blame for Milind's disappearance. 'If we hadn't asked him to quit,' she said, referring to her environmentalist friends, 'this wouldn't have happened. He was so happy with us. And such a good worker! Wonder where he is now.'

Yudi appreciated Gauri's concern. Delighted that she was scoring plus points, she went on. 'The only thing left for you to do,' she told Yudi, 'is to go to Milind's place and find out if he's there.'

This, from Yudi's point of view, was the same myopic thing that Sadiq had suggested. As if she had heard him think aloud, Gauri immediately clarified: 'Mind you, it's not as if I don't know that your affair with Milind is a secret. But then, what alternative do we have?'

Yudi thanked Gauri for her advice, but explained that Milind was dead against his going to their house. One look at him, he said, and his family would grow suspicious. It was his duty to respect his yaar's wishes. Hence, he would leave paying a visit to the chawl to the very end. He would go there as a last resort, only when all other doors were closed.

Before disconnecting, Gauri asked Yudi to be calm, to say a prayer to God for Milind's safe return, and to have an optimistic outlook on life. Then came the catch. She was convinced that if Yudi went over to her place for dinner, or called her to his for lunch, he would feel better; her words of consolation would act as a balm.

Needless to say, Yudi did nothing of the sort.

When people go missing, the way to go about tracing them is to contact their friends; people generally confide in friends more than they do in lovers and family members. Often the friends are the last ones to see them, at such and such place, in such and such clothes. Yudi was aware of this, but realized with a sense of alarm that he didn't know any of Milya's friends—the buddies that he hung about with in his neighbourhood, or even at the workplace. He scratched his head to recall if there was anyone he had seen Milind talk to. Yes! The gutkha-eating boys, with whom he went around sticking posters on lampposts! But where would he find them? He didn't know where they lived, and in all likelihood, they too had been sacked by the eco-feminists. Even if they hadn't been, he was not going to make another telephone call to Gauri to ask for their whereabouts. For any lead that she provided, the woman would demand a meal at a fancy restaurant, not to mention a place in his heart.

Immersed in these thoughts, Yudi suddenly remembered the paan-wala on D.N. Road. His shop was the water hole at which Milind and his mates quenched their thirst. It was also the place, he remembered, where he had created a scene. Yudi rushed to D.N. Road to meet the paan-wala, but was greeted by his younger brother who informed him that 'Ratan bhaiya' would be back in an hour.

'Ratan bhaiya ke saath kya kaam hai?' he asked, as Yudi decided to stay put at the shop till he met Ratan.

'Zaroori kaam,' replied Yudi. The young man thought of asking exactly what that something important was, but changed his mind when Yudi pointedly turned away, making it quite clear that he had no wish to get into a conversation.

Ratan returned earlier than expected, within a few minutes of Yudi's arrival, to be precise. Recognizing Yudi instantly for the scene he'd created outside his shop, he gave him dirty looks and asked gruffly, 'Kya hai?' His hostility didn't vanish when Yudi explained what had brought him there.

'How am I to know where Milind is?' he said. 'It's true he used to buy his Manikchand from me when he worked for Medium Advertising, but he's not with Medium any more. He hasn't come here for almost a month.'

A customer interrupted their conversation. Ratan got busy making the man's masala paan. Yudi felt repudiated. He hung around awkwardly for a few minutes, then turned to leave, when, still working on his paan, Ratan called out to him: 'Hey, mister! Milind said something about modelling. Said he was joining a group that was looking for male models.'

The news paralysed Yudi. That his Milya should confide in a mere paan-wala, and not in him, his lover, wounded him deeply. Milind and modelling! He didn't know whether to laugh or cry. Who on earth would make his dark, skinny Milya a model? He smelled a rat.

Yudi was at the Bhendi Bazaar Police Station, requesting the lady inspector to go over records of the whole of last week to see if any accidental deaths had been reported. The lady's fingers flicked through pages of a register that she ordered one of her constables to bring. Those fingers fascinated Yudi. They were thick in the middle and thin at the ends, and weren't adorned with rings or nail polish. A masculine hand—years of slapping men around must have done that to her.

When she was finished, Ms Gentleman's Fingers closed her register with a bang and informed Yudi that Milind Mahadik's name figured nowhere in it. To rule out every possibility, Yudi flashed his press card and obtained written permission from the lady 'to visit lock-up at police station's backside', just to reassure himself it wasn't there that Milya had landed, thanks to the shady things he did behind his back.

If the murderous eyes of prisoners in the lock-up scared Yudi out of his wits, his next move was even more perplexing. He thanked Ms Gentleman's Fingers for all her help, audaciously remarked that she had done for him what no male cop would ever do, hailed a cab, and through peak-hour traffic on Mohammed Ali Road, headed straight for the J.J. Hospital morgue. There, flashing his press card once again, he gained entry into the hospital's Mafco Cold Storage where the dead rested.

Yudi pulled the sheet off corpse after corpse to verify if any of them was Milind's. Some were mutilated; others had expressions of sadness or joy or anger or horror frozen on their faces. Then came the one—lo and behold—that was Milya's. Or almost! After Yudi had recovered from the shock and retched pitiably a couple of times, he realized, from the manner in which the white sheet gathered between the dead man's legs, from the forest of hair on his chest, that this was not Milya. And yet, the facial features of this one so resembled Milind's that Yudi, perhaps to be absolutely sure, pulled the sheet down to the dead man's knees and gave his dick a long, hard look.

On the night of his visit to the morgue, Yudi was haunted by nightmares. The corpses he had disrobed went for his throat all at once. The one he mistook for Milind accused him of necrophilia, and with blind rage in his eyes, chopped off Yudi's sausage and swallowed it whole. Yudi jumped out of bed clutching his balls and screaming.

Later that day, the doorbell rang at an odd afternoon hour. Yudi rushed to the door thinking it might be Milind. It wasn't

Milind, but a boy more or less his age, height, build and complexion. These days too many people looked the same, Yudi thought. Maybe God was running out of ideas. The boy was from a courier company known as Pigeon Couriers. He carried a letter in his beak for Yudi. Before he opened the letter, Yudi checked out the boy, found he was amenable to 'homosex', and had it off with him in the fucking room in five minutes flat. When one is down in the pits, sex is the best antidote. But the boy was mannerless. He didn't announce that his condom had given way, and allowed his thin semen to spill all over Yudi's backside. Then, having had his own 'discharge', he didn't wait for Yudi to come. Instead, he stood up the moment he was finished and rushed into the bathroom, leaving filthy pugmarks on the tiled floor. Finally, he took off with a radio torch, a present from Yudi's American uncle, which he slipped into his mailbag when Yudi went into the bathroom to clean up.

The letter delivered by the crook from Pigeon Couriers was from *India Magazine*. Yudi's piece on Shravanabelagola had been accepted. However, the editor wanted certain 'unsuitable' portions deleted. Or else, peace-loving Jain Munis, their feet bare and their mouths masked for fear of injuring ants and bacteria, would march to the office of *India Magazine* and set it ablaze. Did Yudi want to see his article lead to arson and looting? As Yudi speculated on the matter, the phone rang. Editor saab himself was on the line. Although he tried to argue out his case with the gentleman, in the end he capitulated. He was low on funds and badly needed assignments, and cheques. What difference did it make if they didn't allow him to say exactly why he cherished the experience of gazing upon Gomatesh? One had to be practical.

Yudi looked at the photographs they would be using. Photos taken in happier times and climes, when Milya was by his side. He wanted to cry! Where, oh where, was Milind? Who in this world of six billion people would understand his pain? When one is anxious, one is seized by colic. Yudi massaged his aching belly and went to the bogs. Sitting on the potty like a meditating Buddha, he tried to think coolly.

Gauri was right. The only way to put an end to his anguish was to make that damned visit to Milind's house. If the chap had gone underground, and returned to blast him for landing up at his home without permission, Yudi would face the music. That would be less bothersome than being in a limbo, as he presently was.

By the time he was out of the bogs, Yudi had made up his mind.

At Chinchpokli, once I return in the evening,
I plot seductions and rapes, plan masterpieces
Of evasions. The loudspeakers blare at me.
Bed bugs bite me. Cockroaches hover about my soul.
Mice scurry around my metaphysics, mosquitoes sing
                              around my lyrics.
Lizards crawl over my religion, spiders infest my politics.
I itch. I become horny. I booze. I want to get smashed.
And I do. It comes easy at Chinchpokli,
Where like a minor Hindu god, I am stoned
By the misery of my worshippers and by my own
Triumphant impotence.

Thus had a poet immortalized the working-class area of Chinchpokli. It was perhaps the only poem on Chinchpokli in the universe. Who, other than an eccentric poet, would bother to write about a smoky, smelly neighbourhood. But Yudi liked the poem. As he read it on the trains that took him from Nalla Sopara to Dadar and Dadar to Chinchpokli, he began to see himself as the minor Hindu god, stoned by misery and impotence.

When the train reached Chinchpokli, it was already late evening. He went to the platform tea stall and drank a glass of chilled lime juice. Then he popped a packet of glucose biscuits into his mouth. The job ahead was arduous; he had to fortify himself well.

Soon after he had climbed the stairs that led him out of the station, Yudi saw the intimidating walls of Arthur Road Jail, taller than a two-storey building. He remembered something Milind had once said. Apparently, his chawl was so close to the jail that the prisoners' cells could be clearly seen from his terrace, just as the Towers of Silence are visible from adjoining skyscrapers. People routinely went up to his terrace to signal to imprisoned relatives. To curtail the menace, the jail authorities had decided to raise the jail walls.

'De daan chhute grahan,' he heard a few beggars cry.

Yudi looked up at the sky and saw that there was indeed a lunar eclipse. What an ominous moment he had chosen to visit Milya's house! The beggars continued to yell, promising deliverance from the curse of the eclipse to all those who gave them alms. They scurried towards buildings from where superstitious people dropped clothes. Yudi quickened his pace. The nearer he came to Milind's house, the faster his heart pounded.

'De daan chhute grahan.'

Beggars on one side, prisoners on the other. An eclipse in the sky above. Yudi felt like a prisoner and beggar rolled into one. Why else was he making this journey to a house where he couldn't be welcome, calling on a family who, if they knew who he was, would be shamed by his presence? For crumbs of mercy? For deliverance from the prison of an emotion he thought he had overcome years ago?

Upon entering the gates of Kasturba Hospital Servants' Quarters, Yudi remembered another of Milind's stories. The quarters were in such proximity to the fortresses of some of Bombay's famous gangsters, that residents were ashamed to tell people where they lived. With Arun Gawli's Dagdi Chawl to their left, and Amar Naik's Amar Prem to their right, the inhabitants of Kasturba Hospital Servants' Quarters were frequently taken for criminals themselves. The police constantly harassed them. Parents found it hard to prevent their sons from being lured by the underworld. Most of the boys weren't even matriculates, were jobless, and inevitably attracted to the idea of becoming millionaires in a week. One of Milind's own brothers regularly called at Dagdi Chawl. Not till the family threatened him with dire consequences did the fellow stop going there. It had all begun with visits to the home of a teacher who lived in Dagdi Chawl, to whom the boy went for 'difficulties'. (Yes, respectable people also lived in Dagdi Chawl, and Yudi recalled what Milind had told him of a petition the residents had signed, imploring Mr Arun Gawli to change the name of Dagdi Chawl because it was turning out to be a liability for people who put it on their CV.)

Yudi took a close look at the Servants' Quarters. There were four buildings, each three storeys high. Each building was the side of a square, and in the centre was a quadrangle where children played. But unlike the quadrangles of convent schools and colleges, this one was littered with muck. The air was malodorous. The buildings themselves were blackened with soot, not painted for half a century. A clothesline ran through every floor, displaying moth-eaten undergarments. Somewhere water dripped from a leaking tap, pit-a-pat, echoing Yudi's own heartbeats.

'Kaun chahiye?' the voice of adolescent kids, playing in the corridor with a bat and ball, alerted him. It took him a few seconds to recover.

'Where does Milind Mahadik live?'

'Top floor, last house,' came the crisp answer. In chawls, unlike in flats, everyone knew their neighbours well. Yudi began ascending the steep steps. It was too much to expect lifts in the Kasturba Hospital Servants' Quarters. When he reached the first floor, the kids shouted to him from down below.

'Milind Mahadik isn't there. He's been missing for the last ten days.'

Yudi turned round to face the bat-and-ball kids.

'Are you sure?'

'Yes. Go to his house and see for yourself if you don't believe us.'

So his worst fears were confirmed. He was hoping against hope to find Milind at home, safe and sound. But now even this glimmer of hope had been destroyed by the sadistic boys.

'Who's at home?' he asked the boys, dejected.

'Everyone. His father, mother, brothers. His mother hasn't eaten since the day he left.'

'Any idea where he could be?'

'How should we know? He was a big bhav-khav. Never talked to us. We too didn't speak much to him. We're actually friends of his younger brother, Dinesh.'

'The guy who was found at Dagdi Chawl?'

The aspersion so unsettled the lads that they didn't know how to react. They defused the time bomb by bursting into laughter. But it was clear that they hated what they heard. Yudi sensed their discomfiture. He took hold of the situation and said:

'I was only joking. Thanks for all your help.'

Then he resumed his journey upwards.

The Mahadiks' front door was open. In chawls, front doors are shut only at night. To shut them at any other time is to suggest one is doing immoral things inside, like fucking. A curtain that looked like a kitchen rag hung from the door shabbily, frustrating peeping toms in their endeavours. Yudi parted the curtain hesitantly, reluctant to touch it, and said:

'Hello, is Milind Mahadik there?'

The entire family was engrossed in watching what seemed to be their favourite TV serial, *Dekh Bhai Dekh*. Milind frequently referred to scenes from the serial and asked Yudi if he enjoyed them, assuming that he too, and in fact the whole world, watched it religiously. It was that important.

Their concentration ruined by the intruder's words, the family came to the door all at once to welcome the stranger. The volume of the TV was lowered although it wasn't switched off altogether, and the tube lights were switched on. There was a hushed silence. Yudi felt as if he had come there on a condolence visit.

'Apan kon? Who are you?' the mother asked Yudi, breaking the silence. She looked like his maid Saraswati's twin. Before he could give them a suitable answer, the adulterous father, still seated on a chair near the idiot box, butted in. He was the only one who hadn't risen from his perch to greet Yudi.

'Give him a glass of water first,' he ordered his family, his words coming out in a drunken drawl. Yudi already knew enough about the man to write his biography. He had a fondness for country liquor. Though he lived with his mistress, he visited his wife and kids occasionally, especially on payday, to atone for his sins. He sometimes wept and farted, both at the same time, when he was drunk.

While the mother went to fetch water from an earthenware pot, Yudi studied the house. It was a one-room tenement which served as bedroom, hall and kitchen. When the common toilets at the end of the rows of such tenements weren't free, a corner also served as a bathing area or a loo. The walls had white patches on them, as if stricken with leucoderma. The most prominent thing in the room was an iron folding cot, followed by the black-and-white TV. His family members, Milind used to say, took turns to sleep on and under the cot, and it mostly fell to his lot, as a late riser, to sleep under it.

'Where is Milind?' Yudi impatiently asked the lady, as she returned with water in a steel *lota*.

'To Pune la gela,' she replied.

'Gone to Pune?' came the surprised query.

'Yes, Pune.'

Milind's three brothers, one older and two younger, stood around their mother in a protective semi-circle as she spoke. Brothers three and four, the former the Dagdi Chawl aide, were ten times lovelier than Milya.

'Stop having adulterous thoughts!' Yudi chided himself, as he found his eyes lingering on their crotches. 'They're your brothers-in-law!'

'Milind often spoke about you,' Mr Dagdi Chawl said. 'You are a Christian padre, aren't you?'

Yudi was astonished by the ludicrous suggestion. A Christian padre! Heaven knows what lies the rogue had inflicted on his family.

'No, I am not,' he clarified. 'I'm merely a friend of Milind's who's trying to find him a job.'

But the mother wasn't listening.

'Please send my Milya back,' she began to weep. 'Tell him not to take to Isaai dharam. We are from the Baudh dharam, the followers of Babasaheb. Don't make him an Isaai!'

Her weeping matured into sobs. The sons consoled her.

'You people are making a big mistake,' Yudi raised his voice and told the family in no uncertain terms. 'I am no Christian padre come to convert your son! I'm a journalist, a reporter, who met Milind at the *Times of India*. After he quit Medium Advertising, he approached me for a job. I got him a job in a friend's recruiting agency, but he disappeared from there without telling anyone. I've come to find out what happened.'

'Deva re deva!' the mother cried. 'If you don't know where he is, then where *is* my son? May god keep him well!'

The father called out from his throne again. This time it was to ask his wife to give Yudi a cup of tea. She seemed to like the idea.

'Yes, yes, sit down,' she said, wiping her tears with the pallu of her sari, and bringing him a chair. 'I'll get you tea.'

The lady withdrew into the rear of the tenement that served as the kitchen. In it were steel utensils and rows of aluminium dabbas of all sizes. Yudi wondered if the dabbas were full, and if so with what.

He turned to the eldest brother and spoke to him for the first time.

'Can you tell me what exactly happened? When did he go away, and in what circumstances?'

Deep down, Yudi suspected that Milya might have run away after a brawl with his family. He frequently complained that there wasn't enough to eat at home (in spite of all those aluminium dabbas); his parents nagged and taunted him, asking him to work before he ate.

But the brother knew nothing. It was obvious that he and Milind weren't very close. He helplessly looked towards his mother who heard Yudi's question, thanks to her sharp ears, and answered from the kitchen, several feet away.

'Aho, he returned from his work in the evening, and said he was going to Pune with his boss and would return after two days. It's now ten days, and there's still no sign of him. Our neighbours upstairs have a telephone, but he hasn't even given us a call to tell us when he is coming back. I hope he hasn't got chakkar and fallen down. I hope he is taking his medicines. Deva re deva, keep my son safe.'

If Yudi derived solace from the woman's words, it was only because they implied that Milind hadn't been killed in an accident outside Sadiq's office. At least he got back home in one piece before he left. However, that Milind had giddy spells and was on a regular course of medicines was news to him. Once again he was pained that the fellow hadn't confided in him.

The mother served him his tea, along with a few Monaco biscuits, which of course he did not touch. Viewing the anxiety on his face, as he sipped his tea in silence, she was puzzled as to why a mere friend, much older than Milind, was so troubled by his absence, while her own family seemed quite unperturbed.

'Don't worry, he'll be back,' she ventured to say to him. 'If you leave your phone number with us, we'll give you a call as soon as he comes back.'

Yudi took out his wallet and searched for a visiting card. (It was Milind who had got these printed for him as a birthday gift when he was at Medium Advertising). But the wallet contained everyone's business cards except his own. Seeing him grope, Dagdi Chawl approached him with paper and pen and asked him to jot down his number. As Yudi stood close to the hunk and wrote out his number (wishing it had fourteen digits instead of seven), he felt an electric current run through his body. Why did God make some people so volcanic?

The tea over, phone numbers exchanged, there was nothing left for Yudi to do, except stand up and take his leave. Yet he felt strangely comfortable in Milind's house, surrounded by his parents and brothers, and would have liked to stay there for ever.

As Yudi headed towards the door, the father's booming voice shook the walls. The man had condescended at last to speak to him directly. He said:

'Tomorrow is 6 December. It's the death anniversary of Babasaheb Ambedkar. If you are so concerned about Milind, come with us to Chaitya Bhoomi Mandir at Shivaji Park and pray for his safe return.'

Yudi liked the idea very much. He had once promised Milind that he would go with him to Chaitya Bhoomi, and here was a chance to fulfil his promise, even if Milind wouldn't accompany him.

'Yes, I'll come with you,' he said without a second thought.

By asking him to join them on this most sacred rite, it was as if Milind's family members were accepting him as their own. It gladdened his heart.

On getting out of Kasturba Hospital Servants' Quarters, Yudi made a discovery. The complex was actually closer to Mahalaxmi (on Western Railway) than Chinchpokli (on Central Railway). Little wonder Milind boarded his trains at Mahalaxmi. Why then did he cumbersomely change trains at Dadar? To experience the Chinchpokli poem live?

Beggars continued to beg. De daan, chhute grahan.

The slow train from Virar to Churchgate took ages. Yudi was compelled to board it because there were no fast trains in the afternoon. As the train meandered, stopping every few minutes for no apparent reason, he changed his mind. He would go to Milind's house first, rather than meet the family at Shivaji Park as was decided yesterday. A rationalist, he convinced himself he was doing this because it was the more sensible thing to do. Where among the multitudes that gathered at Shivaji Park would he otherwise trace his hosts? Rationalists, however, are men whose real motives are irrational. It isn't difficult to fathom what Yudi's irrational motives were. Milind might be back, he intuited, and the only way to connect with him was to go to his house. He went via Mahalaxmi this time, for the Chinchpokli route, despite the poem, had turned out to be unlucky (he hadn't found Milind). He was about to climb the stairs that led to Milya's tenement, his Pentax hung around his neck, when he saw the entire family descending, all of them except brother number one—and Milind. They exchanged pleasantries, but before the exchanges were over, Yudi impulsively asked his question: any news of Milind?

'Nahi ho,' the mother answered, and resumed her cries of 'Deva re deva.' The father asked her to shut up.

They got out of the complex, surrounded by odours of sweat and grime. Yudi tried to be magnanimous and hail a cab. The father stopped him at once.

'What are you doing?' he exclaimed. 'We are going on a pilgrimage. True followers of Babasaheb Ambedkar walk all the way to Chaitya Bhoomi. They don't go there by taxi or bus!'

Yudi apologized. What hell had he landed himself in? He did not dislike walking, was quite a walker himself, in fact, but going on a padyatra with his in-laws was quite another matter. Their presence was soothing as long as they were within the secure confines of their home. To be with them on the streets, exposed to public scrutiny, was a different matter altogether. What would he say to them, having nothing to banter about except Milind?

As it turned out, no one uttered a word throughout the six-kilometre trek to Shivaji Park. This suited Milind's father who believed he was undertaking the most holy journey of his life. What about his country liquor, Yudi wondered, as they ambled along. Was he carrying it in his trousers to have a furtive swig every now and then? And where was his prostitute mistress?

About the only question Yudi managed to whisper into the ears of Dagdi Chawl during the course of their padyatra was: 'Where is your eldest brother?'

The boy looked into Yudi's eyes (almost causing him to die of cardiac arrest), smiled seductively, and said: 'He doesn't believe in things of this kind.'

With every kilometre they covered, the crowds multiplied. People walked not just on footpaths but spilled on to arterial roads and caused traffic jams. In any case, most roads seemed to be closed to vehicular traffic. The Dalits had taken over the streets for the day. It was their day, no one could dictate to them. Policemen did appear on the scene from time to time, blowing their whistles, pretending to direct the flow of marchers to prevent a stampede. But they kept a low profile on the whole; did not say or do much. They frowned upon this audience of Harijans whom they had to oversee. Many of them seemed to believe in untouchability still. They took great precautions to make sure no one's shadow fell on them. Or else they would have to rush home and bathe! In the last analysis, they regarded the lives of these fellows as worthless. What difference did it make if some of them died in the melee, or drowned in the Shivaji Park Sea? The world would be rid of that many Chamars.

The last kilometre of the trek saw every inch of space covered with men, women and children. The procession came to a standstill every few minutes, then moved, only to come to a standstill again. At one point Yudi witnessed a cop beating up a devotee for no apparent reason. The fellow howled as the lathi struck his flanks and shanks. The cop stopped only when Yudi confronted him, flashed his press card, and threatened to have his picture published on the front page of *Mid-Day*.

'Saheb, you don't know what the rascal was up to,' the uniformed brigand said in self-defence. 'He was misbehaving with women.'

However, when Yudi looked around he saw no women claiming that their bottoms were pinched or tits squeezed. It was more as if the poor man was being thrashed to pulp for *not* doing any of these things and feeding the cop's voyeuristic fantasies.

The authority Yudi wielded impressed Milind's family. He could fling a piece of paper and stop a policeman from beating someone up. He was as much of a saviour as their very own Babasaheb! But when he began to click pictures of the procession, they were outraged. This was no picnic or party, they reminded him, but an occasion that was sacred.

'All the newspapers will be carrying pictures of the event tomorrow,' Yudi observed, as even he put away his camera in deference to their sentiments.

If there was one thing that repelled Yudi, it was the odour that came from the crowd. Almost all of them stank. Didn't they bathe regularly? Hadn't they heard of soap, talcum powder and deodorant? Indeed, many of them, judging by the way they were dressed (shabby, ill-fitting clothes), and by their worn out footwear, were not from Bombay but from the rural hinterland where water was perennially scarce. Such people were perhaps used to bathing once a week, exactly like our colonial masters. Slaves, after all, are known to imitate their masters. Yudi thought it would be an excellent business proposition for Lakme India to come here and distribute free samples of their latest beauty aids.

He suddenly remembered what Milind had once told him about Chaitya Bhoomi. It was Haji Deewar Mastan, the notorious smuggler, who introduced the concept of free train travel on this day. Any Dalit who wished to go to Chaitya Bhoomi, even from faraway Nagpur, could board a train without a ticket. The practice continued for twenty long years. The railways incurred huge losses in the bargain, but didn't know how to put an end to it without the government of the day losing out on votes. Trains in Maharashtra were known to be packed to capacity throughout the first week of December, as men, women and children, wearing badges with pictures of Ambedkar on them, clambered for a toe-hold.

The ill-clad, foul-smelling people spat all over the streets as they walked. Some of them ate gutkha; others blew their noses. Yudi was furious. How dare these outsiders come to his city and pollute it! But he couldn't practise his activism here, for they were in the majority. If he gave them a lecture on civic sense, he might be trampled to death.

When the procession came to a halt yet another time, in the vicinity of the Siddhi Vinayak temple, a bored Yudi amused himself with the hoardings on the rooftops of buildings. The titles movie producers gave their flicks were postmodern in the extreme. One film was called *Hasina ka Pasina*. The hoarding depicted the back of a shapely young thing from which drops of sweat trickled down, like pearls. Was it an art or a porn movie? Next to it was a hoarding that advertised a movie by Dada Kondke, famous for his puns and innuendoes. His picture was indecently titled *Bai Hath Aath Ghia*. The hoarding showed the inside of a bus, in which the conductor yelled out to a woman at a window to get her elbows in, lest they were sawed off by oncoming traffic. His words, however, sounded as if he was actually saying: 'Woman, take it in your hand.'

Some hoardings were still being painted. Yudi observed the painters, precariously balanced on scaffoldings. Most of them wore shorts. The hullabaloo down below didn't bother them. They continued to paint their obscene posters, the sacredness of the occasion notwithstanding.

The human train started to move again. It was on the last leg of its journey, past the Catering College. Soon it took a left turn and headed towards the sea. Flower sellers dotted the road on both sides, stringing their marigolds into garlands. A replenishing breeze dried the muggy frames of devotees and sprayed them with salt water. Yudi saw a loo round the corner. The sacred and the profane co-existing nicely.

They reached the temple. This was prime location. Ambedkar was lucky. A flat here would cost five crores at least, Yudi guessed (he would tell the cockroach that). There was a banyan tree in the courtyard that he christened the poor man's Bodhi tree. The temple itself was circular, like the Buddha's Dhamma Chakka, with an ostentatious dome. Devotees first went round the outer circle, then the inner, to garland the statue. Ambedkar seemed pleased with the obeisance of his followers. Saffron-clad bhikshus with clean-shaven heads stood in attendance. When too many garlands collected on Ambedkar's neck, threatening to choke him, they took them off and chucked them all about him in a merry heap. Yudi wondered why people travelled hundreds of miles to garland a statue, knowing fully well that their flowers had a life span of less than five minutes.

Dagdi Chawl waded his way towards him and thrust a garland into his hands:

'Mother says make a wish while garlanding Babasaheb and it will come true.'

Although Yudi felt foolish, he complied. There was nothing he could yearn for, except Milya's safe return.

As Yudi exited from the other side of the temple (that opened out on the beach) it struck him that it was on this day two years ago that a horde of vandals had destroyed the Babri Masjid and set the stage for the Bombay riots. He had found and lost Milya then and was certain the riots had made a martyr of him. Now, in a sense, he was back to square one, with the chap gone again. But would he be lucky and find him a second time, or was he gone for good?

Who could tell?

Yudi's date with the Mahadiks ended at an Udipi restaurant where he invited them for a bite. He noted that the family totally lacked table manners. They greedily shoved large morsels of idlis and dosas into their mouths. The table was splattered with sambar that dribbled down their chins and forearms as they gobbled their food. When the bill came, they didn't offer, even for formality's sake, to foot it or at least share it with Yudi. But then it was he who had invited them.

'Phone me as soon as Milind arrives,' he said to them, and disappeared among the throngs that had gathered to salute Ambedkar.

a.k. modelling agency

But where was Milind? That afternoon, when he told his parents he was going to Pune with his boss, he actually landed up at the office of A.K. Modelling Agency, Goregaon.

A.K. Modelling Agency was a gurukul. At least that was how it's owner, a leading Bollywood star, thought of it. This gentleman was bisexual, but strictly closeted. In a mainstream occupation like Hindi films, where heroes had to be tough and macho (and strictly hetero), he couldn't afford to be open about his sexual preferences. Or no producer would approach him with offers, and his rivals would swoop down and devour all the meaty roles. In order to deal with the difficult situation in which he found himself, the star, Ajay Kapur, floated his agency, nay, gurukul, which gave him a splendid opportunity to lead a double life: to be a hetero by day and homo by night. He appointed half a dozen recruiting agents on monthly salaries that would put IIM graduates to shame. Their business was to go round Bombay's colleges, massage parlours, gyms, discos, locker rooms and loos, to scout and recruit. The recruits were given garish business cards (with all the colours of the rainbow) and asked to report to the agency as soon as possible.

It was no run-of-the-mill agency. Situated on a plot of land just outside Film City, it comprised a set of four bungalows, one of which served as the office. The other three bungalows were said to be holdings of our film star. It was here, evidently, that he carried on his shady nocturnal activities, though it was to his credit that he was never seen in person.

As he never made himself visible to his boys, except on the screen (and how they loved to see videos of his biceps), the agency was actually run by a second-in-command named Menon, and a third-in-command named Mahesh. Menon was a panthi in his forties, Mahesh a koti in his thirties. They issued appointment letters to all the boys picked up by recruiting agents, respecting their choice, even if sometimes they had their reservations about a certain cadet. The appointment letters were terse. They merely informed candidates that they were appointed as 'trainees'. The boys were never specifically told what their duties were. As it was a modelling agency, it was assumed by all and sundry that their job was to model. No one found this hard to believe, considering that all the recruits were reasonably good-looking young men.

The boys rose early. Their day began with exercise, and lessons in the martial arts. Much emphasis was laid on working out. No one could skip workouts, no matter what his excuse. The agency hired the best teachers to train its recruits. It adopted a no nonsense policy with respect to physical fitness. If anyone made a fuss, or proved to be a weakling, he was simply shown the door. Even the RSS was not as stringent.

Then came breakfast. It consisted of cornflakes, omelettes, toasts with plenty of butter and cheese, and fruit. This was followed by a compulsory glass of Complan that none could refuse, even if he threw up. As most of the boys were from Maharashtra, upma and poha were served with breakfast every other day. The agency saw food as an investment. The healthier the grub, the handsomer the men. Thus, mutton, chicken and fish were freely served with lunch and dinner every day.

After breakfast, the boys got ready for work. They were given stylish outfits, all bought from Linking Road. Their T-shirts had slogans that the agency's badshah was said to have invented himself. One such slogan read:

PEN IS MIGHTIER THAN SWORD.

Was PEN IS one word or two? It was one-and-a-half, Ded Galli. There was just that extra millimetre of space between the PEN and IS that would allow their lawyers to argue that they weren't being vulgar.

Anyways.

Another trademark A.K. slogan read:

MY LILLIPUTIAN IS A BROBDINGNAGIAN.

This was too literary, though, and not very popular.

The boys modelled for products ranging from vests and briefs to contraceptives and cosmetics. Their ads didn't appear on TV, or even in glossies like *Femina* and *Society*. They appeared in the vernacular press on cheap parchment paper. But this didn't put them off. On the contrary, it made them euphoric, for had it not been for A.K. Modelling Agency, would any of them have ever got to see their photos in magazines? Besides, each assignment brought them a stipend that they were allowed to keep for themselves. What more could they ask for?

Modelling, however, was not the boys' only work. Perhaps one could rephrase that and say modelling was not their *real* work. For that they had to wait until dark, when all of them doubled up, often literally, as call boys.

A client called, and the boy of his choice was supplied to him. Clients who wished to be serviced by the agency's boys had to leave their name, telephone number and a security deposit of one thousand rupees with Menon or Mahesh. In return, they were shown a photo album (consisting of the boys' photos) and asked to take their pick. Besides being gay or bisexual, all the clients were wealthy, with huge disposable incomes. The customer profile of the agency revealed that most of them were men in their fifties and sixties. About one half were married, while the others were bachelors. Ninety per cent of them were businessmen. They alone could hire boys at prices ranging from one thousand to ten thousand rupees a night, depending on the overall smartness and dick size of the boy in question, of which the boy got to keep 25 per cent. (Only Menon and Mahesh had a table of everyone's dick sizes that they spoke of in terms of shirt sizes: S—Small; M—Medium; L—Large; XL—Extra Large; XXL—Double Extra Large.) If clients wanted boys for a whole week, to accompany them on a holiday to, say, Nainital or Dalhousie, they had to pay five times as much. Prices were also said to vary according to the manner in which a client wished to be serviced. On the whole, penetrators had to pay much more than penetratees. As the agency's CEO had a penchant for hunks (rather than queens), he had to put up with the hostility of those who were made to perform 'womanly' acts in bed. A survey showed that most of his boys didn't think they were abnormal or perverted as long as they were 'active'. They couldn't care less whether what they inserted their organs into was a man's backside or a woman's frontside, especially since the money in this was, by their standards, phenomenal: a recruit at the bottom of the scale made at least ten thousand rupees, and if he reached the top, he could even touch fifty thousand rupees.

After a night of 'duty', a boy was given the day off. This meant there were no modelling assignments for him that day. He was free to do as he pleased, loll about in the agency's sprawling campus, surrounded by hills, or go home to see his folks. Most boys never opted for the latter. They preferred to stay within the secure boundaries of their gurukul, for if they went home and their parents got wind of what they were doing, it would destroy lucrative careers.

Every recruit also nursed one special desire in his heart. It was to sleep with his CEO, the Bollywood matinee idol, at least once. Some of them were lucky, but the number didn't exceed one per cent. Ajay Kapur was choosy. He put every square inch of a fellow's body under the magnifying glass before deciding to take him in.

Milind's tryst with the A.K. Modelling Agency had not happened overnight. It had taken a year.

A couple of months after Yudi took Milind to Testosterone, the boy went there by himself—on the sly, without his lover's permission, for one of the gay world's Ten Commandments is: THOU SHALL NOT GO TO A GAY BAR WITHOUT THY BOYFRIEND. Milya didn't have enough dough for the disco's entry charges, which, as Yudi would say, was a whopping hundred rupees, but he was still in the employ of Parmeshwar, who gave him an advance of three hundred rupees from his next salary. He spent a part of this money to buy the world's tightest jeans, and a black transparent T-shirt to match.

He entered Testosterone's haloed precincts in style, with a cigarette dangling from his lips, hands stuffed into his pockets. Then he leaned coquettishly against a wall, waiting for the crowd. By midnight the dance floor was packed like a Virar fast train. Several men threw desirous glances in Milind's direction. He was thirsty, but no, he was not going to spend his hard-earned money on a beer. If someone asked him to be his dancing partner, he would oblige, but the condition would be, damn it, I'm thirsty, buy me a beer first.

In no time the expected happened. A thirty something guy approached Milind, shook his hand and introduced himself as Ashley Pinto.

He was handsomer than Yudi.

'Can I buy you a beer?' Ashley asked Milind, and before he could answer, held him by the hand and led him to the bar with the high revolving stools. There he bought him the strongest beer on sale, which the boy gulped down in one go. Ashley then asked Milind for a dance. As they gyrated, he drew closer, closer, till they were wrapped in each other's arms. Soon they were smooching, mouth to mouth, not letting go even when the music came to an abrupt halt; making a spectacle of themselves as Ashley's spectacles were pushed off his face and dropped to the floor.

'Haaaa,' Ashley sighed. 'That was quite a mouthful. Would you like another beer?'

The first hour was thus spent drinking and dancing and smooching and drinking and dancing and smooching and so on. Up on the dance floor, Ashley tried to strike a conversation with Milind while the music blared. But his voice being faint and his accent unfamiliar (very different from Yudi's) Milind didn't understand a word. He reacted by smiling and nodding alternately, making Ashley wonder if he'd come from Alibag.

To ensure that he hadn't, he decided to stop dancing for a while, bought more beer, and managed to find sitting space for two in Testosterone's lounging area. As soon as they were uncomfortably seated, he took out one of his rainbow cards. After giving Milind enough time to satisfy his curiosity, he opened his mouth to make a sales speech.

'Seeing how gracefully you dance,' he began, 'I think you have an excellent future in modelling. A.K. Modelling Agency, for which I work as a talent scout, can help you realize your dreams. We can make you a model. We can also fulfil your desires.'

At this point, Ashley Pinto paused for a commercial break and kissed Milind again. (Unlike his first time at Testosterone, Milind was less shy now to kiss in front of everyone else, because it had sunk in at last that sab log aisa hai, everyone's like that only.)

Ashley Pinto resumed his sales sermon: 'I've seen how much you enjoy your "homosex". In A.K. Modelling Agency, you'll get to sleep with the sexiest men in town, like me. (As he said this, he winked.) And you never know! You know who owns our agency? Film star Ajay Kapur. If *he* takes a liking to you, you'll go to bed with the man himself! Your life will be made!'

Milind thought over the matter. To model by day and fuck Ajay Kapur by night sounded like heaven itself. But he'd have to keep everyone, especially his mother and Yudi, in the dark.

'How much will I earn in a month?' he asked Ashley, in a bid to convince himself that the end justified the means, that if the money was good, nothing else mattered.

'I was just coming to that,' said the high-class procurer. 'I won't ask you what you do for a living, or how much you earn right now. But I'll say this much—at A.K. Modelling Agency, you can be sure of earning ten times as much. None of our boys grosses less then ten thousand rupees a month! And that's only the bottom of the spectrum.'

Milind made a few calculations and realized that if what Ashley said was true, his monthly earnings would exceed what he made at Medium Advertising in a whole year! This clinched it for him. Money was life's most important requisite. How long could he let life pass him by, while all his desires to eat good food, wear swanky clothes, and own consumer durables remained unfulfilled?

'There's one more thing,' Ashley added. 'You'll have to live in the agency, treating it as your gurukul. We don't allow our boys to do up-down.'

It suited Milind fine. What difference did it make in a family of four sons if one son went out to earn? No one would miss him.

Ashley Pinto dropped Milind home in a taxi. Both were quite drunk at the time of parting, so much so, they smooched in front of the taxi driver, causing him to yell in protest, 'Kya karte ho sahib!'

For a whole year, during which they stayed in touch, Milind kept Ashley Pinto's offer on hold. Then, tired of the machinations of Parmeshwar and Yudi and Gauri and Sadiq and Ashish Shah, he told his mother he was going to Pune on office work, and left home to join A.K. Modelling Agency. The first few days were awful. Milind felt hopelessly out of place at the gurukul. He was identified as a panthi and made to sleep in the Panthi Dorm, sandwiched between the Koti Dorm in the east and the Hijra Dorm in the west. The Hijra Dorm included hijras, hermaphrodites, and high society blokes who'd had a sex change operation. Milind wondered if the sex change operation types were really different from the hijras—yes, the former had been castrated while the latter been operated upon, but finally it was the same thing, wasn't it? Members slept on the floor on mattresses or sleeping bags neatly arranged in rows. Under no circumstances were they allowed to have sex with each other. If a member violated this rule, and was caught with another member, he ran the risk of being stripped of his membership.

During their first week at the gurukul, as they waited to be picked up by opulent clients in opulent cars, new recruits were required to assist in preparing a directory that comprised names, addresses, telephone numbers and mini biographies of such clients. They were expected to go out into the 'field' with their seniors and look for new suckers so that the agency's directory would swell and resemble the Bombay Telephone Directory. The usual hot spots were five star hotels, beaches, massage parlours and pubs. However, field workers were given strict instructions not to solicit wankers at railway station loos. The agency administration believed that loos were downmarket places, while what they aimed at was an upmarket clientele that wouldn't cringe when it came to parting with hard cash in exchange for hard-ons. Field workers were given a bonus if they managed to entice customers with visa cards, ATM accounts, foreign bank accounts and so forth. Their brief here sounded dangerously similar to an advertisement put out by the Income Tax Department:

'Wanted: men with flats, cars, telephones, club membership, passports, visas, pounds, dollars, etc, etc.'

Milya, then, coming back to him, felt like a fish out of water or a bird out of air. To compound his woes, he failed to land a modelling assignment. One week passed, then two, three weeks passed, then four. Advertisers were convinced that he didn't have the looks of a model, that rather than draw customers to the product he was modelling for, he was likely to put them off. This was because he wasn't conventionally good-looking, though very handsome in the Dagdi Chawl sense. The agency administration seemed to go along with the views of advertisers. They didn't raise a finger to try and get the lad a modelling assignment, even if it was only for zip fasteners. This dejected Milind; indeed, he was dying to see his pictures in print, something that useless Yudi couldn't help him achieve, although he was a pressman. So while the others looked puffed up, Milind looked downcast. His only work was to help in readying their directory of clients, his only entertainment the field trips on which they looked for new bakras.

But then one night he got picked up at last. This was how it happened. A paunchy, fifty something client turned up in a

Contessa, stormed into Menon's office, and called him a cheat.

'I thought this was an agency that supplied homosexual men,' he said in a clipped accent. 'But that scoundrel you sent me last night ain't no homo. I can swear for the life of me he's as straight as a foot rule! The charlatan was totally unresponsive!'

The boy in question was summoned. The poor chicken trembled. On being told of the man's grouse, and asked point blank whether he was this or that way inclined, he claimed he was gay, but not quite attracted to Mr Contessa, who was too old and not of his choice.

'Sleeping with him is no different from sleeping with a woman,' he mustered the courage to say, much to Contessa's indignation.

Menon was amazed.

'Hello!' he said in mock surprise. 'So A.K. Modelling Agency has been set up to cater to the choice of recruits! Not to the choice of clients!'

The boy kept mum. Menon pacified Contessa.

'You see, we can't get inside our boys' bodies to determine if they're really gay, or come here only for the lucre. To date, there are no tests that can provide us with this info. However, I apologize for supplying you with defective goods. I offer you a replacement, free of cost. Take your pick.'

A bell was rung. All the boys present on campus were masqueraded before Contessa. He chose Milind. As he would tell him afterwards, he was turned on by his brain-drain-tube (that he mistook for a thick vein). Nor did Milind enlighten him and tell him what the thing actually was. He took a risk here, for if the man found out on his own, he would break into Menon's office a second time and demand another replacement.

When the man and Milind were alone in the car, he introduced himself as Sameer Shah. 'Call me Sam,' he instructed Milind, inserting his pipe into his mouth. They were driving towards

Malad, where he owned a shack at Madh Island. The shack, he said, was exclusively for this 'shauk', this preference of his, so that his wife and grown up sons didn't smell a rat. Milind asked Sam what he did for a living. He was trying to check out if he was a shareef insaan, decent man, or a kidnapper who was taking him to the jungles of Borivili. Sam let Milind know that he was a copywriter. On hearing this, Milind impetuously asked him why so many advertising people were homos. Sam laughed at the suggestion, and as they continued to drive and blab, it transpired that he knew Milind's former boss, Parmeshwar, who he said was gayer than all Bombay's homos put together.

'Why do you think he's remained unmarried for so long?' he asked, trying to prove his point.

Milind was suddenly seized by panic. What if Parmeshwar came to the agency? He'd sooner be swallowed by Mother Earth, than let the arsehole know where he was now employed.

As soon as they reached the shauk-shack, Sam undressed himself and then undressed Milind. Milya posed his client his million-dollar question: was he a passive koti or an active panthi? Sam wasn't ashamed to admit he was the former. 'You see, I used to be active when I was younger, but now I'm passive, because as a man grows older, his hardback penis becomes a paperback one.'

The joke was lost on Milind, who had little to do with hardbacks and paperbacks. Only Yudi, the journalist, would be able to appreciate its aptness, and appreciate the high-school humour that made Sam one of Bombay's best copywriters. But Yudi was now as far away from Milya's world as the equator is from the poles.

Milind didn't enjoy his 'homosex' with Sam. The fellow had white pubic hair (which he forgot to dye) and more bags of flesh than Milind had seen on any man, even in the movies. He sympathized with his fellow recruit; how could any one be turned on by a man this ugly? The only appealing thing about Sam was his perfume, which smelled good, very, very good. It was this alone that enabled Milind to perform and give the man his money's worth, paisa vasool.

After an overnight halt at shauk-shack, Sam dropped Milind home in his Contessa, giving him a hundred-buck tip for his services. Milya's life returned to its former routine, till a week later he was picked up again.

His new client, Derek, was handsomer than Sam, although more or less the same age. His mini-bio at the agency said he was fifty, but he didn't look a day older than thirty. And he was surprising in other ways too. He had the muscles of a wrestler, yet was more feminine than Rita Faria. For a man so conscious of his looks and his health, he smoked far too much. (He frequently enraged his partners by lighting up when they were cosily inside him.) And though he stank of money (to Milya the sweetest smell of all), his car was a mere Ambassador, a namby-pamby Amby.

Unlike Sam, Derek didn't have to take his lovers to some distant shack, for he was unmarried and lived alone. What he said to Milya in the car was that 'mill-worker types' turned him on. Milind didn't take this as a compliment, for who on earth wants to be told that he looks like a mill-worker? When they reached Derek's flat, he stripped without losing a second, for, as he was in the habit of saying, Time is Money. Whereas Sam had insisted on undressing Milind with his own hands, Derek had no such fetish. He let Milya take off his own shirt, pant, banyan, underwear, while he muttered, 'Time is money.' But then, as the last piece of clothing came off Milya's body, Derek let out a scream. He was what is called a 'size queen' and had chosen Milind not just because he resembled a mill-worker, but because his T-shirt proclaimed he had a PEN IS MIGHTIER THAN

SWORD. Now, inspecting Milya's chilli, he told him point blank that he was a liar.

Milya was deeply insulted. Had the agency administration not taught him that the customer is always right, he might have called the man a chhakka and spat in his face. Luckily for him, the pansy didn't know that the agency gave their clients replacements. Thus he made Milind do it to him anyhow, and even though he was disgruntled, he kept grunting, 'Leave in me a seed, leave in me a seed.'

Back at the agency, Milind still smarted. He approached Menon and advised him to circulate photos of recruits' pricks along with photos of their faces, so that no one was humiliated. Menon pacified Milind, and said that while the law didn't allow them to do that, they were soon going to start having modern-day swayamvars. Recruits would be paraded naked before clients who would thus be solely responsible for what they chose to bed.

Thus the days passed. Milind grew used to his life at A.K. Modelling Agency.

And Yudi? He took ill. With every passing day, his distress increased. He ended up with fever, diarrhoea and vomiting. The sickness, as a local physician explained, defied diagnosis. He did not drink unboiled water, or feast on pani-puri sold on the road. His illness was psychosomatic, directly related to Milya's absence. If only Milind could be brought back ('Bring back, oh bring back, oh bring back my Milind to me,' Yudi often sang in the loo), he would instantly recover.

His diarrhoea notwithstanding, Yudi managed to inform the police that Milind was 'missing'. He wondered why the family hadn't done so all these days. Perhaps they were glad the chap was gone! When the sub-inspector asked for the missing person's full name, Yudi said: 'Milind Mahadik alias Kishore.' Then came the catch. The buffoon wanted to know what Yudi's 'relation' to Milind was. Yudi thought of several options (sex-mate, bed-mate, boyfriend) before saying: 'We are in business together,' and then chuckled, thinking how close to the truth that was.

In spite of all the pills and potions administered by the Nalla Sopara quack, his condition worsened. He was in the loo, vomiting into the shit pot, when Gauri rang. He managed to hobble towards the instrument and pick it up. 'Are you all right?' Gauri asked, and Yudi wondered what karmic connection the lady bore to his vomiting. Many months ago, she was present when he threw up in a horny editor's car. Now when he was sick, she was there again!

Yudi told Gauri of his state; the mother in her surfaced.

'You are giving me your mom's telephone number right away,' she said authoritatively. 'What if you die? I don't want to see maggots nibbling at your body.' Saying this, she went into her now legendary bout of laughter, interspersed with coughing, caused by smoking.

Yudi worked it out in his head. The woman was actually being reasonable. She was asking only for his mother's phone number, not insisting that she would come there herself to look after him. He mumbled the number incoherently. Gauri hung up at once.

Five minutes later, Yudi received a call from his mother. Nothing doing! She was coming there right away to attend to her son. So what if she was old, and Nalla Sopara was in the wilderness.

'Your girlfriend Gauri has agreed to escort me all the way from here.'

Toba-toba!

Yudi's mother took to Gauri like a duck to water. The mad painter kept her promise, took a cab from Bandra to Marine Lines, and then, lo and behold, another from Marine Lines all the way to Nalla Sopara! So what if it cost her (her father, the Colonel, actually) a bomb? It was below her dignity to travel in squalid local trains, exposed to the gaze of men. Moreover, she had now an important person in her charge—Yudi's mamma. It was absolutely essential that she made the right moves.

The guest of honour was impressed. 'It's so kind of you to take so much trouble,' she said to her son's girlfriend several times during the two-hour ride. And indeed, Gauri was bending over backwards for mother and son. She had even thrown her cigarette packets out of the Fiat's window, in deference to the old lady. For Gauri to stay without huffing and puffing for such a long time was not just a sacrifice, it was martyrdom.

Sitting in the back seat like old familiars, the ladies chatted incessantly about the one obsession they had in common: Yudi. The reason for all of Yudi's problems, they agreed, was that he had no woman to take care of him. Heaven knows what the poor boy ate and drank. There was no one to supervise his diet, his nutrition. No wonder he had taken ill.

Prudently, Gauri let Yudi's ma do most of the talking, while she patiently listened. Her dilemma was genuine. There were a host of questions she wanted to put to the senior citizen, but refrained because she had no idea how much the lady knew. For example, she was dying to ask her what she thought of her son's sexual preferences. She was curious to know why, unlike most Indian mothers, she didn't force him to get married, threatening to jump into the Arabian sea if he refused. But if she put her foot in her mouth and blurted out secrets, Yudi would be so angry, he'd fry her alive.

The taxi reached Mate House without faltering even once. That was natural, since it was Gauri who gave the cabbie directions. Didn't she have the map of the place firmly etched in her brain? Yudi was so weak he could scarcely walk to the door to open it when the ladies rang the bell. 'Welcome ma,' he managed to gasp, before rushing into the loo. Fluids were leaving Yudi's body by the gallon, so that he was in real danger of death by dehydration. His temperature too had soared. But now his mother was here. Her love would nurse him back to life.

With Gauri as her assistant, Yudi's mother took charge immediately. She sat by her son's bedside and put a cold pack on his forehead. She gave him glasses of cool Electral water, and allayed his fears that he'd throw the stuff up by working on his will power ('no, you won't, no, you won't'). She cooked khichdi in his matchbox kitchen and insisted that he eat it 'to regain your strength.' She gave him the antibiotics that his quack prescribed, assuring him they would 'destroy the infection in your body'.

After three deadly days of day-and-night vigil, Yudi recovered. His diarrhoea and vomiting stopped, the fever disappeared, and he regained his appetite. His body still felt weak, but there were vitamin pills of all hues to take care of that. The mother had achieved a miracle. She had brought her son back from the grave.

And Gauri? The poor girl travelled back and forth from Bandra to Nalla Sopara because she couldn't spend the night in the flat of an ajnabi marad, a man unrelated to her either by blood or marriage—what would Yudi's mom say! Her fauji dad bore the brunt, with his bank reluctantly giving him an overdraft to pay off her taxi drivers. (At least two of them did offer to drive her for free, though; but only if she allowed them to squeeze her tits as they drove.)

Truth to tell, the love that Yudi's mom showered on him made Gauri jealous. Her heart's deepest wish had always been to take a man under her wing and mollycoddle him. Her first husband had been a beast. When he couldn't stand her overbearing manner, he slapped her around and finally threw her out. Yudi was a man, but then his chromosomes were all messed up. Gauri had resigned herself to the fact that all she could expect from him was friendship, the sort that existed, say, between two schoolgirls. But now, on seeing his mother treat him like a small boy, chhota baba, she suffered a set back. With due respects to the old lady, wasn't she depriving her of a privilege that was rightfully hers? Gauri should have been the one feeding him with her hands, giving him his daily sponge, and sitting on his bed stroking his forehead. Given half a chance, what Gauri would have liked to tell Yudi was that although he prided himself on his originality, he was no different from other Indian men. He was a mamma's boy. If she restrained herself, it was only because mummy was around and he was still convalescing. But one day she would get her point across, oh yes.

The irony, of course, was that Yudi's mother thought no differently. 'If he were married,' she said to herself, 'there would be somebody to look after him and I could die in peace.' She knew why her son was a bachelor, but it wasn't something she could bring herself to talk about, even in her nightmares. 'Where did I go wrong?' she frequently asked herself in moments of despondency. On his part, although Yudi was radically gay, he respected his mother's old-fashioned views and never openly discussed the subject with her. There was a magnificent no man's land between them. Yudi would do as he pleased, and it wouldn't lessen his mom's love for him by even a farthing; but he wouldn't tell her things about himself that disconcerted her. Thus, Yudi could never think of coming out to his mother the way, say, in the twenty-first century, a young and reckless film-maker would—on camera!

Whatever Yudi thought of Gauri (and vice-versa) her presence in the flat made his mom happy. A glimmer of hope rose in her heart: could it be that her son was turning normal? Mummy started to think of Gauri as her bahu and Gauri reciprocated, thinking of mom as her saas. For a few days Mate House, Nalla Sopara, seemed home to a happy little family.

It was the end of yet another day and Gauri was leaving. Yudi was strong enough now to walk to the door to see her off.

'Love to you and yours,' Gauri said, as she negotiated the stairs. By 'yours' she meant Yudi's mom, but it prompted the man to exclaim: 'Don't be vulgar!'

After Gauri's exit, mother and son were alone in the flat. With his fever gone, Yudi's worries returned. There was still no telephone call from Milind's family, which meant he was absconding still. Yudi missed Milind. He recalled all the gay times they had together, ever since fate threw them in each other's way, first at Churchgate, then at the *Times*. That was scarcely one-and-a-half years ago, Ded Galli, yet it seemed light years away. While he was still the same, Milind had changed.

The thought depressed Yudi, and tears began to roll down his cheeks, first one, then another, then a third. His mother approached him with a glass of milk at precisely that moment. It alarmed her to see a middle-aged man weep like a boy of four. She stroked his head and asked him what the matter was. His tears now came down in a torrent. He buried his head in his mom's lap, indeed like a boy of four, and sobbed. His flustered mom caressed his head, and told him all would be well. 'Have faith in God,' she said. She wanted to know what it was that was bothering her son so much, because unless she knew, what could she do? But she also knew it was futile to ask him, because he wouldn't confide in her. Furthermore, she was afraid of finding out, for which mother wants to know things about her children that will bring her pain?

The situation being complicated, Yudi's mother couldn't do a thing but wait for him to compose himself. As he sobbed and she comforted him, she said a silent prayer to her gods: 'Solve his problems. Keep him happy. He is alone. Please be with him. Please protect him.'

When Yudi's crying finally stopped, his mother took away his untouched glass of milk and brought him a cup of tea instead.

'Sorry, mom,' he said, sipping his tea. 'I'll be okay.'

There was a tense silence. The old lady was still debating whether to ask him what was wrong. Observing that the sobbing had had a cathartic effect on her son, she decided to leave the subject alone. She switched on the TV. Both of them began to watch an episode of *Dekh Bhai Dekh*.

That night, however, Yudi's mom didn't have a wink of sleep. She tossed about in the guest bed, shaken by the way her son had broken down. What, oh what, could she do to make him happy?

Gauri arrived as usual the next day on morning duty. In her hands was a bowl of kheer that she had herself prepared. It must have been quite a challenge to transport it from Bandra to Nalla Sopara, considering the state of the city's roads. Yet not a drop of it had spilled over in the cab, such was her love for Yudi! The Mother was also busy in the matchbox kitchen, rustling up a soup that would give Yudi all the nourishment he needed to recoup. She sampled a spoon of Gauri's kheer. 'Delicious,' she cried. Gauri returned the compliment; she put a spoonful of piping hot soup in her mouth, and though it burnt not only her tongue, but also her oesophagus, she managed a look of complete bliss and pronounced Yudi's mom to be the best cook in town. 'Better even than Tarla Dalal,' she said ingratiatingly, not normally used to hyperbole. It made mamma blush, and say out of politeness: 'Don't embarrass me.' (Out of politeness, because the lady indeed had complete faith in her culinary skills.)

While the two were thus engaged, Yudi was busy masturbating

in the shower. One fallout of his mother's visit was that the flat was permanently closed to all the barbers, rickshaw drivers, motor mechanics and chhokra boys he brought home for casual sex. It was, in every sense of the word, a nuisance.

Taking advantage of his absence, mummy dear informed Gauri of Yudi's 'nervous breakdown', and asked her if she knew what the cause might be. In a way, this was the moment Gauri was waiting for. There was so much she wanted to let the venerable old lady know: how she was head over heels in love with her son; how, while she was willing to die for him, he was an ungrateful wretch who had spurned her. Yet she was tongue-tied. Where could she begin? Could she disclose that the cause of Yudi's nervous breakdown (or whatever fanciful term his mom wished to use) was a Bhangi boy with whom he was obsessed? That the Bhangi boy wasn't even a respectable Dalit (creamy layer), whom the government's reservation policy had transformed into, say, a college lecturer, but a mere chaprasi, who until recently went round the city sticking posters on lampposts? The god-fearing lady would probably die of supra-ventricular tachycardia. But the painter was willing to risk even that, if only someone could answer her zillion-dollar question: Did Yudi's mother know that he was gay? If she did not, then anything that she said would amount to outing him, and this she couldn't possibly do because the eco-feminists had pledged to be politically correct always. So she deflected the issue by affirming that there was nothing wrong with Yudi, that it was normal for all sensitive people to be down in the dumps once in a while; and that it was his fever that depressed him, for he was used to being up and about twenty-six hours a day.

The Mother was relieved. 'Please take care of Yudi,' she pleaded with the younger woman. 'He's so lucky to have a friend like you. I'm getting old. Who knows how long I have to live?'

To this, Gauri replied: 'Mummy dear, you'll live to be a hundred. Have no fear. I'll always be there to look after your son.'

To herself she said, sadly, 'I wish the dickhead would look after me too!'

A new month began. Yudi had now recuperated fully. His mother was still around, but unlike before, didn't have much to do. She spent her time bathing, praying, cooking and watching TV. If the programmes didn't interest her, she took up the newspaper and read it from the first page to the last. Once or twice she picked up a couple of Yudi's books—mostly novels—and started to read them, but fell asleep before she reached page ten. One such novel that lulled her to sleep was *Midnight's Children*, another, *In An Antique Land*. The lady was a graduate all right, but didn't have what it took to appreciate a classic. Or so Yudi told her to her face, rudely and crudely, when she accused him of not possessing a single good book in his library. (Her definition of good was *Gone with the Wind*.)

With Yudi being okay, Gauri's visits to the flat also decreased. Her father, the old Colonel, confronted her and told her with a sense of terror that her taxi bills had run up to a monstrous fifteen thousand rupees. This couldn't continue, or their properties would be attached! The embargo that he put on her affected Yudi's mom more than anyone else. She enjoyed the company of her surrogate bahu, and missed the innocent gossip they indulged in every afternoon. When Gauri failed to show up for three days in a row, she turned to Saraswati and tried to chat the housemaid up, but gave up in no time. Though she pretended otherwise, she hated menials, for it was the British who'd shaped her values in pre-Independence India. (This, Gauri had astutely observed on several occasions when the three women were together in the flat. Small wonder, then, that she had come to the conclusion that the old lady of Bori Bunder, nay, New Marine Lines, would die of heart failure if she learnt that her son was in love with a Bhangi boy.)

Pretence was everywhere in the air. Yudi's mom pretended not to be embarrassed by the pictures of almost naked men (including one of Ajay Kapur) that he'd put up all over the house. The sex of the people in the pin-ups bothered her more than their nudity. If nakedness was what he cherished, why couldn't he put up posters of Manisha Koirala? Why did it always have to be men, men and men? On his part, Yudi pretended to be happy, when the truth was that he was anything but, because if he went about sulking, his poor mom would think she was unwelcome in his house.

But this wasn't as difficult to handle as the celibacy he was forced to practice while she was around. For a man who believed that sex was the best prophylactic, this was extremely trying. If the doorbell rang and a casual lover showed up, Yudi turned him away, informing his inquisitive mom that it was the newsboy come for his bill. If he felt horny, all he could do was wank. How long could this go on? Fortunately both mother and son were used to a solitary existence, and both were intelligent enough to sense the other's discomfiture. Hence, at the end of the month, Yudi's mother announced that she was going home, 'now that you are fine.' But her parting wish was that she should see Gauri at least once before leaving. However—'with due respects to your mother'—Gauri flatly refused to travel by train, and demanded the cab fare from Yudi, to which he said no, because 'it's my mom who wants to see you, not I'.

Eventually, the three of them agreed to pool in exactly 33.33 per cent of the total fare each. Thus it was that Gauri came to see Yudi's mom on the last day of her stay at Mate House.

They sat down to a ceremonial meal. Chicken Shahid Ali, Mutton Chomsky, Heroic Cutlet. Bisi Belli Barthes. All prepared by Yudi's mother, with Yudi giving them their innovative names as he helped her lay out the table. The well-meaning old lady had also tried her hand at kheer, having sweet talked Gauri into parting with her recipe one gossipy afternoon. But it was only 33.33 per cent as good.

The meal over, they got ready to leave. Yudi, the dutiful son, carried his mom's belongings, along with a rose plant that she picked up from a Nalla Sopara nursery. 'Take care of Yudi,' she said to Gauri yet again, and Gauri assured her she would. To Yudi, his mother said: 'May you have health and wealth, name and fame.' Yudi responded by reminding her that they were not parting yet, for he was escorting her all the way to Pherwani Mansion. On hearing this, Gauri changed her mind and decided to travel with them by train. A huge chunk of the cash they had collected for her Travel Allowance was thus saved. Yudi divided the amount into three equal shares and disbursed everyone their moneys.

'Good omen,' said his mother, as she took her share.

In the auto-rickshaw to the station, as in the train later, Yudi put his mother between himself and Gauri, because he didn't want the slut to outrage his modesty. Gauri was cut up, no doubt, but she couldn't do a thing (except moan). She alighted at Bandra, while Yudi safely deposited his mom in her New Marine Lines flat and took off on a tour of South Bombay's loos.

He felt like a prisoner released from the Arthur Road Jail.

ten

WEDDING BELLS

It was Milind's sixth month at A.K. Modelling Agency. The days of his probation over, his bosses were planning to confirm him. His track record was good. At least two clients per month, all rolling in dough, asked for his services. His Lilliputian may not have been a Brobdingnagian (as the outfits dishonestly proclaimed), but that didn't hinder him from getting picked up by ad men, mad men, corporates, corporators, and once a retired Army General. Everything from start to finish happened in the poshest of surroundings. They drove in air-conditioned Esteems and Honda Citys. And they copulated in hotels, motels, farmhouses, beach houses, holiday inns and holiday resorts (where they resorted to maximum masti). Milind's sugar daddies treated him to the rarest scotch, the weirdest cocktails, and always, on his insistence, the costliest dish on any menu. At the time of parting, they also tipped the boy handsomely. The lad from Chinchpokli was living a life far beyond his means. Everything a chawl-dweller dreamt of was his for the asking. Even Dagdi Chawl, his brother who had strayed into the underworld, couldn't do better.

Yet Milind was pissed off with himself and with everyone around him. He hated his work, was 'sick and tired' of it, as he frequently told himself, in English. No matter how many Esteems he rode in, his self-esteem was annihilated. He thought of himself as a dhandewala, a whore, and in his scheme of things it was women who were whores, not men. In other words, he was doing womanly work, like sewing and cooking, not manly work as his brothers did. So what if the men he serviced spoke in the passive voice and gave him a chance to speak in the active? It didn't take away from the fact that he was selling his body.

His other worry was AIDS. STD, HIV, AIDS, these acronyms were freely used by everyone in the agency. None of the boys clearly knew what they meant, but were aware that one precaution that each A.K. boy absolutely had to take, whether he liked it or not, was to wear a condom. The agency manufactured its own condoms. The ones available in the market, they believed, were heterosexist: they assumed that dicks entered only cunts. When the A.K. boys used them, they tore half way through, and exposed both user and used to grave risk. The agency thus made its own extra-thick lubricated condoms. They catered to every taste, dividing their 'Esteemed' patrons into two distinct groups: fuckers and suckers. For the latter, they used Dutch technology to manufacture flavoured condoms. The range was impressive: banana and raspberry, strawberry and chocolate.

However, these things mattered little to Milind. He still hadn't learnt to wear his condoms. In his case, the water balloons didn't tear; they simply came off. Nor were any of his old men interested in blowjobs, for whoever's heard of chilli ice-cream? Flavour or no flavour, Milya had little use for rubbers. All rubbers to him were Nirodhs—fifteen paise for three—even if they actually cost the moon. They were useless. He was sure he would die of AIDS.

His only consolation was the money he made, which at last count was no less than a quarter of a lakh. This was princely. He was in a position at last to fulfil his heart's desires, the greatest of which was to own a second-hand Yamaha. He could also give his mother some money to shut her mouth and stop her from nagging the life out of him. Twenty-five thousand in six months was fifty thousand in a year was a lakh in two years (without tax)! Purely in monetary terms, life in the agency was as rewarding as being Harshad Mehta's slave.

There was also the prospect of fame. Milya's surreptitious visits to Testosterone and his dealings with Ashley Pinto had made him a dancer par excellence. He was selected to perform with no less an actor than Urmila Matondkar, in no less a film than *Rangeela*. The song sequence had Matondkar dancing to the 'Mein hoon rangeela re' number, with Milind and a host of others, mostly from the A.K. Modelling Agency, working out in the background. Milind was so pleased with his achievement that he saw the film thirty-two times. Yudi's tale was even funnier. He *thought* it was Milind the first time he saw the film at Bajrangbali, but couldn't be sure: these days God was running out of ideas and making many people duplicates of each other; even Salman Rushdie had a double in Bombay, a car restorer by the name of Firdaus Mistry! Yudi thought his doubts would be resolved the more he viewed the dance number, and with this in mind, bought a ticket for all three shows, three days in a row, last row. But alas! Each successive screening only confounded him further. Made him less and less certain. The ushers thought his brain had given way, because every day they saw him enter the auditorium, only to leave the moment the song was over. Not once, twice, but nine times at a stretch. The last time he did this, Yudi admitted to himself that this was a pointless exercise.

Back at the A.K. Modelling Agency, meanwhile, terrified after a client turned out to be not so passive and tried to rape him, Milind escaped. He stole out one rainy morning and returned home. It was surprisingly easy. All he had to do was wear a raincoat and tell Menon he was off to see a client. He had earned enough goodwill. No one would suspect that he was up to mischief.

His parents couldn't believe their eyes when they saw him. Milind wapas ala! They were in a state of shock. By now they had given him up for dead. How could they be sure he wasn't a ghost, visiting from the neighbourhood cemetery? The brothers were frantically hailed from wherever they were. (The tenement being smaller than a sparrow's nest, they loitered on the streets from dawn to dusk.) When they arrived and pronounced their verdict, namely that this was no ghost but their own brother in flesh and blood, the parents were convinced. They hugged and kissed the prodigal son, and the mother broke into tears. 'Where were you, kuthe hota tu?' That was one question of course that the prodigal son wasn't going to answer. Could he tell them he was busy doing randi-baazi, being a whore, for six months? They would say he was better off dead! Not because they had anything against randi-baazi per se (they were poor enough to be practical) but because it was something that the daughters of the house did, not sons!

Hearing the commotion, all the neighbours on their floor assembled in the sparrow's nest to greet the prodigal son. Everyone was overjoyed. Someone passed a box of pedas around. A fire was lit and they did Milind's aarti. Some boys broke into an improvised song: 'Milya aala re, aala . . .' and there was much whistling and dancing. The father and mother joined their hands before a picture of Ambedkar and thanked him. The prayers they offered at Chaitya Bhoomi had been answered at last.

That night Milya's mother invited everyone to their chawl for Chicken Biryani, made with basmati rice. Dagdi Chawl took care of the expenses. But the feasting wasn't for Milind alone. It was also for the prodigal father, who had given up his wayward ways and come back to his wife and kids. At first, when Milind saw him in the house, he thought the man had only come snooping.

Didn't he do that every now and then, when the guilt pangs became unbearable? But then as night came and the prick showed no signs of going back to his mistress, he realized that something was amiss. Or had the greedy chap stayed back only to hog their Chicken Biryani? The suspense didn't end till next morning, when Milya's mother told him the whole story after her pati parmeshwar left for work. It was Milya who had brought him back, she believed. For, after he ran away, the old man chided himself for treating his family like dirt. Had he given them a father's love, he wouldn't find one son leaving home, another becoming a disciple of Arun Gawli. Enough was enough. It was time he got back and brought things under control, before it was too late. His keep, of course, would hear none of it. She threatened to hire supari killers to finish him off, even if it cost her her life's savings. A pimp from Pimpri intervened. It was agreed that the chudail would let go of their father, provided he paid the witch twenty thousand rupees. They bargained and brought it down to seventeen, and Dagdi Chawl signed the cheque.

The story disgusted Milind. His father's biography reminded him of his own debauched life at the A.K. Modelling Agency. Was he any different from that whore who'd cast a spell on his baba? However, unlike his mother, he didn't believe that the man had come back to turn over a new leaf. In his opinion, the creep was terrified of his sons who'd grown big and strong and capable of reducing him to mincemeat. That was why he was back. No change of heart business for the fart. He was probably too old for that randi, just as he was for his sons: if he messed around with them, they would make baba-curry of him and eat him with chapatti.

Impressed by the achievements of his younger brother, the eldest also began to frequent Gawli's kingdom in the neighbourhood. And Milind too began to toy with the idea.

A week hadn't passed since the return of the prodigal son, when the parents dropped a bombshell. They were getting their first two boys, Rajesh and Milind, married. The two were going beyond the pale. Marriage was the only remedy. When saddled with a wife and kids, the boys would automatically turn away from a life of crime, and sweat blood to make an honest living. Moreover, their aai was getting old. In the absence of daughters, she needed bahus to help her with the household chores, which were so numerous they would fill an exercise book. What she found hardest of all was filling water from the municipal tap and hauling her buckets up the stairs. And her good-for-nothing sons never lent a helping hand, though it was they who used the water for ordinary bathing and drinking purposes.

For these reasons, the elders decided to get the youngsters married.

As to who would marry their wastrels, there wasn't any dearth of girls. Think of train reservations. So thrilled are we to get a confirmed berth on any train, that we don't ask ourselves: what if the train derails? It is likewise with Indian Women. For every one thousand men there are only 933.33 of them. A woman, thus, would rather have a jobless husband, than miss the train.

The girls earmarked for the Mahadik brothers had steady jobs. It was another matter that they were only ayahs. But they were gainfully employed, and that too in the Bombay Municipal Corporation where people were thrown out for working, not for shirking. The boys' parents were delighted to have working bahus who would support their sons. Their only worry was, the girls being identical twins, with almost identical names (Leela and Sheela), what would happen if, God forbid, there was a mix-up or two in the dark? Their fears were genuine. It wasn't as if the boys were going to move out of their kholi once they were married. They would all have to sleep in their one-room nest in a row, and if Milind mistook Sheela for Leela, and Rajesh mistook Leela for Sheela, all hell would break loose! Even so they decided to go ahead with the twin marriage. The problem would be taken care of somehow: perhaps by inscribing the name of each bahu on her bed sheet.

All this did not concern the two boys. They had no thoughts on marriage. It was something that one had to go through anyway, whether one liked it or not. It was no different from one's morning ablutions. What was the point in thinking about it? They would simply do as their parents ordained.

And the parents on their part asked them to get ready to tie the nuptial knot within a month, for there were no auspicious days after that for the rest of the year. The girls weren't willing to wait: if the Mahadik brothers wasted time, they would go find other boys.

Work began at a feverish pace. There was so much to do: whitewash the kholi, buy new clothes for everyone, print and distribute the wedding cards. The younger sons, especially, were expected to help—because tomorrow it would be their turn: in a family of four sons, they had to marry them off two at a time to save on expenses, two in the first round, two in the second. Of course the neighbours in their chawl also came forward with their services: the solidarity of the wretched. In no time, preparations for the big day were complete.

To be fair to Milind's parents, it wasn't their fault if they clean forgot to tell him that a friend of his, Yudi by name, had come looking for him while he was gone. There were a million things on their mind, now that the weddings were fixed, and Yudi wasn't one of them. But one night they remembered, and the first thing they did on waking up was report the matter to him. Adding a dash of mirch masala, they said:

'Milya, who is this Yudi? He came to our house to ask for you. He seemed more worried about your absence than all of us put together! He did not look like any of your other friends, Pramod, David and the rest. He was much older. His hair was grey. He spoke English and looked the high society type. He wouldn't leave when we told him you were not at home. Instead, he came with us to Chaitya Bhoomi and took photos. He gave us his phone number and asked us to ring him up as soon as you returned.'

Dagdi Chawl joined his parents here and corroborated all they said:

'What kind of womanly man is your friend? He was almost in tears when we told him you had left home.'

As he said this, he had a hearty laugh.

Then the father said, 'Whatever it is, Milya, call up the man and tell him you're back. We promised him we would call.'

Milind's reactions to what he heard: wrath, anger, rage. So his worst fears had come true. Yudi had landed up at his place! If only he hadn't made the mistake of giving him his address! But the fellow had tricked him into it, and disregarded his express instructions never to come here, even if the heavens fell. Now he had become the laughing stock of his family. See how the sight of Yudi amused his mother and brother! Look at the way his parents compared the chhakka to macho friends like Pramod and David, and found him wanting! See how they emphasized his age, his grey hair, his hi-fi English! They must have suspected there was something odd about the whole thing! Why couldn't the man stop being an actor? And if he had to be an actor, why couldn't he stay in his own domain, and leave others alone? What he deserved was a thorough spanking.

Milind's anger was greater because he had actually planned to break off with Yudi, now that he was going to be a married man. He hated two timers, like his prodigal father. Besides, he couldn't let his wife know there was this other side to him. And with Yudi in his life, she was bound to know, sooner or later. And getting rid of the man would have been easy. Milind was already out of touch with him for six months. All he had to do was pretend he was still missing. But now, having heard of Yudi's misdemeanours, he decided to thrash it out with him once and for all. Otherwise, the fellow might turn up in his life again and again, like a bloodsucker. It was with this intent that he called Yudi.

Although he wasn't a fatalist, as far as Milind was concerned, Yudi had by now resigned himself to his fate. He had given up hopes of ever seeing his boy-lover again. In the first few weeks since his Chaitya Bhoomi visit, he called Dagdi Chawl (the elder) every now and then to find out the latest. But this couldn't go on endlessly or the brother would grow suspicious. He phoned the brother one last time to say he wouldn't be calling again; that if Milind ever returned, they should inform him of his arrival at the speed of light. No call came; Yudi assumed that his boyfriend was still at large.

Thus, when Milind phoned Yudi, he was quite unprepared for the reunion. It took him a couple of seconds to realize it was his dear darling he was talking to. When he did, his heart raced and his hair stood an end.

'Milya, where are you calling from?' he managed to tremulously scream into the receiver.

'From our chawl,' said Milind.

There was a brief pause. There was so much that Yudi wanted to say he didn't know where to begin. He was busy composing his sentences— where were you, are you okay, I missed you, how come you forgot me—when, taking advantage of the silence Milind spoke, cutting out the frills and coming to the nitty-gritty.

'Why did you go to my house?'

The question flabbergasted Yudi. It wasn't the sort of question he expected a civilized person to ask. He fumbled with his answer, and this only gave Milind the upper hand. He believed he was justified in demanding an explanation.

'Didn't I tell you never to go there?'

'Milya, I was worried about your safety,' Yudi tried to be equitable.

'What safety!' snapped Milind.

'I was worried that Sadiq may have smuggled you to the Gulf.'

'What Gulf! You broke your promise! Seeing you, my family has begun to suspect that I too am a chhakka.'

'My homosexuality isn't written all over my face,' Yudi wanted to say in the face of such prejudice, but decided to keep quiet and mollify his friend. So he said:

'I am sorry. It's wonderful that you're back, and you can tell me later where you were all these months. Or not tell me at all, if you don't wish to. When do we meet?'

Milind wanted to let the man know that he never wished to see him again. Then he remembered that the purpose of making the call was to set up a final meeting to break off with him. He had to find a way, though, of not sounding too enthusiastic; of not giving the fellow the impression that he was dying to meet him. Thus he merely repeated the question like a parrot.

'When do we meet?'

It was agreed that like the good old days, they would meet at Café Volga on Friday. The conversation ended as abruptly as it began. It harried Yudi so much, he travelled all the way to town to buy anti-depressants.

The get together was no less disastrous. Who could say these were lovers, meeting after of six months? On seeing Milind (and marvelling at how muscular he had grown!) Yudi tried to hug him. However, Milind repulsed him by stepping back a few paces so that their bodies didn't touch. The first thought that crossed his mind, as soon as he saw Yudi, was: 'You are the one who has ruined my life. It's because of you that I became a homo. Had it not been for you and your perverse ways, I would never have landed up at a place like that A.K. Modelling Agency and become a prostitute. Shame on you! I wonder whether I'll now be able to lead a normal married life.'

Yudi led the way to the mezzanine floor where they had had some of the best times of their lives. He ordered beer. But when it was time to clink glasses, Milya did so only half-heartedly, or to be precise, quarter-heartedly. He wanted to be done with this as quickly as possible.

Yudi ventured to say: 'My darling, where were you all these months? I missed you.'

It backfired miserably, this voyeuristic inquiry into his affairs, that painfully reminded Milind of his obscene past.

'Doing randi-baazi,' he screamed, causing the old man at the next table to look in their direction, alarmed.

'Hush,' said Yudi. Sensing that the lad was not in his senses, he left the subject alone.

'Okay, where do we go from here?' he asked after a long pause.

This was the moment Milind was waiting for. Fishing out a wedding card from his shabnam bag, he thrust it into Yudi's hands. The card, he realized, spoke for itself; it would save him the ordeal of lengthy explanations, of which the hi-fi journalist was very fond.

Yudi was dumbfounded on seeing the shimmering red card. He didn't have to read its contents, which, anyway, were in Marathi. It was enough that his eyes fell on the bold words MILIND

WITH LEELA. Remembering their own mock wedding, he burst out crying, forgetting the old man at the next table. He had visions of Milya copulating with Leela—that was what the MILIND WITH LEELA meant to him.

Yudi's ululations did not stop. He grew lachrymose. Wisely, the old man at the next table rose and left, while Yudi sobbed and blew his nose into his handkerchief. His tears, needless to say, didn't have the desired effect on Milind. They didn't break his heart and prompt him to tear up his wedding card, proclaiming: 'Okay, I won't get married, balls to my marriage if it hurts you so much. I'll stay with you as your lover for the rest of your life.'

These were tense moments for both males, but Milind's way of dealing with the situation was to opt for the line of least resistance. Accordingly, he gulped down the beer that was left in his glass and got up to go. His farewell words to Yudi were:

'Stop being so weak-hearted. Take hold of yourself. Everyone gets married, and I too have to get married some day or the other. So why not now? I'm leaving. I have plenty of work. Got to distribute all these wedding cards before nightfall. Goodbye.'

Having said his piece, Milind thumped down the stairs of Café Volga's mezzanine floor, just as two years ago he would charge down the stairs of Parmeshwar's office to meet Yudi. It was meeting then, parting now. Yudi thought the brute also said: 'You don't turn me on any more. Rather, you put me off.'

He sat there and ordered a second beer. And a third and a fourth and a fifth. Tonight he would get dead drunk. He was dead anyway, and now he would go ahead and get drunk.

Somewhere in the course of his drinking, a regretful thought entered Yudi's mind: in the midst of all their bickering he had forgotten to ask Milind if he was in *Rangeela*.

Had Café Volga's waiters not told him it was closing time, he would have stayed there all night, drinking. But now a waiter stood before him, arms akimbo, and refused to serve him another beer (even if he paid twice as much).

'It's 8.45 p.m., boss,' he said, 'and the restaurant closes at 9.00.'

'What a bloody nuisance,' muttered Yudi to himself. 'It was never like this in the past.'

Which was true. When Yudi was in college, the café stayed open till 11.00. He frequently landed up there after cruising at Azad Maidan, with or without a partner. It was only after the riots that the owners decided to close early, because as Parsis they too, the old man discovered, were vulnerable.

Yudi climbed down the stairs and landed on the open street. Humid though it was, he felt a breeze on his skin. What were his options? Going to his mother's place was one, to the press club another, and to the Marine Drive Sea a third. Rejecting all three options, he tottered to Marine Lines and took a train home.

It was midnight when he reached his den, but that didn't deter him from picking up the receiver to call Gauri (he would be astonished by this act only in retrospect).

'Can you come here?' he asked her. 'I need you urgently.'

For once Gauri wasn't all charged up with love for him.

'Now?' she yawned. 'It's the dead of night, Yudi. I'll see you tomorrow.'

'Oh . . .' he felt foolish. 'I thought it was late evening. You see, my watch has conked.'

He had a terrible night. Sleep refused to bless him. Obsessed by his MILIND WITH LEELA vision, he wanked half a dozen times and was completely drained by morning.

Gauri, as dependable as the Flying Rani, dutifully landed up at Mate House just in time for breakfast. When Yudi saw her, he buried his head in her lap and cried, and she stroked his head, mamma style, without knowing why he wailed, though she suspected it had something to do with that boy Milind. Yet it felt good to have him crying in her lap. So, he'd begun to see his mom in her, as all hubbies eventually do. Later that day, he told her about Milind's return—and impending marriage. They went to an open-air restaurant for lunch, where she found an ingenious way to humour him. She suggested they boy-watch together. What this entailed was to ogle all the young men around them, from stewards to waiters to eaters. Pass comments on the way they dressed, walked and talked. For starters, they picked on a steward with rather tight trousers; so tight, even his balls showed.

'Isn't he sexy?' Gauri whispered to Yudi.

'Nah! Not my type,' he responded. 'He's too short.'

'But I like them short,' she protested.

They decided that in order to play the game to perfection, they needed to be slightly drunk. With this in mind, they ordered two strong beers, bearing the number 10,000.

The beer arrived; they sipped and zeroed in on their next victim, a thirty something customer.

'Isn't he a cutie?' Yudi made the first move.

'Cutie, sweetly-pie,' said Gauri in baby language.

'For once we are agreed on something,' Yudi observed, surprised.

It didn't last long. For at this point, a middle-aged man walked in with his wife and kids and distracted Gauri.

'Wow!' she exclaimed. 'Subhan Allah. What biceps!'

'Yuk!' cried Yudi. 'Will just about anyone do for you?'

'He's handsome and he looks successful. Not like your wastrels.'

'Look, look, see that waiter there? Wish I could bed him here and now.'

'God!' Gauri grimaced. 'You and your working-class types!'

The game went on. They picked on more waiters and eaters, till their behaviour got so camp people began to notice and give them sidelong looks.

'Time to stop,' sighed Yudi. 'I'm so zapped. Never knew Milind would turn out to be such a ditcher.'

'Yudi, you'll have to forget Milind, you must move on,' said Gauri, assuming the tone of an agony aunt again.

Yudi moaned and was silent. Gauri lit up and blew smoke into his face. They looked at their watches. It was past four. They'd been in the restaurant a good two hours, and the super strong beer had made them tipsy.

'Time to go,' said Yudi, getting up and taking out his wallet to pay the bill.

Then a miracle happened. Gauri agreed to travel by train! She even found out the price of a season ticket and bought one, because, as she said happily, 'now my Yudi would be needing me every day.'

There was no gainsaying the fact Yudi enjoyed Gauri's company. He didn't want her flabby body. But mentally she was on the same wavelength as he. In other words, he could relate to her. He could hardly say this of Milind, and all the working men he slept with, who had great bodies but lousy minds. And this made Yudi realize and accept that monogamy was a fallacy. Every human being needed to fall in love with a plethora of people, each of whom satisfied a specific want. This realization softened him towards Gauri, whom he condescended to view as a wife, provided she kept her hands off him. Thus, when she complained that she found it strenuous to commute from Bandra to Nalla Sopara every twenty-four hours (after all, she had been raised in the lap of luxury), he submitted that they do it by turn; that while she visited him every Monday, Wednesday and Friday, he would visit her on Tuesday, Thursday and Saturday. Sunday would remain a holiday.

The arrangement worked. It ensured that Yudi was kept busy six days a week so he didn't brood about Milind, or attempt to contact him, only to be told he was a leech who didn't let go of his prey.

On their part, Gauri's parents were as gracious as ever. They didn't harbour a grudge against Yudi for not marrying their daughter, for they knew, even if they never said it, that she was hardly the kind anyone would want to marry. It was enough for the old couple that Yudi actually came to their place every other day to entertain their baby girl. The Colonel was still generous with his whisky, which he got from the Army canteen at half the price. The mother, despite her arthritis, still made the most delicious kheer Yudi had ever savoured, and served it to them in silver bowls. Yudi also found to his amusement that Gauri's pets had swelled in number. Shakespeare, her dog, was joined by another poodle, which she named Milton! Then there were a bevy of cats. Since she named the first of these Mao (a most appropriate name for a cat, she had explained), she had no choice but to name the others Lenin, Stalin and Trotsky. Also, the lady now openly smoked in front of her parents, and there was nothing they could do. Being on the same frequency, both Yudi and she said silly things to each other that constantly made them guffaw. This was therapeutic. It helped.

Yudi got a call he least expected. It was from Milind's brother Rajesh, alias Dagdi Chawl (the elder). The purpose of the call was to give him the 'khush khabar' of Milya's return.

'Your khush khabar is as stale as a dead rat,' Yudi wanted to tell him, but refrained. What was the point in being rude to someone who was only trying to be helpful? Rajesh followed up this good news with another: his wedding.

'Stale news again,' Yudi said in his mind, and then as an afterthought, 'only idiots get married.' Aloud he merely said, 'Congratulations.'

'Congratulations won't do, bade bhaiya,' Rajesh replied. 'You've got to come for the wedding.'

Yudi found the 'bade bhaiya' bit hilarious. He contemplated blurting out the exact nature of his relationship with Milind, to see if the man still called him his elder brother. But he did not. He merely dictated his mailing address on the phone, and asked the little brother out of politeness to send him a card.

'Zaroor! I am sending it today, by speed post or courier,' Dagdi Chawl ardently said, before hanging up.

'Zaroor!' Yudi mimicked angrily, as soon as he disconnected the line. 'Isn't that the name of a condom?'

When he narrated the episode to Gauri, she manufactured her own theory.

'Little brother Rajesh obviously knows that you and Milind are lovers,' she reasoned out. 'Otherwise, why did he speak of only his own wedding and not Milind's?'

'Sala gandu,' Yudi swore.

'Cut out the gandu,' Gauri advised. Sala is just right.'

The painter laughed so much at her own joke that both Shakespeare and Milton retreated to a corner and began to bark.

Rajesh's wedding card arrived the next morning by Pigeon Couriers. It was a joint invitation that announced the weddings of RAJESH WITH SHEELA and MILIND WITH LEELA. When Milind thrust the card into Yudi's hands at Café Volga, he had noticed only the MILIND WITH LEELA. Gauri had an explanation for this too:

'Freud said, We see only what we wish to see. We project.'

Yudi was about to tear up the card into a hundred bits and chuck it into the garbage bin. On impulse, however, he decided to preserve it as a relic of betrayal. As Shahjehan looked out of his window at the Taj Mahal and was reminded of his beloved Mumtaz, he would gaze upon the red-and-golden card and remember his heartless boyfriend.

The brother's insistence notwithstanding, Yudi initially decided not to attend the weddings. Why should he? Does a man in his senses go to his lover's wedding? But as the day approached he changed his mind. He wanted to see MILIND WITH LEELA on the dais anyhow. Thus, two days before D-day, he shopped at Apna Bazaar (of all places) for wedding presents. For Milind he bought a camera, something the fucker had wanted ever since their trip to Shravanabelagola. An appropriate gift, he thought, for someone who hadn't learned to preserve the glorious moments of his life. For Dagdi Chawl he picked up a Prestige Pressure Cooker.

Yudi got the presents gift-wrapped and lugged them all the way to Nalla Sopara, going out of breath in the process. It was about time he bought himself a second-hand Maruti. If only he stopped squandering his money on ungrateful unfaithfuls, he might even save up enough to buy a Mercedes!

He phoned Gauri to tell her he was attending the weddings after all. He also discussed his presents with her. Even before the call ended, he was cursing himself for making it. For the mad woman in the attic absolutely insisted on accompanying him.

'Milind is now an enemy,' she argued, 'and I can't let you go into enemy territory alone.'

But Gauri was the last person Yudi wanted to take along to the weddings. She was too upper middle class to attend a working-class wedding. Moreover, to go with her would be to accede that heterosexuality had triumphed, for they would only be seen as the third star couple by all and sundry, after RAJESH WITH SHEELA and MILIND WITH LEELA, YUDI WITH GAURI! Just when Yudi had begun to think of Gauri as the platonic he could depend on, she had shown her true colours. All over again! Could she never think beyond her immediate interests? Couldn't she see that this was a tender moment in Yudi's life, when he wanted to be left alone?

The phone conversation ended in a fight. One of them slammed the phone down on the other (Yudi couldn't remember who), and for the next couple of weeks neither of them bothered to ring the other up.

Meanwhile, the weddings took place as scheduled, and Yudi attended them all by himself. When Milind spotted him among the guests, he gnashed his teeth and muttered: 'Why is this cunt here? Who the hell invited him?' Yudi looked sad and old. His hairline was receding, like a high tide turning low; he was rapidly greying at the temples. Milind was thoroughly distracted by Yudi's presence. He couldn't pay enough attention to well-meaning friends and relatives who went up on the stage with gift-wrapped presents to congratulate MILIND AND LEELA and RAJESH AND SHEELA. What enraged him most was that this dirty old fool, this living proof of his shameful past, had gatecrashed only to spite him. Even in his wildest of fantasies, he wouldn't have imagined that it was Dagdi Chawl (the elder) who was the culprit. Or else, he would have seized him by the collar and asked him what business he had to interfere in his affairs.

'Supposing I sent an invitation to Mr Arun Gawli? How would you feel?' he might have asked him.

So the last nail was driven into the coffin. To Milind's way of thinking, there was no difference between Yudi and Arun Gawli; both were confirmed outlaws, both blood-sucking criminals who fed off young and innocent boys.

Yudi sat down on one of the folding chairs and soaked in the ambience. Here were poor people, trying to look rich. Everyone, from MILIND AND LEELA and RAJESH AND SHEELA down to the humblest guest wore tacky woollen suits and zari saris. It made Yudi look like a delivery boy in his Fashion Street casuals. However, when it came to perfumes, the fakers had no idea what to apply on their rancid bodies. They chose cheap Musafirkhana scents in fancy bottles, giving Yudi the feeling that the smell of their collective sweat would have been less revolting. A group of half-starved men in red jackets sat in a corner and played the shehnai. What an insult, thought Yudi, to Bismillah Khan! Why couldn't they stick to film songs? The men seemed to have read his mind, for soon after they started to play all the songs of that ace wedding video, *Hum Aapke Hain Kaun* (that Yudi and Milind had once thought of seeing together). This was accompanied by the Mahadiks' own version of HAHK, their very own wedding video, photographed by a Saat Rasta passport-size. Eats were passed around in paper plates: laddoo and murukku, chivda and samosa. 'Chakram, give me a chakli,' Yudi heard someone shout out to a waiter, who thrust a plate into his hands. The eats were followed by glasses of Rasna.

Suddenly, Yudi felt so depressed, he wanted to walk out of the ghoulish place instantly. But the presents for RAJESH AND SHEELA and MILIND AND LEELA hadn't been delivered; they sat on the floor in their silver wrappers by the side of his chair. For a moment he toyed with the idea of leaving them where they were, as is where is, and stumbling out. Whoever found them would hand them over to the brides and bridegrooms. If they didn't, but pocketed them instead, so much the better. Then he felt he'd paid for the goods with hard earned money, and his money didn't grow on trees; he was no Dagdi Chawl don. Thus Yudi carried his presents to the dais to give them to his tormentors personally.

The stint at the A.K. Modelling Agency had helped. Milind had learned to act. Courtesy, politeness, joviality, he feigned them all as he accepted his gift from Yudi and introduced him to his Mrs. Inside, though, he seethed. Cursed the day he first met Yudi in the stinking Churchgate loo. As for Dagdi Chawl the elder, he jabbered so much that Yudi wanted to chop off his tongue. Dagdi told his wife that the next wedding in the family would be Yudi's, for his heart's greatest desire was to dance at his bade bhaiya's marriage. All this, as Milind stood uncomfortably near by.

Yudi left post-haste. He didn't think he would ever see Milind again. Another chapter of his life was closed, and now there were enough chapters to write a book.

'Goodbye, Milind,' he said, as he limped towards the door and openly sobbed. The wedding guests stared at him and thought he was a convict from the nearby jail who had lost his way.

a friend in need

Parting is such sweet sorrow. Yudi wept often and for weeks after the wedding, but no tears were as sweet and soothing and reckless as those he shed on the streets and in the train the night he staggered out of the wedding pandal and brought himself somehow to Nalla Sopara. In time—though he would not have believed it that night—he would start living again. Jaise-taise. Anyhow.

Years passed (actually, three). Yudi resumed his single-gay-man-in-Mumbai routine. Milind, too, went with the flow: after marriage, babies. He had thought about or planned for neither. In India marriage is like ablution, like washing one's arse. People marry involuntarily, just as they bring their left hand to their arse after a crap. Ditto with babies.

And so Milya produced one obstreperous baby, then another. There wasn't enough to eat. After his last job at the A.K. Modelling Agency, no job was good enough for him. So he preferred to stay at home, while the wife, Leela, ran the house with her paltry ayah's salary. With the modelling agency earnings, Milind had bought a shack in a Kandivili slum and moved in there with Leela and the kiddies, which was just as well, for Dagdi Chawl (the elder), facing tough times himself, had stopped supporting his parents who had stopped supporting their Milya and would have asked him to clear out had he not done so on his own.

Life in the Kandivili slum was hard. Soon there was almost nothing to eat. It was at this time that Leela had an idea. It came to her in a flash one Sunday morning, when she was watching her second most favourite serial on TV: *Krishna*. She watched poor and wretched Sudama walk into his old friend Krishna's palace. She watched Lord Krishna wash his luckless friend's feet and eat his humble gift of poha . . . At the end of the episode, Sudama made the long journey back home, and his hut was a palace and his wife, who only possessed a single tattered sari, was dressed in silk and gold, like a queen.

And Leela found herself thinking: hadn't her good-for-nothing husband once told her about a rich friend of his?

Milind had told his wife about Yudi, no doubt, but in a convoluted way. It all began in bed one night, when Milind asked Leela if she was a virgin, and she returned the question with compliments. Milind was in a fix. Did men who slept with men lose their virginity, or was virginity merely a thing between men and women? He wasn't sure. After pondering the question for a whole week, he decided he was a virgin and said so to Leela. To his way of thinking, then, all that he had done at the A.K. Modelling Agency hadn't killed his virginity. Nor had his affair with Yudi.

At the same time he wanted to show Yudi off to his wife. Reason? She had challenged him: 'Show me one friend of yours who is worthy.'

'Not all my friends are taporis,' he told her. 'One of my closest friends is a newspaper reporter who writes articles for the *Times of India* and gets paid five thousand rupees per article. People know him even in America. I'll introduce him to you, if you think I'm lying.'

Leela wasn't a detective. Or a lawyer. It hadn't occurred to her that if a forty-year-old journalist befriends a twenty-year-old peon, there is reason to be suspicious. Now, a couple of years later, the only detail that stayed in her mind as she reflected on her miserable plight, having switched the black-and-white TV set off, was that Milya had a friend who earned five thousand rupees for every article he sent to the *Times of India*. If that was the case he must be rich, filthy rich. Of course, she did not think the man would be a Krishna to her family—for gods were gods and men mere men—but where was the harm in asking for help anyway? She was not to know that unlike Krishna and Sudama, her husband and the journalist—corrupt mortals, after all—were both more and much less than friends.

Though times were so hard, even had she known, she might still have done what she did.

She ordered her husband to go and see Yudi. For the sake of the children.

Milind's face fell as soon as he heard his wife take his boyfriend's name. This was not because Yudi was male and Leela his wife, and what did it mean for her to talk of a man not related to her. His face fell because deep down he had the portentous fear that if Yudi and Leela came together (for whatever reason), his secret would be exposed. Imagine his wife getting to know he was AC/DC! He wouldn't be able to face her for the rest of his life. He would have to go to the roof of the Oberoi Towers and dive into the Arabian Sea!

So Milind hit back at his wife.

'Don't drag my friend into this,' he warned. 'He doesn't own a bank to lend us money. Besides, he lives such a posh lifestyle that his earnings are insufficient even for him.'

That night, however, as he thought over the matter, he felt that his wife was right. Who else bothered about him as much as

Yudi? But then again, did he really? Hadn't he refused to let Milind move in when he lost his job at Medium Advertising? If, at that time, he had said, 'Let us live together from today,' Milind's life might have been different, might have been less wretched.

Then he remembered the pocket money Yudi gave him, and decided he would ask him to revive this on a permanent basis, and if not, then . . . But hat-teri-ki, blackmail wouldn't work. Yudi was as open about his sexual inclinations as the Azad Maidan!

In the morning, Milind pretended he was coming round to his wife's point of view, but only partly. His male ego didn't permit him to agree with her entirely. If he did, they would call him joru ka ghulam, a hen-pecked husband. He told his wife he would see Yudi, but on one condition: he wouldn't ask him for anything.

'I have my atma sammaan, my self-respect,' he claimed.

Of course he remembered well that three years back he had vowed never to see Yudi again. Well, so what! Life was full of contradictions. Besides, they were friends once, weren't they? Carpe Diem. Sieze the day.

But how could Milya go to see his estranged friend empty handed? The world thrives on presents, he knew. Apart from sex, Yudi loved beer, but a bottle of beer seemed inappropriate to Milind as a present. He considered alternatives. A bottle of whisky? A bottle of rum? Monginis pastries? Devgad mangoes? Mithai from the nearest sweet-meat mart? But he dismissed each of them. Had there been money in the house to buy these things, where was the need for him to see Yudi in the first place? He decided he would take something homemade for his bachelor friend. When he said so to his wife, she was aghast. Had her husband taken leave of his senses? Would Yudi touch food prepared by Untouchables? Milind was at pains to explain to her that Yudi wasn't that kind of person, that touchables and Untouchables were the same to him. Even though she didn't believe her husband,

Mrs Leela Mahadik finally zeroed in on puranpolis, the ultimate goodwill dish for the Marathi-speaking. She would prepare the puranpolis with her own hands, then, and send them to Yudi. But again, this was easier said than done. The young Mahadiks were experiencing their worst time ever, financially. There was nothing to make the puranpolis with. So, as she always did in times of need, Leela turned to her neighbours.

She borrowed freely from her neighbours. Not just a spoonful of dahi to set the curd, but money, provisions, even toys for her children. The result? The neighbours refused to oblige her this time. Not until she settled previous debts. Leela Mahadik begged: 'One last time.' The neighbours refused: 'Sorry, sister.'

In this hour of need, it was Mrs Mahadik senior who came to the rescue. Leela made a day-trip to her mother-in-law's place to pick up all the stuff needed to make the puranpolis. Of course she had a sense of arithmetic: she knew that 100 grams of maida would cost much less than a return ticket to Mahalaxmi. But then, she travelled in the ladies'. 'Without' . . . It's possible on Western Railway.

The puranpolis cooked, she stuffed them into a plastic carry bag, and when Milind returned home from another day of loafing, she handed him the carry bag and told him to embark on his journey at once.

Travelling ticketless, Milind reached Nalla Sopara. But when he went to Mate House, he found Yudi's nameplate replaced by one Arthur Lund's. Sniggering, confident he'd come to the right place, he ventured to ring the doorbell all the same, only to be told by Lund—not his weird ex-friend with a new name but a bald white man who did indeed look like a dick—that Yudi had sold the flat and gone away god knows where. The watchman from Paranoid Security Systems seemed to know where. Or hazarded a guess. Yudi, he said, had probably gone to live with his mother in her South Bombay apartment. It was to this watchman's credit that although he had never seen Milind before (the society couldn't afford his services during the times Milind frequented the place), he did not shout 'Chor, Chor' and shoo him away, as others of his ilk might have done. This was especially commendable since Milind, like any unemployed youth, had begun to resemble a thief, with uncut hair and ruffled clothes. Remembering the day he was thrown out of the Taj, Milind wanted to tell the watchman that he deserved the Bharat Ratna for his politeness. But there were more important things on his mind. What he knew of Yudi's mother's flat was that it was opposite Liberty. If only the old fox hadn't blindfolded him the one time he took him there! How was he to find the place now? He couldn't exactly go to Liberty Cinema and ask the manager to flash a message on the screen. WANTED: YUDI'S ADDRESS. Nor could he go to Café Volga and ask the old Parsi about a chhakka. Ultimately it was a postman from the New Marine Lines Post Office who came to his rescue. Milya spotted him after two full hours of loitering at Liberty, and got the address from him. The postman was moved to tears by Milind's story: the young man was dying of cancer, and wanted only to return the money he owed kind Mr Yudi, his ex-boss, so he could die in peace. His heart aching with pity, the postman gave Milind meticulous directions to Yudi's flat.

A speechless Yudi welcomed his Milya with open arms. He wasn't at all bitter about the manner in which Milya had dumped him. He was too old for self-respect, and too much in love. Tears flowed down his cheeks. His heart was full of gratitude and joy, so that when his prodigal lover complained about how long he had walked, Yudi sat the boy down and knelt before him to massage his chapped and weary feet.

From the far end of the room, a cold pair of eyes watched

Yudi risk rebirth as a cockroach or a shit-worm by touching the feet of a Bhangi. The eyes belonged to Gauri. She hadn't succeeded in reclaiming Yudi, but one day it had occurred to her that she must think of him as her sister. That did it. From that day onwards, Gauri's brain was conditioned, at last, into viewing Yudi as a non-sexual object. For sex, and a fat allowance, she turned her attention to a widower of sixty who was looking for a wife. Although Gauri didn't marry him, they went on the occasional date, after which they retreated to his bungalow at Versova. However, Gauri made it a point to visit Yudi almost every day. She didn't tell her widower (his name was Shitole), or he would have died of jealousy. Yudi referred to him as old man number two, old man number one being, of course, the Colonel. And it was Shitole who, without knowing it, now paid for Gauri's cab rides to New Marine Lines.

So Gauri stood and watched the reunion as it became even more bizarre: having kneaded and tickled Milind's feet, Yudi rushed to the bathroom, rushed back with a half-bucket of water and a mug, and began to wash the boy's feet. She was jealous, but quiet.

His feet washed and dried with a towel, Milind sighed and leaned back in the chair. His mind was full of questions. Why had Yudi sold his Mate House flat and come to live in Pherwani Mansion? Where was his mother? Had she gone to South India again, to attend the wedding of another nephew? How had Yudi managed to make his peace with Gauri?

Yudi answered the questions one by one. His mother, he explained, hadn't gone to South India, but to the other world, from where no one returns. It happened suddenly one night, and the doctors diagnosed it as, what else, a heart attack. After her death, faced with the option of selling the flat, he decided to sell his and keep hers, as a sort of memorial. (A thought, then another, and another, crossed Gauri's mind here. Was it truly for memory's sake that Yudi had kept his mom's flat, or was it that if a man chose to stay in Nalla Sopara instead of New Marine Lines, people would doubt his sanity? Besides, weren't all the newspaper offices and cruising areas within arm's reach from here, while from Nalla Sopara they were as far as the moon? Above all, if he lived in New Marine Lines, didn't it mean that Bombay's suburban trains, hell on earth, were no longer a part of his life? Gauri thought all this, but did not open her mouth.)

As for Milind's third question, concerning Gauri, Yudi let it remain unanswered. Some questions simply didn't have an answer.

It was time now to exchange gifts, for both men knew that the world thrives on presents. Yudi emptied a whole sachet of Manickchand gutkha into Milind's mouth. Milind gave him his puranpolis. This inspired a fresh round of crying. And Gauri stifled an urge to hit Yudi.

Sobbing, Yudi said to Milind: 'You are so thoughtful. You know I freak out on puranpolis. Remember how Saraswati made them for us at Mate House? This is the best gift I've been given in all my life!' To prove that he meant what he said, Yudi swallowed a puranpoli there and then, even if it didn't seem very appetizing, given the carry bag in which the gift was wrapped.

Then something made him sad and he stopped munching. Leela, who had stolen his boyfriend from him, had cooked the puranpolis, after all. Ought he to be eating them with such gusto?

Gauri stood by, a silent spectator still. Yudi didn't offer her a puranpoli. The painter was appalled. In childhood, it was clear, no one had taught him manners. What school did he go to? A village paathshala? Not bloody likely, for had that been the case—and to hell with political correctness here—would this sister of hers have scored minus point after minus point, first by washing a Bhangi's feet and now by eating his puranpolis? And this boy wasn't even a hygienic, educated Bhangi. He was the worst example of his kind! Shame!

Jealousy brought such thoughts to poor Gauri's mind. To be fair, she had nothing against Bhangis, even though some of her best friends were not Bhangis; it was Yudi's abject love for the boy that made her think such thoughts.

But why such rage now? Hadn't she known of her sister's affair with a peon for years? Seeing, however, is believing. Not until she saw, with her own two eyes, Yudi's fingers entwined in Milind's toes had she ever imagined anything physical between them. Now, her mind was bamboozled by the ultimate heterosexist question: *What do gay couples do in bed?* For heterosexual men, nothing was more erotic than two women in bed, Gauri had heard. She was now discovering, to her discomfort, that likewise, for heterosexual women nothing was more erotic than two men in bed!

Milind spent the night at Yudi's. There was no guest room in this flat (Yudi's mother didn't get any guests), so Milind slept in the master bedroom on an antique four-poster, Yudi by his side.

Gauri took her leave: her sister forbade her from hanging around at her pad beyond sunset. That, then, was the only witness gone, for Milind had noticed there were no watchmen in this building to spy and to gossip. He felt better.

But he didn't sleep soundly. For one thing, he hadn't informed Leela that he was spending the night at Yudi's. She would nag him to death when he got home, assuming that like his vagabond father, he too had acquired a mistress.

For another, Yudi didn't allow him to sleep, resuming his jhop mod-palang tod tactics with a vengeance. He hadn't exactly starved himself of sex all these years, but no errand boy, no waiter, no loo attendant had matched up to his Milya. Not until dawn did the old lovers stop, and then they fell fast asleep, waking up only at noon, exactly as they did in Mate House years ago. When Milya awoke, it hit him like a thunderbolt: his wild bachelor days were permanently gone. He was a married man now, with a wife and kids. What was he doing here?

Milind made preparations to leave.

'Blockhead,' he heard his wife nag him. 'Ask, ask.'

And he did. Without directly connecting it to the sex they had, Milind asked Yudi for his pocket money (arrears plus interest). After his assignment at A.K. Modelling Agency, he wasn't going to let anyone touch his body for free. Not even his wife, who paid for it by doing his cooking and washing.

When Gauri arrived the next morning, she saw Yudi giving Milind a bunch of currency notes. Because Milind was receiving for what he had given—the puranpolis included—he did not feel like a beggar. He had his atma-sammaan. Ignoring Gauri, who had once assaulted him and whom he'd contemplated marrying, he thanked Yudi for his hospitality. Yudi hugged him, but did not weep at this parting. Nor did he say, 'Come again—nakki pucca-shambar takka.' This time he was certain they would meet again.

On the local train home, Milind re-lived his experiences at Yudi's house. What did it mean to him, his meeting with Yudi? He wasn't sure. Yudi had offered only when he asked, but so what, he was content . . . He would keep going there again and again whenever he was short of cash . . . As one of A.K. Modelling Agency's T-shirts proclaimed: A FRIEND IN NEED IS A FRIEND IN NEED . . . He laughed: How the man washed my stinking feet . . . how he said he had missed me, as if he hadn't been hunting around for other dicks all the while . . . how he shed crocodile tears, ha, ha, ha . . . how I fucked him on the fancy bed on which his mother once slept . . .

Then he heard his wife's haranguing voice: 'You fool, what have you brought for me and the children? Wasted my puranpolis!'

(This because Milind had already decided to keep all the pocket money for himself without giving them a paisa.) But Milind was imperturbable. What did the bitch know anyway? Why couldn't she wash dishes in someone's house and allow the master of the house to fuck her, if she was that desperate for pocket money? 'Must flog her with my belt again,' he told himself. She should know her place; she didn't own him. No one did, not Yudi, not she . . .

Needless to say, when he reached home, his hut wasn't transformed into a palace. Leela and the kids didn't run towards him in Versace outfits. For Yudi was no God to effect overnight changes.

Gauri tapped Yudi's shoulder. 'Stop brooding,' she admonished her sister. 'Your boyfriend is back and you should rejoice. You started out at Pherwani Mansion, and now he's here again. The wheel has come full circle. Look forward to your next meeting with the dirty bugger—if you must!'

Her words pepped Yudi up. He opened a bottle of vodka and fixed them a Bloody Mary each.

'You know, Gauri,' he began, then paused. 'You know, I have come to the conclusion that life is beautiful.'

'It is indeed,' she agreed.

They clinked glasses. As they sipped their vodka-with-tomato juice, they became nostalgic. Reminisced about their first meeting in Bhatnagar's office. The drive in Bhatnagar's car, Gauri cleaning Yudi's vomit with her bare hands. Her cab rides to Mate House. The showdown at Yudi's door, with Milind and Saraswati as supporting cast. Gauri's dogs Shakespeare and Milton. And so on.

Suddenly Gauri said: 'Yudi, I've got to make a confession.'

'Not again,' he stuttered.

'No, you must listen to this one,' she insisted. 'It's out of this world.'

'Go on, then.'

'You know, hearing you go on and on, I've started feeling attracted to women!'

'Really!' Yudi exclaimed. The news made him laugh as if tickled to death in the armpits.

'I am not joking,' Gauri continued, her face growing serious. 'I mean it. For starters, how about introducing me to Milind's wife? I've even done a painting depicting the four of us.'

'Perfect arrangement,' declared Yudi. 'While Milind entertains me, you can humour his wife! Keep her busy so she won't miss her husband.'

It was past the embargo hour, but Yudi didn't ask Gauri to leave. This, after all, was an exceptional day, a day on which the boyfriend had returned. They sat up all night, drinking, nursing each other's wounds.

PENGUIN ONLINE

visit our author lounge

•

read about your favourite authors

•

investigate over 12000 titles

•

subscribe to our online newsletter

•

enter contests and quizzes and win prizes

•

email us with your comments and reviews

•

have fun at our children's corner

•

receive regular email updates

•

keep track of events and happenings

www.**penguin**books**india**.com